Copyright Matthew Ca
Edited by M
All rights reserved. No
reproduced in any form o
inclusion of brief quotations in a review, without
permission in writing from the publisher

.

This book is a work of fiction. The characters and situations in this book are imaginary. No resemblance is intended between these characters and any persons, living or dead.
This book is sold subject to the condition that it shall not, by way of trade or otherwise, be lent, resold, hired out or otherwise circulated without the publisher's prior consent in any form or binding or cover other than that in which it is published and without similar condition including this condition being imposed on the subsequent purchaser
Published in Great Britain in 2023 by Matthew Cash
Burdizzo Books Walsall, UK

The Society

The Society

Raven Taylor

Burdizzo Books 2023

The Society

PART ONE

Chapter 1

2009

"Thank you for taking the time to see me, Mr. Bergman," she extended a thin hand and he took it rather nervously.

Quinn Bergman was a slim, elderly man, with dark circles around his eyes and a distinct air of uncertainty. If she could have picked one word to describe her first impressions of her subject it would have been *haunted.* He looked like he had not slept in days, and there was a definite air of fear and a nervous energy radiating from him. Quite understandable, she mused, given what she knew of what he had been through. When her assistant had shown him into her office he had entered like a mouse; creeping on his toes, glancing back over his shoulder towards the door as if to check that he was not being followed. He had a point. *They* were well known for employing spies to follow those who they considered a threat.

"Do sit down, won't you?" she gestured to the leather upholstered chair across from her desk as she sank back down into her own seat. She watched Mr. Bergman clumsily pulling out the chair and perching on the very edge, as if ready to flee at any moment. She noted that he had not said a word since he arrived.

"Really, there's no need to be nervous," she assured him. "Would you like a glass of water? Tea? Coffee?"

Quinn shook his head and swallowed hard. He gave another brief glance back at the door. Her assistant had now closed it and she observed how his body seemed to relax a little, satisfied that no one would overhear the conversation they were about to have.

"I really am very grateful that you have agreed to do this," she reiterated.

"Yes, well," he said at last in a small, strained voice, "with all that's come out recently, I thought it my duty to come forward, I could hardly decline your invitation to share my own experiences of the whole subject."

"And anything you can tell us *will* help," she leaned across the desk and fixed him with an empathetic stare. "Anything, no matter how small, that we can learn about these people will be invaluable. We only want to help, do you understand?"

"I... well... yes, of course," Quinn nodded.

"As we discussed, I am a private investigator. I was originally hired by a family who were concerned about the disappearance of their daughter, but it's become about so much more since then. It's about bringing a stop to them once and for all- exposing their crimes and hopefully, God willing, one day bringing criminal proceedings against them."

Quinn shifted in his seat and gave a slight nod of agreement. He had not been surprised when she had reached out to him. She wouldn't have been the first to try and get him to talk about his experience. Generally he turned all such offers down, but she had been persuasive, and he had been thinking about coming forward anyway. He'd been hiding for too long, and it was selfish of him to continue to do so when what he knew could potentially help other victims. She genuinely seemed to want to do something, to hold them accountable, unlike the others who just wanted a grisly story to sell under a sensational headline. Anyway, he was getting old now, and the closer he got to dying, the more he wanted to unburden himself so he did not have to carry this secret with him to the grave.

She gave him an encouraging smile. "I must say it is a pleasure to meet the man who once enthralled the country with his literary genius. Mind, it took me a long time to track you down, you've become infamously reclusive, and it's been years since you had a book out."

"Yes, I have been a bit of a hermit," he agreed, "and I haven't really written anything since it all ended. They saw to it that my career was ruined when I left."

Quinn sat back in his chair and tried to relax, to still his heart which was hammering in his chest. There was nothing to worry about. The whole thing happened years ago. There was no need to be so afraid. He had to do it, to tell his story, for the sake of the investigations.

He looked around the room. The office was bright and airy. The window was open allowing a fresh summer breeze to waft in. There was a distant sound of children playing in the park peppered with bird song. The setting seemed all wrong. Such disturbing tales as the one he was about to tell seemed in complete contrast to the safe, cheerful surroundings. He let his cap fall into his lap. If he continued to twist it and fuss at it with his fingers it would end up ruined.

"All right then, so how does this work?"

"I'd just like you to tell me the story, in your own words; everything and anything you might feel is relevant, or not, just let it flow. Though I'd imagine with your talent for storytelling this should be easy."

Easy? Nothing about this was going to be easy.

Quinn gave a deep sigh.

Might as well just begin at the start.

"Here we go then," he gazed off out the window and added quietly, "for you, Sonny,"

The Society

Raven Taylor
Chapter 2

1965

My introduction to The Society began with an advert in a writers and artists magazine. I was slumped at the kitchen table in my small London flat, drinking black coffee, and nursing yet another hangover, when the bold black header text asked me 'have you lost your creative spark?' This immediately caught my attention. Since the success of my debut novel, 'Marked for Sorrow,' I had not written a single thing of merit. I had gone from being tipped by the critics as the most promising young authors of the decade, to being all but completely wiped from the nation's collective conscience. At first the literary world had waited with great anticipation to see what I would do next, but when nothing was forthcoming, the hype slowly died down, and they forgot about me.

Concluding that I had indeed lost my creative spark, I proceeded to read the advert.

Chyanvean House is a stunning hotel and centre for enlightenment set on the beautiful Cornish coast. We offer a series of retreats designed to help ailing artists, writers and musicians rekindle their inspiration and get their creative juices flowing again. Our team cares deeply about the arts and understand that in this current climate, creatives are undervalued and often discouraged from pursuing their dreams. We recognise that such struggles and hardships can often result in an array of mental health problems such as melancholia and drug addiction, which further impede the creative process. Our programs are designed not only to

The Society

provide fresh inspiration, but also to treat any underlying psychological conditions which may be interfering with your ability to work. We count top actors, musicians, artists and writers among our clients, many of whom are household names, all of whom owe their success to us. Contact us today and see what we can do for you. And remember, our retreats are always free, for the right kind of person.

"What nonsense," I scoffed. "Household names indeed!"

I didn't give it any further thought and left my home to run a few errands. However, later that evening, when I returned home drunk again, and saw the magazine still lying open on the kitchen table, I began to wonder if it might be worth looking into this further. London had not been kind to me this past year, and to simply take off and leave behind all my problems, and the constant reminders of what a mess I had made of things, was very tempting.

There was a grainy photograph accompanying the advert of a fabulous old Victorian house perched on the cliff tops. I stared at it for a moment; at the towering gothic pillars, rambling architecture, and the gorgeous rolling sea stretching on to the horizon where a low sun hung in the sky. Partly driven by drink, and partly by nostalgia for the family holiday we had once had in St Ives when I was a youngster, I decided to call the number. It was gone ten pm, I half expected an answering machine, and was surprised when a woman's voice answered. My memory of the phone call itself is blurry, though I do remember being asked a lot about my writing career, my mental health, and the details of the recent difficulties I had been having. Some of the questions seemed very personal, and the lady appeared to read them from a script in a monotone voice. As I answered, I heard the scratching of a pen on the other end as she took notes. It felt a little like an interview. As the interrogation closed, I was informed flatly that someone would be in touch.

The next day, on sobering up, and still feeling intrigued by the promises of the advert, I decided to run the idea by my editor, and lifelong friend, George. George was aware that I had been going through a period of terrible depression and ill health, and I told him that this retreat offered to help with both creative blocks and mental health issues. Hearing myself put it into words, I began to feel a slight sense of doubt. It sounded quite foolish when I tried to explain.

"And it's free," I said lamely, "for the right kind of person…" I trailed off and I heard George laugh harshly.

"No one gives away anything for free, Quinn," he insisted, "it must be some kind of scam."

I don't know why, but his scornful tone made me reluctant to back down and my resolve began to strengthen again.

"They were very thorough with their questions," I told him, "I got the impression that they know about these things, and if nothing else, it could be a chance to escape to the countryside for a bit, get some sea air."

"Please tell me this isn't about what happened," George groaned, "because nobody thinks any less of you, Emily and I love you dearly, and this seems a little like you're looking for a reason to run away."

Was I running away? Perhaps I was.

Later that day the telephone rang and I was greeted by an unfamiliar female voice.

"Am I speaking with Quinn Bergman?" she enquired.

"Yes, this is Quinn."

The Society

"This is Fern from Chyanvean House," the voice replied, her tone brisk and businesslike, "I'm calling to inform you that after reviewing your questionnaire answers, you qualify to attend our retreat free of charge."

I was a little taken aback. I had assumed the offer of free help was just to make them appear charitable, to reinforce the message that a love of the arts came above all else. I had been expecting a sales pitch, and even then, I was willing to listen, because the way I felt, I would have given all I had if I thought they could help get my life and my career back on track.

"Oh, I see," was all I could manage to say.

"Details will follow shortly in the post. We will be seeing you very soon, Mr. Bergman."

Before I could respond she hung up.

Well, I thought to myself, it seems I am indeed, 'the right kind of person'.

Chapter 3

1965

Despite George's continued reservations and warnings that I was clearly walking into a scam, I left for Cornwall the following week. In our last meeting he gave me strict instructions to stay in touch, because if I didn't, he would assume the people who had posted that ad were crazed lunatics and he would be forced to come looking for me.

The letter arrived two days after the telephone call. It immediately stood out from the other mail that landed on the mat that morning (mostly bills in brown envelopes) because it was sealed with red wax bearing a stamp of a bird in flight. I picked it up, ignoring the bills, feeling the rich texture of the expensive off-white paper, scanning the address which was handwritten in sloping, looping letters in shiny red ink to match the seal. On closer inspection the seal also bore the motto 'the arts above all,' confirming my guess as to where this had come from. It was from them, the people at Chyanvean house. As I broke the brittle seal I felt a sudden thrill which cut through the heavy lethargy that had hung over me for months.

The letter did not say much. It was written in the same slopping hand on the same high-quality paper as the envelope. Once again I was expecting some kind of sales pitch, a caveat to it being free, like a suggested donation, but there was nothing. There was no brochure explaining what exactly I was signing up for. Nothing to give me any details of how the retreat worked, what I could expect from it. It simply reads as follows.

The Society

Dear Mr. Bergman,
We are delighted that they have decided to join us. Please arrive at the address given above this coming Monday. We know that with our help, you are going to do great things and we cannot wait to welcome you.
Kind Regards
Dante Lewin-May
Course Coordinator, Chyanvean House.

An address for the house was printed in the top right-hand corner, a place called St Morlyns, and that was it.

I decided that I would give myself a few days before I was due at Chyanvean House to make my way slowly down the coast, making some stops along the way. I set off in my car, and soon left behind the grey smog of London, and found myself rolling through the pleasant English countryside. The more miles I put between myself and the city, the better I began to feel.

Britain was going through a cultural revolution, whose epicentre seemed to be the capital, with pop music, gaudy fashions and television seeming to take over. Often I thought I had been born in the wrong era, because despite being a young man myself, I was baffled by what was happening around me. Suddenly it was all about colour televisions, transistor radios playing the Beatles and The Rolling Stones, miniskirts, recreational drugs, psychedelic prints, and all I could do was watch from the sidelines and wish that I too could be so easily entertained. I ached for quiet, for classical music, for soft lighting and a log fire. Sixties society was alien to me, I simply did not fit in. What was it my father had always said of me? That I was an old man trapped in a young man's body. Yes, escaping London was probably for the best.

I took my time, working my way along the south coast- Bournemouth, Weymouth, Torquay- taking lodgings wherever I could in guest houses beside the sea. It being October, and outside the holiday season, it was not difficult to find places to stay, and although I began to feel a little better, that heavy sadness that had plagued me this last year remained, trailing behind me mile after mile like a persistent black dog.

It was four days after my departure that I crossed the border, leaving England and entering Cornwall.

The October weather had so far been kind to me, the country roads offering the perfect autumnal backdrop as I drove my beloved 1953 Magnette. It was unusually mild and sunny as I progressed along the southern coast. It could almost have been summer, had it not been for the orange leaves on the trees, and the hedgerows heavy with a harvest bounty of berries in hues of red and black.

I stopped for lunch in the charming village of Polperro, in a peculiar little inn called 'The Crumplehorn,' then continued on my way down towards Lands' End, stopping whenever it took my fancy to stretch my legs, or have a pint of local ale in one of the many quaint old village pubs I passed. I was making good time and was on track to arrive at my destination in the late afternoon.

St Morlyn was a small and picturesque village, which clung to high on the cliff tops overlooking the Celtic Sea along the coast from Porthleven. It had one main street on which I counted three pubs, a small grocery shop, and a post office. There were also several souvenir shops, which all appeared to be closed for the season. It was a pleasant enough place, with an assortment of old whitewashed cottages, each different from the next, and all of them possessed a quaint old-world charm. Then something caught my eye.

In the distance, set apart from the rest of the village, and perched precariously on the very edge of the cliffs, was a very large, impressive looking Victorian structure, with turrets and rooftops reaching into the sky, and countless windows.

That must be the place, I mused, hardly even able to imagine the views out to sea it must command.

A little further down the main street I came to a hand painted sign pointing off down a side road which read 'Chyanvean House: Guest rooms, fabulous sea views and the captain's tearoom: home of the best cream tea in Cornwall!'

I took the turn and followed the narrow road until it ended abruptly at a set of tall metal gates set into a stone archway in the wall which surrounded the building's grounds. The gates were open, and a sign on the post read 'visitors most welcome.' A long driveway cut across a large, well maintained, lawn, and there was a gravelled area for vehicles at the front. Getting out of the car, I noticed the flag flying from one of the turrets. It had on it the same symbol which I recognised from the wax seal on the letter- some kind of bird in flight, with what appeared to be the outline of a blazing sun above it and the words 'the arts above all'.

This can't be right, I thought, checking the address I had written down, *it's even more magnificent than in the picture.*

On passing through the huge arched doorway with its heavy oak doors, I was met by a rather grand entrance hall with polished wooden floors and opulent silk wallpaper patterned with an endless design of intertwining gold vines. For a moment I simply stood, taking in the grandeur of the place. Ahead of me a wide staircase swept up to the floors above, drawing my eyes to the countless gilt framed paintings that adorned the walls on the way up to the landing. There were lush green ferns cascading out of huge antique Chinese vases dotted around the foyer. The rugs were clearly expensive Persian and woven with the most intricate designs. I was convinced I was in the wrong place. How could somewhere like this be offering free residencies? One thing that did strike me as a little odd was the piped in birdsong that filled the air and the strong smell of lavender, as if they were trying just a little too hard to suggest a sense of tranquility. A console table against the wall contained an assortment of framed photographs, many of which showed smiling guests all shaking hands with the same dashing man. I found myself drifting over to the table so I could look more closely at the pictures.

'Satisfied graduates of The Program' a small notice told me. I picked up one of the photos so I could examine it.

"Good lord, isn't that…"

"Yes," a voice cut me off. I hadn't even noticed the woman at the reception desk in the far corner. "Kevin Bambridge. Are you a fan of his work?"

"Oh, I'm sorry…" I said, putting the picture back, feeling like I had been caught out doing something I shouldn't.

"Don't be sorry. Welcome to Chyanvean House, my name is Magda." Although she smiled at me there was something a little off about her expression, as if her pleasantries were not genuine, and were merely rehearsed to create the desired impression.

The Society

"My name is Quinn Bergman," I said as I approached the desk, "I'm not sure I'm in the right place, I'm booked in for some kind of creative retreat?"

"Of course Sir, you are in the right place, don't worry." She opened a large leather-bound ledger and began to leaf through it. "Ah yes, here we are, you're the writer, aren't you?"

"Yes, I am," I confirmed.

"Can you fill this in please?" she slid a guest registration form across the desk, "you are a little early for the course though, yes?"

"I wanted time to get settled in first."

"I understand."

I filled in my details and passed the form back to her. As she glanced over it my eyes wandered to the painting on the wall behind her. It was illuminated by a spotlight and framed in a fancy gold frame. It was painted in acrylics and seemed to show some surreal looking landscape with psychedelic colours and naked people dancing, while in the blood red sky above them was a silhouette of a bird, much like the one I had seen on the flag when I arrived. For some reason I found I couldn't stop staring at it, and the people dancing with the blissful expressions on their faces seemed to draw me in. I could almost hear their merry laughter.

"You are admiring the painting," Magda observed, startling me from my thoughts.

"Oh yes, it's quite remarkable how the artist has captured the colours of the sunset."

"Sunrise," she corrected me, "we do not have sunsets here at Chyanvean, only sunrises full of new beginnings."

"Oh," I said quietly.

"As it's out of season the house is very quiet so we have upgraded your room to one of our best, with glorious sea views at the back of the house. I think it will be to your liking."

I was still marvelling at the splendour of the place. I had not imagined for a second that I would be staying anywhere so magnificent. I had expected tired, dated decor, stale musty smells, a run down, falling apart building with damp and mold, but it was as if I had stepped into a stately home from years gone by.

Magda stood up and came out from behind the desk.

"For the right kind of guest, there is no charge," she said with a smile, as if she knew what I was thinking, "the owner likes to do all he can to assist those involved in the arts. This way please, I'll show you around."

She walked ahead of me as we crossed the foyer to an open door on the right, and she ushered me into the splendid room beyond.

"This is the bar and restaurant. The kitchen serves dinner between seven and nine, if you'd care for it. Through that door at the back is the owner's private living room. Chyanvean is first and foremost a family home, and that is how you should think of it, as a home, not a hotel, in which you are a most treasured guest."

She spun on her heels and marched back out into the foyer. Bemused, I followed her.

"That is also the owner's private quarters up there," she pointed at the grand staircase. "The guest accommodation is this way."

Magda pushed open a set of double oak doors to the left of the stairway and led me into a room which I can only describe as stunning. As we stepped in the whole place opened out around us with massive floor to

The Society

ceiling windows looking directly out to sea where the sun was already starting to set. There was a fireplace at either end of the large room, with sumptuous high-backed sofas huddled around them. More comfortable chairs and side tables were dotted around the room, some of them occupied by other guests who all seemed to be reading books. Just like in the foyer, the air was alive with the sound of taped birdsong. I could not help but notice more psychedelic paintings like the one behind the desk. They seemed to be everywhere. I wondered if the owners were somehow part of the whole new age hippy movement.

In the centre of the room was an elegant dining table which could have easily seated 30 people and whose surface was adorned with endless, complex carvings. My hostess paused beside this table.

"Do you know anything of the history of Chyanvean House?" she inquired.

"No, I don't," I admitted.

"Well, you have much to discover while you are here. It was built in 1871 by a man called William Thomas, a celebrated Victorian engineer and spiritualist. He was quite a lover of eastern mysticism, and if you look you will see various pieces around the house that he collected on his many trips to India, including this table. He had this specially carved by a craftsman he met out there. The carvings are supposed to depict the journey of the soul through its many earthly incarnations, and the lessons it must learn along the way. William Thomas was quite a believer in reincarnation, which was deeply frowned upon in those days when Christianity was seen as the only true way."

She shrugged dismissively and started towards a second staircase in the far corner of the room, before I had the chance to get a really good look at the table.

"Do feel free to use this whole area to relax in," she said, "and your room is up there on the first floor, number 157."

She handed me a key on a large wooden keyring, and that was where she left me.

I made my way up the stairs and along the hall on which hung more of the bizarre paintings, all in heavy gilt frames which would have been far more suited to classical pieces. I found my room easily enough, and after a bit of a struggle with a rather stiff door, I managed to push my way in, all but falling into the room. I was not disappointed. The room was enormous, vast compared to the poky guest houses I had been staying in of late, with a huge antique four poster bed with red velvet hangings, and a leather sofa by a beautiful fireplace. But best of all were the glorious bay windows, huge and sweeping with uninterrupted views of the craggy Cornish cliffs and the dramatic ocean beyond. By the windows, looking out to sea, was a writing desk.

I put my bags away in the wardrobe and surveyed the room again, marvelling that such accommodation had cost me nothing. I was not surprised to spot another painting hanging above the fireplace. This one depicted what appeared to be the house itself, rising proudly from the cliffs with the psychedelic colours of the sky all clashing with each other, and a bird flying high above.

I sat myself down in the chair at the desk to watch the rapidly setting sun.

"Always a sunrise, never a sunset," I mused to myself quietly.

The Society

Then in my mind George's words came echoing back to me.

No one gives anything away for free, Quinn.

Raven Taylor
Chapter 4

1965

At around eight pm, after the sun had gone down and the sea had turned an inky black, I decided I would go down to the dining room to get some food and drink.

I ordered from the menu a meal of rare steak and seasonal vegetables with a glass of red wine in the pleasant dining room. There were a number of other guests in attendance, dotted around the room, carrying out private conversations in hushed little groups- other guests of the hotel I assumed. I wondered if they were also here for the artists' retreat or were they just holiday makers here for an autumn break before the weather turned really bad. I glanced curiously at them but none of them looked at me or made any effort at conversation. The thing that struck me as a little odd was that rather than background music, we were once again being serenaded by birdsong. It was a little quirky, but with the soft lighting and elegant decor, the atmosphere in this room was strangely relaxing and comfortable.

By the time I had finished eating most of the other guests had moved through to the lounge area or had retired to their rooms. I approached the bar and ordered a large brandy before retreating to one of the high-backed chairs in the bar next to the open fire which was crackling away merrily. On the coffee table in front of me a large glossy book had been placed for guests to peruse. It was entitled 'The Life and Works of Sonny Newton,' and the cover showed a photograph of a handsome young man with shoulder length, tousled

The Society

copper coloured hair, and intense green eyes standing in front of an artist's easel. I leant over and began to leaf through the volume. The foreword announced.

'For over ten years Sonny Newton has been living and working as artist in residence at Chyanvean House in St Morlyn, Cornwall, where much of his work is displayed in an ever-evolving exhibition. Sonny helps to run a number of retreats and courses for artists at the house. In recent years his work has won much acclaim among critics, and his pieces are becoming highly sought after in the art world.'

The body of the book was filled with fantastic colour prints of the artist's work, the style of which I recognised immediately.

Well, that explains why those strange pictures appear to be everywhere you look.

Satisfied that a mystery had been solved, I closed the book and sat back in the chair, a glass of wine in my hand, and I at last began to feel at ease. It seemed as if all the anguish and mental torment that had plagued me was being washed away by the warm glow of the fire. All thoughts of George, and that terrible evening when I stood outside of his house in the rain, screaming up at his window, were driven away by the hypnotic dancing of the flames. I felt time no longer had any meaning, and nothing existed outside of that fire. In those moments it didn't seem to matter that my behaviour had almost cost me my two best friends, that my father was longer talking to me, that I couldn't seem to write anymore… I couldn't tell you how long I had been sitting there, looking at the flames and listening to the birdsong, when a voice interrupted my dreaming.

"Would you mind if I sat down?" The voice was pleasant, soft and un-intrusive, and rather than startling me from my trance it seemed to gently guide me back to consciousness.

I looked up at the man who was gesturing to the armchair across the table from me.

"Oh no, by all means."

"Thank you."

The lighting was low in the bar, and as he settled himself into the wing backed chair, his face was hidden by the shadows his cap cast across his face. He was dressed rather shabbily in a blue shirt, a black knitted tank top, which had spots of paint on it, a jacket whose cuffs were fraying, and rather worn looking cord trousers. With his face turned towards the fire, he reached into his jacket pocket and pulled out a silver case from which he took a cigarette and lit it. Without looking at me, he extended his hand across the table and offered the case to me.

"Thank you, no, I don't."

"Suit yourself," he dragged on his cigarette and exhaled a cloud of smoke which drifted in front of his face, obscuring his features.

As he lowered the hand holding the cigarette, and the smoke cleared, I was at last able to get a proper look at his face. His features were elegant and young, with high cheekbones and a slender nose which had a spattering of freckles across it. I guessed he was around my age, and I was sure I had seen him somewhere before.

"Why, you're the artist," I tapped the book on the table, "I didn't recognise you at first."

"Guilty as charged," he chuckled, turning to look at me.

He really did have the most intense green eyes.

"Sonny Newton, glad to meet you, friend," he reached out again and I shook his hand.

The Society

"Quinn, Quinn Bergman."

He sat back again, puffing on his cigarette and stared at me for what seemed to be the longest time.

"So how are you enjoying Chyanvean?" he asked at last.

"I've only just arrived this evening, but I must say it is a beautiful building, and the location is simply superb."

"Yes," he agreed, "it is quite a remarkable place with a fascinating history. I simply love it here; the views, the sea air, the unique light that always changes. What more inspiration could an artist wish for?"

"Yes, I have been admiring your paintings, they are quite original."

"Well, I'll take that as a compliment," he smiled, and stubbed his cigarette out in the ashtray. "And you, you're a writer I believe?"

"You recognise me?" I asked in surprise.

"No, no!" Sonny slapped his knee and laughed, "Dante told me we were expecting a writer."

"Well, yes, I'm a writer. I mean I was a writer; I haven't written anything for quite some time. I'm not sure what I am these days."

"Nonsense! You don't simply cease to be a writer just because you are going through a bad patch. In fact, Chyanvean could be just what you need, it is the most inspiring place I know. I believe you are here for our artist's retreat?"

I was starting to feel a little uncomfortable. I had never been any good at making small talk with strangers, and I wondered if I could politely excuse myself and go back to my room.

"I am. I saw the ad in the paper and thought, why not?"

"Why not indeed! Chyanvean is a very special place my friend," he said. "It is as if she were built to inspire the creative side in every artist who visits. I've created some of the best work of my life since coming here and slew many a personal demon!" He leaned in close to me and whispered, "maybe you could too…"

He sat back with his fingers steepled under his chin as he observed me curiously. I didn't quite know what to say so I just nodded and smiled, too polite to do anything other than humour him.

"Well, since we are friends now I simply must show you the artist's studio I have here, come, come, I'll get you another drink on the way past the bar."

I hesitated. He was now standing up and waiting for me to follow.

"Yes, that would be very interesting," I found myself saying, cursing myself for my awkward inability just to say no thank you.

At the bar an elderly lady with a blue rinse perm and expensive looking diamond earrings was laughing hysterically at something the man behind the bar had said. Sonny laid a hand on the old lady's shoulders and she turned around and grinned at him adoringly.

"Oh, Sonny you do look well tonight," she commented, "your poor face has completely healed up. I do hope you won't get into trouble again; black eyes and busted lips really do spoil your handsome looks."

"Oh, you know me," I watched the exchange, slightly bemused, "Can't seem to stay out of trouble these days. Paul, can you get another glass of wine for Mr. Bergman here?"

"Oh, but Dante loves you," the old lady continued to ramble, "we all do, you know that don't you?"

The Society

"And I love you too, Ethel my dear, and you yourself look ravishing this evening."

"It's this place, isn't it? I've honestly never felt better in my life!"

"What did I tell you?" Sonny turned to me and handed me the glass of wine. "Ethel is one of my most valued guests, and a collector of my paintings!"

"Oh, I should say I am your biggest fan!" she exclaimed.

"I'm taking Quinn up to see where I work," he told her.

"You are in for a treat," Ethel gushed.

"Ethel my dear, I'm going to bid you goodnight. I'll see you tomorrow, you have an appointment with Dante, don't you? I'll come and fetch you at 9?"

"Yes, that will be fine."

"Dante runs the house," Sonny explained as he led me away.

"Yes, his name was at the bottom of the letter I received."

"He and his wife Kerrigan are in charge of everything that we do here, all the activities and courses. I imagine you'll get to meet them tomorrow, they are lovely people, huge fans of William Thomas and his work, they've been running this place for twenty years now. They've been very good to me, honestly I don't know where I would be without them...dead most likely..." For a moment he paused and a troubled look crossed his face, but then he clapped his hands, and his smile returned and he said, "but let's not be morbid! Come!"

We were out in the foyer now, and he held open for me a small door to the right of the main staircase, behind which there were some narrow, stone spiral steps dimly lit by low watt bulbs set into the curved walls.

"Please, go up first, and take your time on the stairs, they're a bit steep."

Up I began to climb, feeling a little lightheaded from the wine, and trying my best not to trip on the stone steps. The plastered walls had been painted, clearly by Sonny himself, with an endless, curving fantasy landscape, in which trees and leaves could be any colour he wished, and the grass was never green, and where strange figures danced and more black birds flew. I could scarcely imagine how long it must have taken him to paint such a massive piece.

"The artwork on the wall is inspired by William Thomas's table downstairs," he explained, "did you see it?"

"Yes, the receptionist told me something about it depicting reincarnation?"

"That's right, it does, as does my little piece here. It shows man's journey through many lifetimes, each with a new lesson to learn, and his eventual ascent to paradise."

We reached the top of the stairs, where there was a small landing with a steep set of wooden steps leading up to a trapdoor.

"Here we are!" Sonny climbed the steps and unlocked the hatch at the top, pushing it open and disappearing up into the space beyond.

I hesitated for a moment, feeling a bit awkward, before I followed.

I found myself in a large circular room with tall, narrow windows interspersed around the circumference. It appeared to be some kind of observatory. The room was elevated above the rest of the house and gave three hundred- and sixty-degree views of the surrounding

The Society

landscape. The night sky peered down at us through the massive glass domed ceiling. The half-moon rode high in the heavens and its reflection rippled on the surface of the calm ocean, while along the headland I could see the twinkling lights of the next village.

"It's extraordinary," I said quietly, trying to take it all in.

"Isn't it?" said Sonny, closing the hatch on the floor. "It's the perfect place for an artist to work. So much natural light. Such views. It's also the perfect place to just relax, so calming!"

There were a lot more paintings lying about up here, and pots filled with brushes, and tables littered with tubes of paint. I was impressed.

"Please sit down, make yourself comfortable, anywhere you like."

There was a collection of mis-matched chairs scattered about the place, most of them speckled with splashes of dried paint. I chose a low armchair with threadbare cushions facing out to sea.

"You know you are quite lucky to see this place," Sonny remarked, pulling a wooden, paint-stained dining chair towards me so he could sit opposite. "I don't show just anyone my workspace, especially with so many unfinished and substandard pieces lying around. No, it takes a fellow creative to really appreciate something like this. Someone like you, but I fear your spark has gone out recently, hasn't it?"

"I suppose it has."

"I can tell," he said, and as he gazed at me I felt it would be all too easy to get completely lost in his deep green eyes. "You have such a creative soul, but you've lost touch with it…"

"I'm afraid I may have lost it forever…"

Raven Taylor

"Nothing is lost forever, it's still in there somewhere, we just need to find out what's holding you back and suppressing that talent."

"I don't know. I've just been feeling so incredibly down, like I'm being smothered by some heavy blackness."

I had no idea why I was telling a stranger all this. Perhaps it was the wine loosening my tongue, or something about his soulful gaze, but suddenly I wanted to tell him everything, all of my troubles, things I had never before tried to put into words. I wanted to tell him about my breakup with Emily, my infatuation with George, how I had disgraced and embarrassed my family so that they would no longer speak to me...

"Ah yes, the horrible black emptiness. I know it well." Sonny gave an understanding nod and patted me on the knee, letting his hand linger there. "Without your writing you have completely lost your direction, haven't you? I see it in your tired eyes. You are lost, you are desperate, there have perhaps even been times when you wished you were not here at all. Believe me, I know what it is like not to want to live."

This man was incredibly perceptive. It made me feel a little uneasy. For a moment my mind went back to the source of my anguish; I saw myself yelling up at George's window that I was going to end it all, saw the glint of the straight razor as it dripped with ruby red drops, and the ambulance screaming round the corner, lights blazing blue in the darkness, come to take me away as Emily held me, the rain soaking her long dark hair, and George looked on, dripping wet with an anguished expression on his face.

"Yes, I've lost a huge part of myself this last year, and in doing so have fallen into deep despair. I am no longer living, just existing. But it isn't just the writing..."

The Society

Sonny let out a deep and troubled sigh. "It is the curse of the creative mind, I'm afraid, to be burdened with mental unrest. But we can help you."

"You really think so?"

"Oh, I'm sure of it," he looked intently into my eyes, and much like I had when staring into the fire earlier, I was once again lost to a peculiar feeling of drifting away.

"The doctors couldn't help," I found myself saying.

"What is offered here at Chyanvean is not something you will find in a doctor's office, or at the bottom of a pill bottle," he insisted. "I was just like you, an artist without a spark, miserable, depressed, full of demons, until I came here, and now look at me. I'm prolific. The ideas and the inspiration just flow from me now." He stood up and gestured to the countless paintings.

He picked up a bottle of wine which was sitting on one of the tables, topping up my glass and sitting down again.

"And you live here at the house full time now?" I took another sip of wine.

"Since I was seventeen years old," he sounded proud, "ten years now."

"Ten years?"

"Yes, Dante brought me here from Bristol."

My curiosity was piqued now. Just how did a seventeen-year-old end up in a place like this? It was very unlike me, but I found myself wanting to know more about his story.

"Is Dante a relative?" I asked.

"Goodness no!" he chuckled.

"A family friend perhaps?" I pushed. I hoped I wasn't getting too personal, but I got the impression that he *wanted* me to ask questions and draw the story out of him.

"Not quite. More a friend of a family friend. I'm not entirely sure of the connection, an acquaintance of a friend of my parents I believe. I met him at a party not long after my parents passed away." He was gazing at his glass of wine now, a reflective expression on his face.

"I see."

"Yes, they died in a car accident. Quite tragic really. By the time I met Dante as I was in the middle of throwing away my inheritance on drink and drugs and wild parties. In truth I'm still quite fond of the drink and the parties!" He laughed and drained his glass. "More wine?"

"Oh, no, I think I've had enough…"

Ignoring me, he leaned across and topped up my glass again.

"I had been accepted into art school not long before the accident," he said, "but nothing seemed to matter anymore, least of all painting, so I never attended."

"I've never really believed art can be taught anyway," I admitted, "it's too subjective, what one person finds attractive another might hate."

"And do you like *my* paintings?" he asked with a smile.

"Yes, they're very interesting," I said politely, not wanting to admit that they were not to my taste at all.

"And what about writing? Have you had any formal training?"

"No, it's just something I've always been able to do since I was a small child."

The Society

"Perhaps you're right. But it helps to have some encouragement, something to help you focus, and someone who can get you noticed, and that's what Dante did for me. If he hadn't been at that party I don't know where I would be now."

"He liked your work then, and offered you a place on one of his retreats?"

"Yes, although the workshops were not anywhere near as refined as they are now. It was in the early days; I suppose I was sort of a test subject for the techniques Dante was developing. I still remember the first time I saw him."

He stared wistfully off into the distance.

"I think I might have seen him in some photographs downstairs, he was shaking hands with Kevin Bambridge, the musician, in one of them."

"That's right, he's quite dashing, but pictures don't do him justice. Yes, I was at a party being hosted by one of my late parents' friends when I first spotted him. It was one of those high society things, you know, all posh accents and pearls and three-piece suits, people drinking Brandy, that kind of thing. I was finding the whole thing incredibly boring, then I saw him, he was standing staring at one of my paintings."

"One of *your* paintings?" I asked.

"Yes, this friend of my parents had me paint something for their hall. It wasn't very good, and to be honest I was surprised they still had it hanging up. But on seeing this striking looking man looking at it so intently, I decided I had to go and speak to him. I'm afraid I was drunk and high on God knows what and I made a bit of a fool of myself."

With that he took another hearty swig of his wine. I sipped mine slowly, hoping there would be no more unsolicited refills.

"I thought Dante was terribly handsome, you see, and I made a silly pass at him. God, it makes me cringe to think of it even after all these years."

It surprised me to hear someone talk so openly like this. My expression must have betrayed me because he hastily added, "Oh, no, I'm past all of that now, it was just a stupid phase, you know."

"Well, you were young, we all make idiots of ourselves at that age…" or at any age, I thought, trying not to picture that rainy night some months before.

"You're very kind, Quinn," he patted my knee again which made me feel slightly awkward. "Anyway, despite that, he must have seen something in me, and in my work, which made him think I was worth saving, so he brought me here. He knew that I would thrive if I was removed from all the bad influences in the city and given a calm and nurturing environment in which to work. And he was right, being here proved to be quite the tonic."

Perhaps this was exactly what I needed. Sonny's tale had caused the cogs in my head, which had been jammed for so long, to slowly start to turn again, and I began to feel a little bit of hope, like a tiny fragment of the piece of myself I had lost had been returned.

"I wonder if there could possibly be a story in this, I'm starting to see a new character, a lost young man struggling with addiction…" I hadn't meant to say it out loud.

"I think perhaps the magic is starting to work already," Sonny said as he watched me with a curious smile.

The Society

"I do feel a little better," I admitted, and, feeling bold, I added, "I wonder if you'd feel comfortable telling me more about your life before you met Dante sometime? I'm quite intrigued by the mention of these wild high society parties."

"Someone wants to write a book about me," he teased with a wink.

"No, no," I said, suddenly embarrassed and feeling my face turning red. "It's just, how I usually work is I come up with a character first. My process is odd that way. I'll meet someone I find interesting and from there I form a character in my mind and then, I, well, build them a story."

He didn't say anything, just continued to stare at me.

"I mean, usually the finished character bears no resemblance to the person who first inspired them, it's just a starting point, a sort of…" I was fumbling for words now, growing quite flustered, and I cursed myself for having drunk so much wine.

"A spark?" Sonny finished my sentence for me.

"Yes, I suppose so."

"I'm not sure I've ever been someone's spark before." There was something endearing about his crooked smile. I looked away quickly and finished the rest of my wine in one gulp.

"I'd be happy to tell you more about my younger days," he said, "but it's getting late and I think we've both had too much to drink. Anyway, before I let you go, I usually like to welcome new guests with a gift."

He crossed the room to a pile of pictures which were all painted on thick boards and leaning against the side of the desk and began to go through them.

"These would usually go for a couple of hundred in a gallery," he mused as he sifted through them. "Lesley Holmes, John Lennon, Michael Caine, all own pieces by me, you know. In fact, why take my word for it, have a glance in that cabinet over there and you'll see some pictures of me with some of my dear friends, many of whom you will recognise."

I went to take a closer look at the framed photographs behind the glass doors of the cabinet, and sure enough there was Sonny beaming out, pictured with a range of well-known actors, musicians, writers and artists.

"Ah yes, this is the one," I heard him say.

When I turned back Sonny was holding a board of about sixty centimetres squared, onto which he had painted a colourful forest with a silver path winding its way through the trees and disappearing off into the distance. The trees in the foreground were dark in hue, and the colours grew more vibrant the further into the distance they were. And of course there was a bird.

"This is perfect for you; I would like you to have it."

I was a little taken aback. That painting was not really to my taste, but it *was* artfully done, and I could see it had taken many hours and a great deal of skill to produce, and if they really were as collectable as he had me believe then this was a very kind gesture.

"Oh no, really, I couldn't."

"You can and you will," he insisted. "This picture represents the beginning of a journey, a new path from darkness into light, very appropriate, don't you think?"

"And the birds? I feel I must ask, why do they all have the same bird?"

"Why isn't the bird the perfect symbol of freedom?"

The Society

I followed him as he picked up the painting and made for the door. We made our way slightly unsteadily back down the spiral staircase, Sonny with the painting tucked under his arm.

"Magda, my lovely, would you please have this painting taken up to Mr. Bergman's room?" He addressed the receptionist when we returned to the foyer, "It is my gift to him from one creative to another, and get him another drink on the house, whatever he fancies."

I soon found myself back in the high-backed chair by the fire with a whisky in my hand, reflecting on this bizarre escapade.

"I'm going to leave you in peace now my friend, I've taken up quite enough of your time for one night," Sonny said, "but before I go, I have one more thing for you."

From his pocket he produced a brass key suspended on a long silver chain.

"This will get you into the observatory," he spoke in a low voice as if sharing a secret. "Feel free to treat the space as your own while you are here, use it whenever you need a quiet moment or some inspiration."

I took the key and turned it over in my palm, feeling that uncomfortable awkwardness pressing in on me again. Why was he giving this to me? It was heavy and the old brass was tarnished. The bow was shaped like a flower and leafy engravings of vines spiralled around the stem.

"I should probably mention that it's a skeleton key," he added in the same low tone. "It will get you into most places in the house. You'll probably never need it, but I'd suggest you keep it close, because you never know…"

Chapter 5

2009

"So that's how you met Sonny," she looked up from her notes on her subject.

Quinn looked just as nervous as he had when he first entered.

"I think perhaps I cared for him the moment I saw him," he said thoughtfully. "Stupid, isn't it? But something about him just struck a chord with me. In the weeks that followed I would often find myself in the bar with him, sitting by the fire, chatting until long into the evening."

A small smile tugged at the corner of her lips. She couldn't help but feel a warm feeling creeping over her as he described how the two of them would find themselves up long after everyone else had retired, the fire dying away to dancing embers, fine wine flowing, as they both shared stories from their past.

"Some of the things he described," Quinn had taken on a distant look, lost in his memories. "The parties, the sheer amount of money that was lavished on him growing up. Our backgrounds couldn't have been more different. He came from a wealthy family and I from modest stock who had only just lifted themselves above the working class by my father's generation. He attended a prestigious boarding school, his every whim met by his overindulgent parents, while I went to the local comprehensive. And yet he suffered from many of the same troubles that I did. He'd led me to believe on the first night that it was the death of his parents that had started him on the downward spiral, but it began before that. He was already experimenting with drugs long before the accident. In recent years I myself had been abusing alcohol as a way to deal with my feelings, and that was just one of the things we had in common. We were both bullied as youngsters and grew up feeling we were somehow different. We had both been through unsuccessful and unfulfilling relationships with the opposite sex. We had both lost our families, albeit in very different ways- his had passed away while mine had disowned me- and we both found something in Chyanvean that we thought we'd never have again; a family…"

Quinn trailed off. He was getting ahead of himself.

"Anyway," he said briskly, "you must think me a terrible, gullible fool to have just run off like that to take part in something in which I had no idea what was involved!"

"There is really no need to be so harsh on yourself," she said, "this is always how these things start, it's been seen time and time again. A person who has grown dissatisfied with his life will often make snap decisions and jump at a chance that seems to offer him a change, something more than his current lifestyle is providing, and predators can always spot the weak."

"But I can't to this day tell you how it happened, how I allowed myself to be taken in like I was, and so quickly. It was as if the moment I entered that damned place I was bewitched or something. It was like wandering into a thick fog that impairs all your rational senses…" he faltered and shook his head in frustration.

"They know the types to prey on," she reassured him, "none of this was your fault."

"Maybe not," he admitted, "it's incredible that something so small as an ad in a magazine can change your whole life. Do you know that I still have nightmares about the whole thing? I feel like I've never stopped running from it."

"This is why it's important to talk about it," she encouraged, "especially now that so many people like you are coming forward. You've been living for years without any kind of closure, and this is your chance to get that."

"Part of me knew something was amiss from the very start. I woke up in the middle of the night that first night, filled with panic, and sat bolt upright with the most horrible feeling that I was making a terrible mistake. I felt fine again by the morning, but there was always something a little off about the place. It was like a beautiful, calm river that hides a vicious, dark under current. Part of you knows what is waiting beneath, but the water just looks so inviting, and in you go, only to be sucked under and never seen again. That's what happened to me when I entered Chyanvean. I really should have listened to George; he knew something wasn't right."

"Often when a person objects to something we want to do it just makes the whole thing seem even more appealing," she interjected. "Perhaps it *was* a little rash to run off like that without really knowing what you were getting into, but your urge to get away was perfectly understandable, and this just provided a convenient way to do so."

He seemed to relax a little more and he sat back in his chair. Everything she was saying was exactly what he had told himself over the years, and he felt vindicated in hearing another person confirm it. He was starting to warm to this woman. She seemed kind and non-

The Society

judgmental. That had been his worst fear when he had agreed to take part in this interview, that he would be ridiculed, laughed at and questioned as to how anyone could be such a complete idiot. Of course, signing up to a little self-help course for artists was a minor thing compared to the catastrophic levels of stupidity he would stoop to in the time following this. Still, her calm supportive nature gave him hope that he might actually get through this, and somehow, he found the strength to continue.

Raven Taylor
Chapter 6

1965

The next morning, as I looked out across the grey October day at the dramatic, craggy coastline, my anxieties had faded like morning dew, and I was once again convinced that this was a good place for me to be. It was the perfect escape from the city, and if it offered help for troubled people like myself, then surely that was a good thing.

As for the painting that Sonny had given me, I was not sure that it would really fit in my London flat. It was, however, exactly the kind of thing Emily liked, and I decided I would send it to her as a gift. Dear, sweet Emily, my childhood friend, who had been so forgiving when I broke off our engagement. I retrieved some paper from the desk and my fountain pen from my luggage, intending to pen a letter to her over breakfast.

There were a handful of diners in the breakfast room when I arrived. The waiter, a young chap in a cream linen suit, showed me to a table by the window where I could once again gaze out at the sea. I noted that the birdsong was still being piped from the speakers in the corners of the room. I ordered a full English, and once I had finished eating, I started on my letter while sipping a strong black coffee.

My Dear Emily,

I hope this letter finds you well. I myself am feeling quite improved already. Chyanvean is quite an impressive place, and I believe I am due to start on my course tomorrow.

The Society

Anyway, you will see that I have sent you a rather curious painting. It was given to me last night by this odd chap who is apparently the artist in residence here. He told me he has been helped greatly by the programs at the house. He tells me that his work is quite sought after, and he showed me some pictures of himself with various celebrities whom he claims collect his paintings, but I would take all of that with a pinch of salt, I doubt they are worth what he would have me believe or else he would hardly be giving them away to strangers just for signing up to a course! All in all, he was a very intriguing fellow. It was a very surreal first evening, I don't think I've quite got the measure of the place yet, but I think there might just be something in what he said- I think the place may have inspired the beginnings of a story! Tell George all may not be lost, I might have some new work for him soon.

All my love
Quinn

After breakfast I decided I should probably call George and let him know that I had arrived, and that so far everything seemed to be ok, if a little surreal, and that I had survived my first night without anything untoward happening.

As I was returning to my room I found Ethel, the elderly lady Sonny had chatted with the previous evening, sitting alone in the guest lounge. Her tiny, frail figure looked absurd sitting in the high-backed chair at the head of the massive, carved table. I noticed that she was swaying back and forward slightly, and waving one hand as if she were moving to music only she could hear. I approached her, but she did not acknowledge me or stop her swaying even as I came up right beside her. She had a dazed look on her wrinkled old face and the corners of her thin mouth were turned up in a blissful smile.

"Are you alright?" I questioned and she turned her head to look at me, still swaying.

"Oh yes," her smile widened, "it's such a wonderful feeling to have all of the negative thoughts just plucked from your head. So freeing! That's why I come here!"

I considered the possibility that she was perhaps a bit senile and decided to leave her to it.

I thought I would take a walk into the village to find a post office so I could send the painting off, and I should probably try and find out a bit more about this course I had signed up for too.

When I returned to reception with the letter and the painting to ask about the course, I was approached by a tall gentleman in an expensive-looking three-piece suit who I guessed to be in his mid-forties. He had black hair which was oiled back so not a single hair was out of place, a pencil moustache, and piercing blue eyes which unashamedly looked me up and down. I began to feel quite shabby in comparison in my worn tweed jacket with the loose threads hanging at the sleeves. Then he broke into a wide grin which revealed rows of perfect white teeth.

"Mr. Bergman!" he addressed me with an eloquent voice that echoed around the foyer. "It is a pleasure to meet you and add you to our list of famous guests."

"I wouldn't exactly say I was famous," I said, shaking his hand.

"Maybe not yet," he agreed, "but perhaps you could be. I understand you are a writer, how fascinating! To be able to pull stories from thin air is quite a gift. But where are my manners? I am Dante Lewin-May, and I

The Society

welcome you to Chyanvean. I hope your stay with us so far has been pleasant?"

Sonny was right. The pictures did not do him justice. In the flesh he was far more impressive, his presence seeming to dominate the room, towering and tall and so immaculately turned out. He left me feeling a little intimidated.

"Yes, it's quite an impressive place," I managed to say.

"Isn't it? When I saw it come up for sale I just had to have it, especially given its history and who built it. It was just what my wife and I were looking for, it's perfect for our project."

"Project?"

"You mean you don't know about the work my wife and I carry out?" he grinned.

"If you mean the residential courses then I'm actually here to take part in one."

"Excellent, I am very pleased to hear this. If you'd like to come with me I can give you a little more information about what we do here."

"Actually, I was just about to go for a walk into the village," I told him.

"The village? Oh, you don't want to bother with that. I don't want to sound unkind, but St Morlyn is an odd little place, a very tight knit community, funny and suspicious when it comes to outsiders. They were not overly welcoming to myself and my wife when we came to the house, despite all our efforts to help the community. In fact, they are unfriendly and downright rude when it comes to anyone who wasn't born here."

I found this a little strange as so far I had found the Cornish people to be nothing but accommodating and pleasant.

"Unfriendly or not, I need to go to the post office so I can send this off to a friend of mine in London."

"Don't worry about that, Magda will have it wrapped and sent out with the hotel mail," he insisted, before folding his arms and saying in good humour, "though I'm not sure how Sonny will feel about you giving away his gift to you."

"Oh, it's just that it's exactly the kind of thing my friend likes and…" I felt my face growing red.

"I'm only jesting my good man," he chuckled as he took the painting and the envelope from my hand, "it's yours to do with what you will, I hope it will bring your friend much joy."

He handed it across the desk to Magda, glancing at the envelope and adding, "A lady friend. Are you romantically attached?"

"Not exactly, it's complicated."

"Human affairs usually are," he said knowingly. "There, now you are free to indulge me, come, let me show you the study room, you should know where it is if you are going to be attending our program."

"Yes, about that, when exactly does it start? How is it structured? Is there a timetable?"

He put a hand on my shoulder and guided me across the foyer.

"The Program starts whenever the time is right. Some might even say it began the moment you arrived."

He took me through a door off the foyer which was marked with the words 'SOS Department of Study and Well Being' and down a long corridor papered in green and decorated with more of Sonny's paintings. We passed a lot of closed doors, all with gold plaques (a few of which I managed to read: 'Cleansing Room,' 'Workshop,' 'Admissions'), before we finally came to one marked 'Study Room.' I was quite surprised when I

The Society

was first shown into the study room. What I had seen of the house so far had all been traditionally decorated in period style; all dark colours, fancy silk wallpaper, antique furniture, but the study room's decor was rather jarring in contrast. Everything was white, the floors, the walls, the furniture. There were also no paintings here, just a small reproduction of a portrait of a stern-looking Victorian gentleman. One of the walls was lined with bookcases filled with books which were all uniform in size with white spines printed with gold text. There were ten desks, each with a plastic chair, all of which were also white, and the lights were bright and clinical.

"Quite different, isn't it?" Dante must have caught the surprised look on my face. "We find it's best to have minimal distractions when learning how to apply our methods. Sit here."

He pulled out a chair from a desk in the front row, and I took my seat obediently as he went to the bookshelf. He came back with a white ring binder and a cardboard documents wallet. He pulled out a pen and wrote my name on the front of the folder.

"This will be your file," he said, "it's where we will keep track of your progress within the program. There's a form you need to fill in to officially sign up."

"All right."

"Have a read of this," he put the ring binder down in front of me. "When you're done, if you still want to sign up, just fill in the form in your folder. If for any reason you don't think the program is for you, then you are free to leave, no hard feelings."

Just then there was a knock at the door, and a young girl in a maid's uniform entered carrying a tray with a pot of tea. She sat it down on the desk next to me without looking at either of us and gave a nervous little bow to Dante before backing out of the room.

"Such good staff we have here," Dante remarked, "all hand-picked by my lovely wife. We're just like one big happy family. I'll leave you to it, I'll be back very soon."

He opened the door, but before leaving he turned to me and added, "You really could do great things Quinn, with a little help."

It all felt a bit strange, but I was curious, thinking if nothing else I could at least write about my experiences here at a later date. I opened the ring binder and began to read. The first page was an introduction to the house. There was a little bit of historical information about the construction, and a message of welcome from Dante and his family urging guests to treat Chyanvean like a home rather than a hotel. There was a family photograph of Dante, a beautiful red-haired woman who I assumed was his wife, Kerrigan, and a little girl of about seven who could only be their daughter given the strong resemblance between her and Dante. Next was a passage about the family themselves and the courses offered at the house.

Dante and Kerrigan Lewin-May bought the house in 1948. They were both fans of the writings of William Thomas, especially his texts on the importance of the creative arts in society, treatment of mental illness, and his unique programs for self-help and spiritual betterment, which he developed using his own experiences while traveling in India. When his estate, including all of his original works, was put up for sale, Dante and Kerrigan were keen to obtain it. Later generations of the Thomas family had shown little interest in their ancestors' works, and the couple thought it important his legacy be taken into the care of those who appreciated it. They

The Society

were able to purchase the house with the help of good friend James-Anthony Broadbent. Although not a permanent resident in the house, James-Anthony played a crucial part in helping the couple to sift through the extensive original texts written by William Thomas and make his teachings and philosophies more accessible and more workable within the modern world. These writings, which are still housed in Chyanvean's library, form the basis of the self-help programs offered today.

The couple soon discovered that the wealth of knowledge contained in these texts was not the only thing that could be utilised in helping creative people overcome the range of conditions that can hold them back from their work, but the house itself has a sort of subtle magic that seems to inspire creativity. Because of this, it was decided that this special place should be made available for all to enjoy, and so it was opened up as a hotel and retreat for artists with a range of valuable courses and workshops that make up The Program for Better Living.

In wider society the teachings of The Program have been made available in various centres outside of the house. Whilst the courses offered at Chyanvean focus on helping artists, the outreach centres offer alternative forms of help for all kinds of problems such as addiction and mental health issues, this side of things being handled by James-Anthony. In 1960 The Program for Better Living was granted charitable status for the good work it carries out in local communities. All of this is thanks to the remarkable discoveries and knowledge of William Thomas.

"I can't say I've ever heard of it," I muttered to myself, pouring myself a cup of tea.

The rest of the folder I just flicked through. It was mainly just more detailed information on the various courses offered as part of The Program for Better Living, both the ones available in the hotel and ones held at various other sites. Which one was it I had agreed to sign up for anyway? Leaving the binder sitting open, I picked up the file with my name on it. Inside was a slip of paper which said that I was agreeing to take part in the 'relighting the creative spark' course. I thumbed through the binder to see if I could find anything about this particular course.

"Ah, here we are, 'relighting the creative spark.'" The description was brief and read as follows.

We know that there comes a time in every creative person's life when the spark seems to go out. But do not fear, the spark has rarely gone for good and this course will equip you with the tools to ensure whenever that spark dwindles you can effectively identify why and tackle the problem in a practical and effective way, restoring your ability to create. Many have found that this course not only teaches the creative mind to overcome such obstacles but can actually enhance your talents far beyond what they were, rebuilding your confidence in your work and ensuring you will achieve success beyond anything you have had before in your chosen career. Here are just a few of our well-known participants who have gone on to have glittering careers after applying the skills taught in this program.

"Surely not," I said to myself in disbelief as I read the list of well-known actors, musicians and writers, "this can't be true, it's just a marketing ploy."

But most of these people were in the pictures Sonny showed you last night, so maybe there's some truth in it, and if it's a marketing ploy, why are they offering their services for free?

The Society

Chapter 7

1965

Dante returned to the study room shortly after I was done reading the brochure and drinking the tea.

"Well?" he enquired, "How did you get on?"

"It all seems very interesting; it certainly seems like you and your good wife are very generous and do a lot of good work."

"We do, we do," he agreed. "When a person is born into money like myself, I feel it is one's responsibility to help out wherever one can. It's only right to give something back after all and bringing the invaluable teachings of William Thomas to the wider public, and opening my house to people who have creative potential is just my way of doing that. It keeps me humble. Money should be used for good if you have it. Just look at Sonny. I'm sure he's filled you in on what a hopeless predicament he was in when we found him, and we've thankfully been able to cure him of his addictions and give him a life free from the misery in which he existed. He's since very much become a part of our family."

"Yes, he did mention that. It was very good of you to take him in."

"Thank you. I would very much like you to meet my wife, would you like to join us in our private quarters for dinner tonight? I like to get to know a person a little before we begin our course work, so I can tailor the sessions to fit them individually, that is if you are still planning on taking part?"

The Society

He picked up my folder and the sign-up sheet and nodded in satisfaction at my signature.

"Yes, I still plan to take part and I would love to join you for dinner."

"Excellent," he smiled as he tucked my completed form into my file and picked up the ring-binder. "Come down to the bar at 7.30 then and I'll meet you there."

After we parted company I returned to my room, as I was overcome by the sudden urge to write. It was such a welcome feeling after so long, like the return of a much-loved absent friend. What happened when I sat down at that desk by the window with my notebook and pen was quite remarkable.

For a year now, every time I sat down in front of a blank page, be it my old typewriter or a notebook, I had been gripped by a sense of sheer panic. A sick feeling would wash over me, and I would feel as if the page were mocking me, and there I would sit, for hours and hours, but the words would not come. The fear that the words would not come grew and multiplied over the months to the point where I couldn't even look at a blank page without feeling ill. I had fully believed that I was doomed, yet when I sat down at that desk I found that at last the words came.

A couple of hours passed and I did not pause. It was over, and I was filled with joy, the horrible block had been broken at long last. I was so excited that I rushed downstairs to the telephone in the foyer to call George. His receptionist answered and put me straight through.

"Hello Quinn," said a familiar voice, "it's good to hear from you, I'm glad you called, Emily was getting worried that you'd fallen foul of some horrible scheme down there. How is it?"

"It's a little unusual so far," I found myself admitting. "The house itself is beautiful, my hosts are all rather eccentric. I met this artist fellow last night who lives here in the house, an odd chap, but he does paint the most remarkable pieces. He insisted on showing me his studio where he works, which was in this big glass domed observatory at the top of a tower."

"Sounds interesting."

"It was a little bit awkward if I'm honest, I seemed to be the only one out of all the people in the bar singled out and given this private tour, and he kept giving me wine, I ended up a little drunk."

"Perhaps he took a liking to you," I could almost hear the smile in George's voice.

"Either way, he did give me an idea for a new character," I could hardly keep the excitement out of my voice. "And you know how it goes with me once I get a character in my head…"

"Yes, I've always thought your way of working was a bit unusual. Didn't you tell me the whole idea for 'Marked for Sorrow' came from the ten minutes you spent talking to some woman you ran into in a coffee shop?"

"Yes, in Camden Town, she was remarkably interesting, and that's all it took, Arabella Swan was born and from there the whole story just grew around her."

"Well, let's hope something similar happens this time."

"But it already has!" I said happily. "I'm actually writing again George."

"Quinn, that's fantastic news, it makes me so glad to hear that."

The Society

"It's this place, there's just something about it."

"This is truly the best news; I don't think I've heard you sound so happy in months."

We chatted a little more, George telling me about a new author he was working with and me describing some of the places I had stayed on my way down to Cornwall. It was the easiest and most natural conversation we had had since *the incident* last year, and we talked like we always had without there being any of the underlying awkwardness there had been of late.

"I'll be in touch to let you know how things are going," I said as we wrapped up our conversation. "Oh, and give my love to Emily, won't you? Tell her to watch the post, I've sent her a little something from this place. Anyway, I best get going, I'll be in touch."

After I hung up, feeling like I needed some air, and knowing that I would be dining at the house with Dante and his family that evening, I decided to ignore the warning and have lunch in the village. I had a bracing walk along the coastal path which snaked along the high cliffs and eventually wound its way down to the harbour and the village. All around me seabirds cried as they wheeled overhead in the endless, clear sky. The path was rather steep and rocky in places. At times, it seemed to come perilously close to the edge where the land fell away and the sheer cliff face plummeted dizzyingly down to the jagged rocks below. The waves rolled in and clashed with the rocks, their foamy jaws waiting for me to put a foot wrong and come crashing down so they could consume me, their voices echoing through the caves in the cove below. It brought to my mind images of wreckers and smugglers, of stranded ships caught on the rocks and cargos being loaded onto waiting carts by grisly characters who would batter to death any survivors that came ashore. It would be impossible not to be inspired by such a place.

The village of St Morlyn was a pretty little place, and I was able to take it in better than I had from the car the day before. Squat little fisherman's cottages hunkered down and braced themselves against the elements, weather worn and hardy little structures that I imagined would be quite cosy inside once a fire was lit in the hearth. Around the harbour, lobster pots were stacked and little coloured fishing boats bobbed peacefully on the gentle waves of their safe haven, waiting for the next morning when they would bravely forge a path out to sea. At the very end of the harbour was an old clock tower, standing proudly as if it were the gatekeeper to the village, an ever-observant watchman and last line of defence against the ocean. And looking over it all, a looming and ever dominating presence high on the cliffs, was Chyanvean House. It struck me at that moment how out of place the grand structure looked in such quaint surroundings. From this distance its dominating presence seemed somehow threatening. I found myself staring at it. A sudden gust of wind sent a handful of autumn leaves scuttling into the gutter and I pulled the collar of my coat up and hurried on.

Soon I found a pub called The Red Lion, which had a board outside stating that they served food. It was gaily decorated with many bright hanging baskets of late violas and looked quite inviting. Just what I was looking for.

Inside it was a typical country inn with bare stone walls, low ceilings with varnished beams, and collections of maritime memorabilia such as old lobster pots, ship compasses, gas lanterns and old pieces of rope hanging from the ceiling and stuck to the walls. Perched

The Society

on the edge of the bar was an old-fashioned diver's helmet and a bowl with a goldfish swimming about inside it. There were a few people enjoying lunch, and a lady behind the bar called to me to take a seat, telling me she would bring me over a menu.

I settled down in the corner and the plump barmaid with a shock of blonde hair brought me a leather-bound menu.

"What can I get you to drink?" she asked in a strong Cornish accent.

"Do you have any local ciders?"

"We have a Cornish scrumpy?"

"Yes, I'll have a pint of that please."

"Of course, I'll be back over dreckly."

While she was away getting me my drink a voice addressed me, asking, "On holiday, are you?"

I looked up from my menu to see an old man in a knitted fisherman's smock and a wooly hat sitting by the fire. At his feet lay a shaggy dog stretched out, enjoying the heat from the flames.

"Something like that, though it's turning out to be a bit of a working holiday actually, I'm writing a book you see."

"A book, eh? Staying locally?" His face was craggy and lined, grizzled from countless mornings spent out at sea. There were wisps of white hair curling from beneath his hat and his watery eyes seemed to look at me with a hint of suspicion.

"For now, yes, up at Chyanvean House."

The man scowled and turned abruptly away, standing up and muttering to himself as he shuffled towards the bar where he began to whisper to the blonde-haired woman. Then the barmaid strode briskly back to my table, her friendly smile had vanished.

"I'm sorry sir but we don't have any cider left."

"That's all right, I'll just have a pint of bitter instead, and I think I'm ready to order," I wondered why her attitude had suddenly changed. What had the old fellow said to her?

She pursed her lips and looked distinctly uncomfortable.

"I'm sorry sir but you've just missed lunch, we've stopped serving now, we're just getting ready to close for the afternoon."

"That's absurd, you just gave me a menu!" I protested, baffled.

"I'm sorry, I must have lost track of time, but we really are closing."

Confused, I watched as a young waitress brought out plates of food to a young couple at another table.

"Well, I know when I'm not welcome!" I stood up and gathered up my coat.

"I'm sure they'll feed you at the house," the old man who had addressed me earlier said, before adding, spitting out the last word like an angry, venomous snake, "and good luck with the *book*."

The Society

Raven Taylor
Chapter 8

1965

In the end I got a pasty from the bakery, being careful not to mention where I was staying or that I was writing a book and ate it on a bench on the cliff tops. On returning to Chyanvean I spent the afternoon blissfully lost in my newly emerging work, scribbling away like a man possessed until dinner time stole upon me out of nowhere, and it was time to get changed to meet with Dante.

I had not really brought anything fancy to wear, and I wondered if I would be expected to dress for dinner. I made my way down to the bar, once again feeling inadequate in my slightly worn and creased clothes, and a little nervous about having dinner with such wealthy and fancy people. What on earth would we talk about? I reasoned that we probably had nothing in common, and I was bound to make a fool of myself in some way by saying the wrong thing, which is if my neglected appearance didn't do that for me first. I found myself wondering when I last had a haircut. Was there too much stubble on my face? Were my shoes too scuffed? When did I last polish them anyway? I told myself to stop being so ridiculous.

Dante was already there when I reached the bar, sitting on a stool and looking as dapper as ever in his blue suit and perfectly groomed hair which made me feel self-conscious all over again.

"Ah my dear friend," he greeted me, standing up and shaking my hand. "I trust you have had a pleasant day?"

The Society

Without asking he poured a glass of wine from the open bottle he had sitting on the bar and handed it to me.

"I'm afraid I went against your advice and went into the village," I confessed. "It was most peculiar. I went into the pub, The Red Lion, to get some lunch. At first everything was fine, then suddenly the land lady came out with some nonsense about forgetting the time and them being just about to close. Funny because her attitude seemed to change as soon as I mentioned I was staying here."

"I did warn you," Dante shook his head. "The locals of St Morlyn are prejudiced and small minded. They don't take too kindly to outsiders, especially outsiders with money."

"Is that so?"

"Yes. They took great offence for some reason when we purchased Chyanvean, wanting it to remain in the possession of locals or something, as if any of them could ever hope to be able to afford such a place!" he scoffed, shaking his head. "But we were generous, opened our doors and tried to share it with them, even offered residents of the village free places on our programs, hosted a Christmas ball and invited everyone in the village."

"It does sound like you made an effort."

"A huge effort! But do you think any of them took us up on the offers?" He paused and ran a hand over his oiled hair as if to check it was still sitting perfectly. "No, too bloody stubborn and ignorant, they'd rather hold their petty grudges than allow themselves to take advantage and actually come and enjoy the place. It's sad really."

"But what does that have to do with me? I'm just a guest staying here. Surely, they don't object to tourism and the money it must bring in."

"I'm afraid this grudge runs so deep that they tend to shun anyone associated with us!"

"That hardly seems fair."

"It doesn't, does it?" he shrugged. "How was your day other than that?"

"Wonderful, actually. I had been suffering from the most hideous period of writer's block, then today I started writing again, just like that."

"Well, I'm not surprised," Dante said, "Chyanvean has that effect on people. Come now, dinner will be nearly ready and I'd like to introduce you to the family."

The east wing of the house apparently held the Lewin-May's private living quarters. I was taken to a large formal dining room where the table was set for dinner with extravagant silver candlesticks and expensive china and crystal glasses, and I began to feel quite out of place. The lighting was soft, and a fire crackled in the hearth, sending shadows dancing across the waxed floorboards and the thick rug.

"Darling?" There was a tall, slender woman standing with her back to us at the far end of the room by the window, Dante's wife, Kerrigan, no doubt. She turned at the sound of his voice, "I'd like you to meet Quinn Bergman, the writer I was telling you about."

The woman stepped forward. She was exceptionally beautiful with her olive toned skin and waves of auburn hair that fell about her shoulders. Dante sidled over to her and put an arm around her waist. As the two of them stood, side by side, each grinning and showing rows of perfect white teeth, I

The Society

thought they looked like they could have stepped off a red carpet in Hollywood.

"I'm delighted to meet you Mr. Bergman," she said.

"Please, Quinn will be fine."

"All right, Quinn, I'm Kerrigan," she said and we shook hands.

"And where is Astrid?" Dante asked.

"Astrid is our daughter," Kerrigan informed me. "Astrid is with Sonny, I'm sure they will be along soon."

So, the artist was going to be joining us. The news pleased me, I had hoped to see him again. As she spoke the dining room door opened and Sonny entered. I felt myself relax because I was no longer the shabbiest person in the room. His wavy copper hair was all messed up, and his shirt sleeves were rolled up to the elbows, his top button was undone and there were splashes of paint on his clothes. At his side was a little girl in a green pinafore with her hair tied up in a matching ribbon. She too was spotted with daubs of paint.

"Ah, Quinn," said Sonny, "it's good to see you again, I'm so glad that you're joining us for dinner."

"Nice to see you again too. And what's your name?" I asked the girl.

"I'm Astrid," she said and she did the most adorable little curtsy.

"I'm very glad to meet you. I'm Quinn. Your parents have kindly invited me to dinner tonight, I hope that's ok with you?"

She smiled and nodded, "you can sit here."

She took my hand and guided me to the chair to the left of the head of the table.

"Papa always sits at the head, Mama at his right, the guest of the evening on his left, me next to the guest and Sonny next to Mama."

"That's right my love, that's how we do it," Sonny pulled out my chair and motioned for me to sit.

"So, I am the guest of the evening?" I said as I sat down.

"Oh yes," Astrid confirmed, taking her place next to me, "we always try to find someone we like among the guests and then ask them to join us at our table. Someone with a creative mind Papa says, so we can learn a little more about them and see how we can help."

"Do you think I need help?" I asked.

"Everyone needs help," Dante interjected as he took his place at the head of the table.

The same young man who had served me at breakfast came into the room and poured wine for us all.

"Dante tells me you are here to take part in the restoring the creative spark course," Kerrigan said. "A wise choice. Do you know we tackle problems such as yours by addressing all aspects of your life? Generally if the creative process has ground to a halt it tends to be because of other negative things in one's life, bad influences and such, toxic people, the wrong environment. It really is a must to identify what it is that a person is struggling with and provide them with the means to tackle it."

"If you don't mind me asking, why do you do it? If the courses are as good as you say they are, why do you not charge for them?" That had come out wrong and I was afraid I had offended them. "Sorry, I didn't mean it like that, it's just there's so few people in the world who would do something simply out of the goodness of their hearts. Not that I'm saying that isn't exactly why you do it…"

The Society

"Not all of our courses and services are free, only some, and only to a certain kind of person. But as I explained earlier, we don't want for anything, we have enough wealth to keep us in our accustomed lifestyle with bags left over, and we are both very, very passionate about the arts," Dante informed me. "Can you imagine a world without art, music, literature, theatre? Life simply would not be worth living. Yet our society, our government, seems hell bent on crushing the arts with a program of systematic neglect."

"So very true," Sonny nodded sagely.

"It starts when our young people are at school," Dante continued. "Everything is geared towards maths and science and preparing for a mundane career. Children are not encouraged to use their imaginations, instead they are expected from an early age to conform, their natural free spirits are broken to make them good little citizens."

I could relate to what he said. I remember being told by a teacher at school that I should stop daydreaming and start living in the real world when I mentioned that I would like to be a writer. At home, I was constantly being told off by my father for spending too much time reading novels and writing stories. I should be focusing on getting myself a real career, not wasting my time on such fanciful things.

"That's why we homeschool Astrid," Dante gave his daughter a smile and continued. "And it goes on for the rest of your life. No one encourages you to go out and be a writer or an artist, they steer you towards far more menial careers, because it suits them to have everyone meek and under the thumb and not thinking too much."

Raven Taylor

"I know exactly what you mean," I told him. The young waiter had returned and was dishing out bowls of soup. "My father pushed me into a job at the bank where he worked as soon as I left school and it was excruciating. I hated every minute of it."

"I can only imagine someone as remarkable as you would have felt stifled, would have wilted like a hothouse plant out in the cold in such an environment," Kerrigan observed.

"I think that accurately sums up how it was. I felt like life was being slowly sucked out of me, I almost went mad from boredom. Thankfully, it didn't last long as a good friend of mine had started working as an editor at a small publishing house, and with his contacts I had soon released my first novel and was able to leave the bank, much to my father's disapproval. Despite my initial success he still insisted it was not a reliable career choice, it was liable to crumble and leave me with nothing to fall back on."

"Do you know why our government is so keen to keep suppressing creativity among its citizens? Because it keeps the population dumb, stops them from having free thoughts and ideas of their own, makes them into good little drones for the factories, the shipyards, the mines," Dante banged his fist on the table angrily.

"I suppose I've never thought of it that way," I said as I sipped my soup.

"But you escaped the machine," he told me earnestly, "your creative spark was so strong it could not be put out."

He kept using that phrase, 'creative spark,' over and over, they all did, like it was some kind of mantra.

"It must have been wonderful to have such an opportunity," Kerrigan said, "people who have escaped the system with their creative mind intact are very

The Society

special indeed, our world needs them, and that's why we feel so strongly about helping them. Be that by encouraging alternative ways to educate our children or helping people like yourself to get back on track when they become a little stuck."

"I'm glad to be a part of it, the world is a better place with such generous and caring people in it like yourselves," I said.

"Here's to your next great piece of work then," Dante raised his glass.

"May it be your best work yet," Kerrigan added.

"And to the start of new friendships," Sonny chimed in.

We all clinked glasses, even little Astrid with her glass of apple juice.

Throughout the main course the conversation was a little more casual and relaxed. General, getting to know you, small talk, which usually I would do anything to avoid, but with these people seemed easy and natural. I learned that Dante had inherited his vast fortune from his father and his hugely successful engineering business. Kerrigan was apparently of Polish descent. They did not say where they met. I found their company to be very pleasant, and they were easy to talk to so that I found myself freely offering up details about my own life, much as I had with Sonny the previous night. This was most unlike me, as anyone who knows me will tell you that I am generally quite shy and often socially anxious, but it was as if I were among trusted company, and I felt entirely at ease.

I told them all about growing up in London with my father working in the bank, and about my younger sister who had passed away when she was only five. I told them about my relationship with Emily and, without going into specifics. I talked about how I had always written little stories even as a child, and about George and his job at the publishing company. I even told them how George and Emily had become a couple since the two of us separated.

"Yet you all remained friends?" Sonny enquired. He had been relatively quiet and unengaged throughout the meal but he suddenly looked interested. "That must have been very difficult for you."

"In a way yes, it was. But the three of us grew up together and had always been very close, and the nature of our separation was, well, complicated..."

Sonny raised a knowing eyebrow, tilting his head to one side, and pausing with his fork hovering above his plate. I stopped myself. I couldn't believe I had almost been about to tell them some of my most private secrets.

I had first had suspicions that I might be gay when I was around 13 years old and began to develop feelings for George. Admitting such a thing in those days would have been unthinkable so I eventually struck up a relationship with Emily in an effort to have a normal life. It was true that I did love her dearly, and so I convinced myself that I could make things work with her, and that perhaps I was not gay after all, merely just a confused adolescent. I told myself what I felt for George in my youth could be put down to a sort of hero worship, for he was everything I was not; confident, handsome, strong and athletic, intelligent, well liked and would heroically come to my defence whenever I was jumped upon by local bullies. In contrast I was the thin, weedy one who loved books more than sport, was always plagued by anxiety, and suffered from panic attacks. I found it surprising that Emily preferred me to George when it came to romance. I told myself I should

The Society

consider myself lucky that such an attractive and wonderful girl was interested in me. It was as if I was being thrown a lifeline by someone, a chance to save myself from drowning in my own immoral thoughts. Our relationship lasted three years. I even asked her to marry me, but that was just a desperate, last-ditch attempt at a normal life, because by that point, my secret feelings for George were threatening to consume me.

Sonny was still staring at me across the table, but when it became apparent I was not going to elaborate further he looked down and started eating again.

"I think perhaps you should tell me about this in more detail some time," Dante suggested, "it looks like it is something that still troubles you, and helping you to dispel the demons that are interfering with your work is one of the things we are here to help you with."

"I recommend it," Sonny said, "Dante is a wonderful listener, he has this way of looking at things, at people, and at life and its problems, and seeing them in a way that no one else can. From there he is able to gain a unique perspective that few have and give the most superbly helpful insights. You'll come out of a session with Dante feeling so much lighter, so much more focused and generally happier and more at peace. He's done far more for me than any doctor ever could!"

"Such high praise Sonny, you're embarrassing me," Dante smiled. "But doctors, like our government, and in particular mental health professionals, are just out to suppress us, keep us quiet, nice, easy to manage cogs in the bigger machine. But here we operate a machine of our own and ours is run on love and compassion. Tell me Quinn, with all your troubles have you ever had any dealings with the mental health profession?"

Raven Taylor

I thought of the bottle of pills in my luggage upstairs. I would not usually dream of sharing my medical history with strangers, and yet I once again felt oddly compelled to do so.

"I've had my bouts of depression for which I've sought treatment," I admitted.

"And you were given drugs I assume?"

"Yes."

"As I thought. Any electroshock therapy?"

"No, nothing like that, just a short hospital stay."

"Tell me my friend, when was the last time you felt truly alive?" Sonny leaned forward, studying me again.

The smart young waiter was clearing away our main course dishes and no one paid him any mind. I considered how the drugs made me feel numb, how I held them part to blame for my recent inability to create.

"I think that's enough of the serious chat for now," Kerrigan said before I could answer and Sonny sat back, looking a little annoyed.

But his question had me thinking. When *had* I last felt truly alive?

The Society

Chapter 9

1965

Off the same corridor as the study room, was another room called 'The Disclosure Room.' It was very similar in decor to the study room, with everything being white, but it was much smaller in size, and almost claustrophobic. I was sitting at the single table and Dante was sitting across from me with the file he had assigned to me, an open textbook, a stack of some kind of cards, and a notepad and pen. There was also a metronome on the table, and a small pocket tape recorder.

I was summoned early that morning, woken by a loud rap on the door at the ungodly hour of five am. After dinner the previous night I had found myself once again alone with Sonny, sitting by the fire in the guest lounge, talking until late. It was past midnight when I finally retired and I did not appreciate being woken so early. I was groggy and irritable as I opened the door to find Magda who told me curtly that I was to get dressed and follow her, that it was time for me to begin the program. She had taken me to the small white room where Dante was waiting.

Before he had sat down, Dante had left me alone in the room with a pot of tea, which I drank, to read over a page in a textbook which he had set before me. As expected, the writing was by William Thomas, and was a list entitled 'Common Misdeeds of Mankind'. There was a short explanation which informed me that the following was a list of acts and conditions which would negatively impact a person's life and should be avoided at all costs and dealt with if already committed. It stated it was by no means an exhaustive list, and there could be other things in a person considered 'immoral', and that it was up to the practitioner leading the disclosure to identify any other potential 'blocks.' Some of them did not differ so much from those considered to be 'sins' in the Christian faith. Some were more bizarre and seemed to make little sense at all. It read as follows:

- *Taking that which is not given.*
- *The taking of mind-altering drugs (mild stimulants such as caffeine or alcohol are acceptable)*
- *Sexual misconduct*
- *Associating with 'non-beings'*
- *Telling lies*
- *Suicide*
- *Homosexuality*
- *Delusional emotional attachment*
- *Suppression of one's own or another's creative spark*

Dante was back within a few minutes, and he took the book from me and leafed through it to find the page he needed. There was something oppressive about the atmosphere in that room and Dante looked very serious.

"Now then," I shuffled uncomfortably in my seat as he spoke, "we are about to take the first step in The Program for Better Living. No matter what particular course within the program the participant is currently taking part in, this is a common first stage which everyone has to undergo, called disclosure."

My mouth was dry. I tried to nod to show I was listening but I felt strangely disconnected from my own body.

Raven Taylor

"Disclosure is necessary for everyone to move forward and tackle their problems," he continued, "whether the end goal is enhanced creativity, spiritual enlightenment or something else, none of the other tools or guidance will be effective unless the main transgressions and misdeeds of a person's life are dealt with. Disclosure will be a regular part of your time on the program for the duration of your participation, and throughout any and all courses you may choose to study."

He glanced down at the textbook. I was starting to feel quite nervous and on edge. I could hardly believe this was the same generous and charismatic man who had played host at dinner the previous night.

"Of course, the program was not devised by me, I am merely a practitioner, we are working from the guidance set out by William Thomas, our founder. He devised these methods while trying to help his wife who herself suffered from significant mental afflictions. In Victorian times sickness of the mind was usually dealt with by throwing the individual concerned into the madhouse, but Thomas was adamant that this was not going to happen to his beloved wife. And so he found far more effective ways of dealing with mental problems, and these methods can be applied to conditions far less severe than those which his wife suffered from.

"These days the approved treatments have changed slightly, but they are no less barbaric. A patient might be strapped to a bed and have electricity fired into his brain. Or he might be given something like these."

Dante reached into his waistcoat pocket and took out a small brown bottle and set it on the table. I squinted at it and realised the label had my own name

The Society

on it. This was my medication! He had actually had someone go into my room and take it!

"But those are mine!" I protested indignantly, "Why do *you* have them?"

"Because my dear chap, this is one of the very first rules of the program: no drugs. You heard what I told you last night, these are designed to keep you dumb, to stop that creative spark from burning, how can you expect to get well again if you allow yourself to be drugged and numb to the world around you?"

"I can sort of see your point, but you can't just stop taking these, it has to be done gradually, you have to consult a doctor."

"A doctor who will tell you just to keep taking them. You will be fine, trust me, I have guided many people through withdrawal from all kinds of things far worse than these, cold turkey is the only way, and you'll find it will be much easier than you think because you'll receive something far better in its place. Have faith, you don't need them."

This was unexpected. I had thought that I was signing up for a creative course and here I was being asked to give up my medication.

"The road will be long and you must work hard, stick with it and do exactly as I say. Great things await you if you stay the course."

He looked at me seriously and, without dropping his gaze, reached out and started up the metronome. It's slow, steady, hollow tick filled the small room.

"For a few minutes we will just sit," he told me, "just look into my eyes and try to relax. It will feel a bit uncomfortable at first, unnatural even, but try to just pay attention to any random thoughts that come into your head."

Raven Taylor

It was some form of hypnosis, that much was obvious, but it did have a relaxing effect. What I found myself thinking about was the drugs. The inability to come up with ideas for my writing, could it potentially be a side effect of the medication? They had, after all, made me feel numb to the world, experiencing neither pain nor joy, just a constant, flat and unfulfilling sense of mediocrity.

"Now, often as we go through life we pick up negative things. Every time we do something morally wrong or embarrassing, even the smallest of indiscretions, they all attach themselves to our soul. This forms a thick sludge, as if your spiritual being is weighted down, coated in a heavy, tar-like substance. This tar is made up of every transgression that has ever occurred in your life, and often they will follow from one lifetime to the next, so that each new aspect we take on still has the misdeeds of past lives stuck to it. Do you understand?"

I wasn't sure I did. I didn't believe in souls or reincarnation but I nodded anyway.

"So you see, often we are doomed to fail from the start, especially if our soul is older and has been through many, many lives. On the program we are able to cleanse the soul with our methods, beginning with current life misdemeanours and working our way back."

He turned the page in the textbook. The feeling of being disconnected, the sense of unreality was growing as the metronome ticked on endlessly.

Was there something in the tea?

"The treatment is split into two parts. This is the first- disclosure. The second is cleansing. Disclosure must always take place before cleansing can be administered."

I was starting to feel lightheaded.

The Society

Perhaps it's in the wine too. Why are they always giving me tea and wine?

"There is no secret to Disclosure. It simply requires you to be open and honest and look carefully at yourself and admit any and all misdeeds that you have committed, simply speaking them out loud is the first step to dealing with them."

Can't be, he said himself they are totally against drugs of any kind.

"In a way it is a little like a catholic confession but without the punishment or the judgment," he told me, "there is no judgment here. That's not the point in this, this is a simple unburdening. I do tape our sessions, but that's because I may need to go back over some things to fully understand. Is that all right?"

I nodded and watched as he reached into his jacket pocket again, this time he brought out a small pendulum. It was gold, and shaped like a cone with the point hanging down when held suspended on the chain to which it was attached.

"This, I suppose, is a bit like a dowsing rod. An experienced practitioner such as myself can use it as a tool to tap into his subject's subtle energy and ascertain if they are being truthful. The pendulum will swing clockwise for the truth, anti-clockwise for a lie. Erratic swinging can often indicate confusion, extreme emotions, bad thoughts and misdeeds. A still, calm pendulum shows clarity of mind, clear thoughts, spiritual calm."

"So, it's a bit like a primitive lie detector?" I asked.

How could this man possibly determine if I was telling the truth using only this piece of metal?

"I suppose it is. I will ask you some of the basic questions from these sort cards which are taken from

William Thomas's writings, and then we will dig a bit deeper into any potential misdeeds. But first we will start with a few test questions, things I know the answers to already, just to warm things up and make sure I'm correctly aligned with your energies. Please answer at least one of these test questions falsely so I can get an accurate calibration, do you understand?"

"I think so." Another wave of lightheadedness had struck me.

Before doing anything else he pressed the record button on the small tape player. He then set the metronome in motion and I watched curiously as he held the pendulum in his left hand, suspended over the table, and picked up the pen in his right. The little shiny piece of metal was still as Dante stared at it intently. The metronome ticked steadily as the seconds passed by.

"Is your name Quinn Bergman?" he asked at last.

"Yes," I said, watching the pendulum.

At first nothing happened, but then it started to move, ever so slightly, in a clockwise motion, mapping out small, invisible rings in the air above the desk.

"Truth," Dante confirmed, for the benefit of the recording. "And you are twenty-five years old?"

"I am." The pendulum seemed to be picking up momentum.

"True. And are you a writer?"

"Yes." The circles it was mapping out were growing larger as it swung with increasing strength.

"True. Which room number are you staying in here at the hotel?"

"Number 35," I lied.

The pendulum which, mere seconds ago, had been swinging furiously in clockwork circles stopped abruptly and then, to my amazement, changed direction. From what I could tell Dante's hand was entirely still.

The Society

That did not mean, however, that he was not subtly manipulating the thing.

"Untrue. Did you send the painting Sonny gave you to your friend in London?"

"Yes." There was another abrupt change in direction.

"True."

Next, he turned over a card and read the question from it.

"Have you ever taken recreational drugs?"

"No."

"True. Any other kind of mind-altering drugs?"

"Well, I suppose if you count those ones the doctor gave me then yes."

"True," he turned over a new card. "Have you ever stolen anything?"

"No."

"Lie." I watched as there was another change in direction.

I had been telling the truth!

"No, that's definitely true," I insisted.

"Your energy says otherwise, you are repressing something. Search Quinn, think, it's there, no matter how small."

I stared at the frantic anticlockwise swing and racked my brains. I was pretty sure I had never so much as taken a towel from a hotel room! Dante was staring at me now and I began to feel extremely uncomfortable.

"I swear, there's nothing!"

"There is! Just relax, clear your mind and it will come to you."

The metronome ticked steadily. I tried to do as he said and clear my mind. Then it came to me. I saw myself as a young boy, around ten years old, helping myself to a bottle of fizzy pop from the back of the lemonade van that used to come around the houses when the driver had left the doors open and turned away for a few minutes. I saw myself running home, feeling a rush of exhilaration from having done something bad. My parents had been very disappointed with me when they found out and had made me go back and pay what I owed and apologise to the van's owner. I had forgotten everything about it until that second. Could that be it?

"Yes," I said slowly, "I stole a bottle of pop from a delivery van when I was ten."

"True," he read from the pendulum, "is that all?"

"Yes, I think so."

"True. You're doing well, keep it up. Have you ever had thoughts of ending your own life?"

"No."

"Lie."

"All right, yes, I admit it. I have considered suicide before."

"True. Tell me about it."

"I attempted to kill myself once, after my break-up with Emily."

I felt my eyes closing as the unpleasant memories attacked my brain. It was like a dam had burst and I wanted to let it all out. It would be such a relief to tell him everything.

"True. Are you still in love with her?"

"No. I love her but I'm not *in* love with her."

"No, I see you aren't. I think this is part of a big block for you, the tip of an iceberg perhaps. A lot of your recent problems come directly from this situation; I fear. Why did the relationship end?"

"She wanted to be with George."

The Society

I opened my eyes again and looked at the pendulum. It was no longer spinning but was sort of swaying back and forth, as if not able to commit to an answer.

"That's only half true, there's more to it. Remember that to get the benefit from this, to allow us to identify and help you deal with problem areas you have to be completely honest not just with me but with yourself. Unburdening can be so liberating," he said, then quickly added, "have you ever been in a relationship with someone of the same sex."

"No."

"True. But you have had feelings for people of the same sex?"

"No."

"You're lying," I watched as the pendulum betrayed me and wondered how the hell he was doing this.

"All right, yes. I was in love with George. That's why Emily and I broke up."

"See, telling the truth isn't so hard."

I was sweating now and my hands were shaking. This was nothing like a Catholic confession, it was an interrogation.

"Have you ever had sexual relations with a member of the same sex?"

"No, never."

This is not somewhere I can go. I absolutely cannot go there with this stranger. It's just a trick, that piece of metal can't possibly know what you're thinking, and neither can he.

"Come on Quinn, you're doing it again, telling lies. Only through disclosure of your misdeeds can we begin to deal with them. If this is something that is affecting you negatively it's better to get it all out, clinging onto things which shame us holds us back terribly."

"All right, all right, yes!"

"And this, I sense, could be your biggest stumbling block, the thing you struggle with most, but we can help you, just keep going, we can help you deal with all of this."

"But it's worse than that," I found now that particular box was open I couldn't stop. To say it out loud, to confess to what I had done, simply to share would surely bring great relief. "These weren't just casual affairs. These were people I found in Soho...People I paid! These were sordid, desperate, shameful encounters in public bathrooms...and all while I was still with Emily..."

I stopped abruptly, feeling horrified. I had never told any of this to anyone. I never would. Yet here I was...

"It's all right," Dante said, "nothing that has happened in the past will ever be held against you here and by letting it out, by simply talking about it, you have already started to deal with it."

I slumped back in my chair, my head spinning.

"And that's today's disclosure over, it wasn't so bad, was it?" He put down the pendulum and turned off the tape recorder.

"No, not so bad." If the pendulum had still been in his hands it would have told him this was a lie.

"You won't feel better instantly, this was just us readying you for the next stage in the treatment which is the cleansing." He closed the textbook. "The time that must be left in-between disclosure and cleansing is always different, but I will know when you are ready to receive it. Cleansing is where the real magic happens.

The Society

After that you will feel better than you ever have in your life."

I was shaking and feeling strangely weak as I left the small room. I felt somehow like I was losing my grip on reality. Yet I did feel ever so slightly lighter for having told someone about these things. Perhaps there was hope for me after all. I had admitted to someone just exactly what I was and the world had not ended.

Chapter 10

1965

I was aware from the itinerary I had been given that morning that next on my list was the supervised creative class. As no one had told me specifically what time or where this would happen, I returned to my room following the disclosure for a lie down. I had barely laid down on the bed when there was a sharp knock at my door. I opened it to find Sonny standing there.

"Good morning, Sonny," I said brightly, feeling cheered by the sight of him.

"I've come to take you to your class," he said with a scowl.

I was a little taken aback by his sharp attitude. We had talked like old friends for hours last night and I wondered what had happened since to put him in such a bad mood.

"Ah Yes," I said, trying to be as pleasant as possible, "let me just get my work, I'll be needing it won't I?"

He hovered in the doorway as I retrieved my notebook and pen from my desk.

"How are you this morning?" I asked as I stepped out into the hall and closed the door behind me. "I have to say I enjoyed our chat last night."

"This way," he said abruptly, without answering my question. I thought better of trying to voice more pleasantries as I followed him to another of the white rooms marked 'Project Room.' Clearly he was not having a good day.

The Society

There were already two people in the room waiting for us. One was Ethel, and another was a middle-aged woman whom I did not recognise. Both were sitting at easels- Ethel was waving her brush in slow strokes across the canvas, a dreamy look on her face, and the younger woman was stabbing frantically at hers as if it had offended her in some way.

"You can work over there," Sonny snapped at me, pointing at an empty desk at the back.

I sat down and waited for further instruction. This was an odd set up indeed. I watched as Sonny went to each of the busy artists in turn and praised their work, offered them advice about light, and used colour to achieve the illusion of depth, and how to keep things properly in perspective. He was perfectly pleasant as he spoke to them.

Must just be me he's annoyed with. But what could I possibly have done to offend him since we parted last night after a perfectly pleasant evening?

"Quinn!" He barked at me, slapping his hand on the desk, making me jump and causing the other two to stop and look at us in alarm. "Stop wasting time. We don't tolerate wasting time."

"Sorry," I said, quite alarmed, "I'm just not sure what I'm meant to be doing."

"For heaven's sake!" He exclaimed, rolling his eyes. "You're a writer. This is an open class where you come to work on your project. So, in your case, you write!"

He grabbed my notebook, opened it, slammed back down on the desk, and glared at me.

"But I usually like to be alone when I write," I told him, thinking this couldn't possibly work. How could I sit and write when he was going about talking and giving advice to people painting pictures?

Raven Taylor

"The whole point in this supervised time is to make sure people aren't procrastinating, which is all too easy to do when you're on your own. This way we make sure people actually get things done, as well as offering constructive criticism. At the end we all share something of what we have made. Even John is being supervised by Kerrigan in the music room."

I had no idea who John was. I really wanted to ask what I had done to upset him so much, but I thought better of it. Best to just give it a go, I had signed up and agreed to adhere to their methods after all. I put my head down and put pen to paper.

To my surprise the words continued to flow. I found I was able to block out the background chatter about colours and different types of brushes and was soon lost in my fictional world. I found myself continuing to draw inspiration from Sonny's tales. Last night he had regaled me with stories of excess about the parties Dante used to throw for all of his rich friends at the house in the early days, rattling off a list of names, all of whom held noble titles such as lord and count. It seems there was all kinds of drunken debauchery in the beginning. Apparently, this kind of thing did not happen so much now, he told me the revelry was now saved for one big party which was thrown annually. After that he had grown a little morose as he spoke about a relationship he had struck up with the daughter of an earl he met at one such party. It had ended badly, for similar reasons my time with Emily had come to an end, because he was in love with someone else. He was vague on the details, but little things he threw into the conversation hinted to me that that someone else was in fact Dante. It was a subject I wanted to know more about, but I wasn't bold enough to push the matter given we were still strangers, really.

The Society

The lavish lifestyle he had led was a stark contrast to my own humble beginnings, but I found the world he had described to me last night a great source of inspiration while I worked during that morning's study time. We had been there for two and a half hours, and the words had been flowing freely, when I started to feel a little unwell. I knew the symptoms well; the slight feeling of nausea and the weird jolts that would periodically zap my brain; I had experienced them before on the odd occasion when I had forgotten to take a dose of my medication. I wished that Dante had not confiscated my pills. I realised I had stopped writing and was rubbing my temples. Sonny was straight over demanding to know what the problem was, why had I stopped? Had I run into a block? Did I know what was causing it?

"Yes, actually," I told him, "I'm overdue for a dose of my medication, but since it has been taken away I'm experiencing withdrawal symptoms. It's not very pleasant."

His expression softened and he appeared to have temporarily forgotten that he was angry with me.

"That's something I'm familiar with. Poor Quinn," he patted my head like you would a child, before he remembered he was supposed to be annoyed and snapped, "right, well maybe I can look over what you *have* managed to produce."

He snatched the notebook off me and strode off to a chair in the corner where he started to read. I put my head in my hands as my brain experienced another zap. It was a horrible feeling.

"Right students," said Sonny standing up, "I'm going to go and get John, and then we are all going to share some of our work and have a little discussion around each person's contribution."

When he had left the room I tried to talk to my course mates about the class to take my mind off the sick feeling and the shocks in my brain but was told abruptly by the younger woman that we weren't supposed to discuss with other students how far along we were on the program.

Sonny soon returned with Kerrigan and a man who I assumed was John. He was probably in his sixties, had long grey hair in a ponytail at the back while the top of his head was shiny and bald. I noticed he was wearing sandals. He was also carrying an acoustic guitar.

First we had to listen to the middle-aged woman, who Sonny called Sarah, trying to justify how the sickening jumble of colours on her canvas represented the struggle of the working classes. She rambled on and on, and she was painfully boring and full of self-importance. My head ached and I felt sick. Next Ethel showed us her atrocious painting of a vase of flowers that looked like a five-year-old had drawn it. Thankfully she did not have much to say about her work, just that she liked flowers because they were 'so pretty and good at chasing away negative thoughts.' Sonny gushed about what wonderful progress they were both making, and what fine artists they were going to be. Kerrigan nodded in agreement. Following this we were subjected to some excruciating music that John had written. He wailed and strummed his way in a high, off key, whiny voice about love and peace, his head thrown back and his eyes closed. It was all I could do not to burst out laughing at this ridiculous charade. There was not a shred of talent to be had among these people, yet Sonny and Kerrigan praised them all highly.

The Society

Finally it was my turn. I felt dizzy as I stood up and opened my book. I wasn't sure I was going to be able to make it through this given how unwell I felt. I began to read. I had performed readings of my works before in various small bookshops around London, sometimes to crowds even smaller than this one if you can believe it. I read them a passage in which my young hero, an opium addict living in 18th century Cornwall, had found himself faced with a bunch of ugly wreckers, a ship in distress, a lot of plundered goods, and violent fighting on the private beach of his family's estate. Towards the end I started to sway a little and had to sit down as the dizziness threatened to overpower me.

"Thank you, Quinn," Kerrigan said when I had finished, "that was very powerful, beautifully written. I felt as if I were actually there. I'm so glad to see that this beautiful part of the world is playing a part in your new story, and dare I say that your Denby Hall is perhaps heavily influenced by Chyanvean? Sonny, what did you think?"

I glanced at him hopefully, feeling nervous and a little excited, wondering if he had drawn any parallels between himself and my main character.

"Over romanticised nonsense. Nothing that hasn't been done a million times before. I expected better," he said dismissively.

I was hurt. I had really wanted him to praise me the way he had the others.

As the class packed up ready for lunch before our afternoon study time, Kerrigan held me back as the others left.

"This really was very good," she said, picking up my notebook. "Dante will want to read over this."

"Oh, no," I protested, "nobody reads the first draft, only my editor."

"This is how we do things here," she insisted, "Benjamin Lovell wasn't too sure at first either, but he persevered, stuck with our methods, and now look at him."

"Surely not *the* Benjamin Lovell, the author of 'Starting Out'."

"The very same. He owes his meteoric rise to fame to correctly adhering to our methods."

"You're telling me Benjamin Lovell stayed here?"

"I can see how my claims might seem fantastical. I'm worried this class might have given you the wrong impression about our services here and what we are trying to do," she looked troubled. "Those other three people we have studying with us are completely talentless, and I'm under no illusions that they are anything more. They're just paying guests passing through who we try to help as much as we can, but ultimately, they won't go on to achieve anything. I mean, our methods are fantastically effective but they need some raw ingredients to work with. Many, many of our students pass through and that's all. But you're different, you're exactly the type of person we, and the world, needs, that's why we are not taking any payment from you for your course. It's always such a joy to find a genuine talent among the rough. We hope that you will do a little more than simply pass through. Come with me, I want to show you something before lunch."

As I followed her back to the corridor where all of the rooms associated with their services were, I asked her if she knew why Sonny had been so unimpressed with me today.

"Oh I wouldn't worry about him," she laughed, "he's in a bad mood because he found out this morning

The Society

that you sent the picture he gave you to your friend in London."

"Is that what it is? I had no idea it would offend him, Dante said it would be fine."

"And it is fine," she confirmed, "Sonny's simply acting like a petulant child, just ignore him, it's only because he really likes you that it's bothering him that much, he'll come round."

"Maybe I should apologise," I thought perhaps it had been a little tactless to give away a gift like that.

"That's up to you. Come on."

She ushered me through a door and announced, "This is our room of success."

It was dark at first as there didn't seem to be any windows, but when she turned on the light I was able to see why she had brought me here. The walls were covered with pictures of well-known artists, actors, musicians, writers, many of whom I recognised, some I did not. There was a bookcase filled with books, and a table in the centre on which sat what appeared to be a large scrapbook.

"I'm going to leave you here for a little while," she said, "please feel free to look at anything you like, take your time. When you are done, come back to the restaurant where lunch will be waiting."

She left, closing the door behind her, and for a moment I simply stood and stared. So many celebrities!

I picked up the ledger off the table and sat down in a comfortable chair in the corner. Leafing through it I found a collection of letters written by the same celebrities whose photos lined the walls, all gushing with thanks about how much they owed to the program, and how it helped their careers and changed their lives. I could have passed the letters off as mere forgeries had it not been for the corroborating photos in which the various celebrities posed with Dante, Kerrigan and a third man who I did not recognise.

I put the ledger back and went to the bookshelf. The shelves held many and varied titles. I selected one that I was familiar with, a copy of 'Tomorrow's Sunset' by Grace Hibbert, and opened it to the title page.

"To Dante, Kerrigan and Sonny, thank you so much for allowing me to stay in your beautiful home, and for helping me to reach spiritual enlightenment, love Grace."

Grace Hibbert, whose works had won countless literary awards, had been a part of this same program that I was about to embark upon? The few other novels I looked at all contained similar notes of heartfelt thanks. I could not help but be impressed, the desire to be part of something that so many of my hugely successful peers had been involved in seemed too great an honour to turn down. After my unexpected experience of the disclosure, and the unorthodox supervised creative time, I had been beginning to have doubts. That and the curious ambiance of the place, and the eccentricity of my hosts, had left me wondering if I might be better simply giving up on the whole perplexing set up, and heading home. This had, however, leant Chyanvean and its courses a fresh and irresistible appeal.

But why had I never heard of it? This program? If it had helped so many famous people why were they not talking about it?

The Society

Chapter 11

1965

When I returned to the restaurant for lunch, I found Dante, Kerrigan, Astrid and Sonny waiting for me. They sat around a table on which there was a platter of sandwiches, cakes and scones. I found I wasn't really hungry as the effects of missing my medication were still making me feel a little sick and dizzy. There were a few other guests dotted about including my classmates from this morning's workshop.

"So, what did you make of our room of success?" Dante asked me, his voice swelling with pride.

"It's very impressive," I nodded, "you really helped all of those people?"

"Most of them wouldn't be where they are today if it weren't for the teachings of William Thomas," Kerrigan grinned.

"And you can have it all too," Dante said encouragingly.

I noticed Sonny shooting me a scowl. I wondered if I could get him alone after lunch to talk to him about the painting.

"Success beyond your wildest dreams. Happiness. Contentment. Freedom from negative thoughts and mental illness," said Kerrigan.

"We think you should consider staying with us a little longer," Dante said, picking up a scone, "at least until our annual conference at the end of November."

"I'm not really sure I'll be able to stretch to that," I said doubtfully.

The Society

"You really must," he insisted, "you'll get a better idea of what we are all about, most of the people you saw in that room, your peers, the top creative people in the country, will be in attendance. Just think of the connections you could make rubbing shoulders with actors, musicians, and great writers."

"And the head of our group always attends, our personal friend who'll you have read about in the welcome brochure, James-Anthony Broadbent. You simply have to meet him, some of our people would give anything for an audience with our leader."

"Well, I'd have to speak to my publisher, they might want me back in London…"

"You see what you can do," Kerrigan encouraged, "I don't believe you should just pass through the way the likes of John and Sarah will, I think you have far more potential than that, you've already started to make great progress, but I don't think two weeks will be long enough for you to fulfill your true potential."

"Please stay," Astrid added, smiling at me from across the table.

I resolved to call George and see what could be done. I already had a good few chapters I could send him as proof that I had started to work again if need be.

Sonny, who had so far been silent, suddenly burst out with, "You gave away my painting!"

He glared at me. He looked absolutely furious with his fists clenched on the table and his face turning a deep shade of scarlet.

"I'm sorry, I didn't mean to offend you," I felt taken aback, "it was just so beautiful and I knew that Emily would really appreciate it."

"It wasn't meant for her, for some unenlightened, dull outsider. It was meant for you!"

"Now, now Sonny," Dante stood up and placed a hand on his shoulder, "you need to calm down, you know how bad for you all of this negative energy is."

"But the painting was for him!" he spat.

"I know, I know, come on."

Sonny got to his feet, and Dante started to guide him away from the table.

"Remember how we talked about anger and infatuation and what a terrible block they can cause in the creative channels?" he said in a low tone, "I'm disappointed, I really am, I thought we had started to deal with all of this. I suppose we are going to have to go back and work on things a little more, hmm?"

I watched them leave in disbelief.

"I'm sorry about that," Kerrigan sighed. "Sonny has always been difficult. He has never really taken to all aspects of the program the way most do. He simply has too many problems that we haven't been able to crack, and that's why he's still here, we've never really been able to get to the point where we can allow him to take his talent out into the world. Of course we tell him his paintings sell well out there, but in reality, Dante gives them away to our celebrity friends or buys them himself. The tragedy is that he really is a brilliant painter, but he still has misdeeds that he simply cannot deal with no matter how many disclosures and cleansings he attends. His stubbornness stops him from fully embracing the program. Yet we love him anyway."

"Do you mean to say you actually keep him here?"

"Oh goodness no, Sonny could leave whenever he likes, but where would he go? There isn't anything

The Society

out there for him, no family, no friends, no money, no job. So, he stays. He's our terminal case."

Just then Dante rejoined us.

"I'm sorry about that," he said as he sat down, "all taken care of now though. I'm sorry he got so angry at you Quinn."

Before afternoon study time I decided that I would call George again. I couldn't wait to tell him about some of the literary giants who had stayed here and attended the same course I was currently taking, or the conference that would actually allow me to meet some of them. When I reached him he was suitably impressed as I rhymed off the list of names.

"Are you serious? These are some of our own personal idols, and they've all studied there, at that house you're staying in?"

"I'm telling you! I wouldn't have believed it myself but there's pictures of them all with the people who run things here so it's definitely true! And if I stay on and attend the conference I'll actually get to network with them. George, this could be huge!"

"It sounds like quite a remarkable place! And the writing is still going well?"

"Incredibly well, so far. It's early days, but I think being on this course will give me the structure and discipline I need to keep at it. I should get in a good few hours every morning during the supervised work sessions, and another few hours in the evenings after dinner."

"Well that leaves you the afternoons free then, I hope you'll make good use of them and get out and about, see the sites."

"No time," I confessed, "the afternoons are study time."

"Well, try not to push yourself too hard…" George said doubtfully.

"No, I'll be fine, I've never felt better," that wasn't entirely true, I was really starting to feel the effects of having not taken my medication. "George, as there's a chance I might be staying here a little longer, there's a few things I need from you."

"Yes, go on."

"I need you to send me my typewriter, and if I call my doctor, can you pick up a prescription for me?"

I reasoned that if I could get some more pills sent through, I could go on taking them and simply not tell Dante, because really the withdrawal was becoming highly unpleasant and was only going to get worse.

"Yes, Quinn, I think I can manage all of that."

"Thank you so much George, this means a lot to me, honestly this place is doing me the world of good and I'd hate to have to come home so soon."

"You're my oldest friend, anything I can do to help I will, you know that," he assured me, "oh, Emily received the package. She absolutely loves the painting. I however think it's hideous so thank you for ensuring I have to look at it above our fireplace every day for the rest of my life." He chuckled and we said our goodbyes

The Society

Chapter 12

2009

Quinn had so far painted quite a picture of his introduction to this controversial group. While he had at first been nervous, speaking of his experiences with the caution of a man who was frightened he might step on a mine, now he was becoming more animated, and at times seemed completely lost in the tale. It was good that he was starting to trust her. That was important.

So far what he had told her was peculiar, but not exactly traumatic. She would need him to entrust his complete confidence to her if he was to talk about the events which came later. What she really wanted to hear about was what had happened at the infamous November 1970 conference. Tracking down people who had been in attendance at Chyanvean that evening had proved almost impossible, and understanding what had taken place then was essential for her investigation. Still, this was his story and it would not be a good idea to rush him, she should just let him tell her everything. It was vital that if she were to share his complete confidence he should feel reassured that she understood and did not place any blame or judgement on him.

"It's interesting to hear the circumstances around which you were recruited," she said. "It's certainly a very cleverly orchestrated system they have; their use of celebrity endorsement to reinforce their promises of a glittering career, clever but subtle hypnosis techniques, the confiscation of your medication which must have completely interfered with your thinking. Not to mention the general charms of your hosts; the dinner,

The Society

the drinks, the luxurious surroundings, the impression that they really were friends looking out for you, and perhaps, dare I say, the beginnings of a romantic attraction to the artist?"

She watched his reaction and surmised she had assumed correctly, as his face turned red and he shrugged his shoulder as he looked off out of the window.

Outside the sun had slid behind a cloud and a breeze moved the curtains. He had spent his whole life unsuccessfully trying to forget Sonny, but he was always there. He still saw him sometimes. It has been happening more and more recently. He knew he wasn't real, and he didn't believe in ghosts. No, it was just his overstretched imagination, or perhaps some kind of madness, brought on by the years of solitude. But still, every time he caught a glimpse of him his heart would ache and he would have done anything to hear him laugh again, to feel his fingers brush his face.

"All of this, and the fact that the place had also jolted you out of your writer's block," she cut through his thoughts. "It must have had an effect on your ability to think rationally. It's perfectly easy to see how you got carried away with it all."

"They knew what they were doing, and they were clever. They had hooked me just like they hooked Sonny all those years ago, and just like they had hooked all of those celebrities. You're right, it was easy to be blinded by it all. As time went by, the world they created for me, and the way they gradually isolated me, soon left me so far removed from reality that I was completely out of touch with anything that was going on outside of The Society. But of course I'm getting ahead of myself, I had not yet been introduced to The Society, I was simply on the lower levels, a mere participant of the program."

"Yes, the program, tell me about it…" she scribbled something on her notepad.

"Each day I would spend hours writing while one of the three of them watched my progress and while other guests worked around me. The afternoons were spent in the study rooms, reading the self-help books and spiritual enlightenment texts written by William Thomas. During these study sessions we were usually joined by members of staff from the hotel who were all, it seemed, also given time to read the texts. For them it was a requirement of their job."

"And what were these texts like?" she pressed.

"Hard to describe. The man had written countless books. He was stark raving mad, but I couldn't see it at the time. Many of them read like simple self-help guides and talked a lot about positive thinking and techniques on clearing the mind, things like that. Much of it was wild and hard to understand ramblings about the suppression of the arts and the evils of government. A lot of it was like some kind of religious dogma with endless passages about past life regression, reincarnation, lists of 'misdeeds' which a person should avoid committing."

"It's hard to tell exactly what kind of group they are, isn't it? I've read some of the texts myself, the ones that are not so closely guarded, and I still can't fathom it. They claim to be a religious group, gained recognition as such in the late 70s, but they appear on paper to be more of a business corporation selling their services. They don't appear to have a God or anything like that."

"No, no God, no church. Just old souls, new souls, workers and non-beings, and the Grand High Master at the very top of it all," he said thoughtfully.

The Society

"A dangerous cult, I think we can both agree on that, at least."

"Well, yes. I will come back to this, to the beliefs of The Society, but not yet. I know you want to know about Sonny and the 1970 conference, or the enlightenment as they called it, and we'll get there, but now I'm telling you about my first really troubling experience at the house, which happened on the evening of my first day on the course."

Outside the window a crow cackled harshly and Quinn gave a visible shiver.

Chapter 13

1965

That night a storm rolled in off the sea. I could not sleep owing to the constant brain zaps I was experiencing from my lack of medication, and I lay awake listening to the wind howling frantically around the house, shaking the windows in their frames, and making the old building creak and groan in protest. The rain lashed against the glass panes, and down below I could hear the waves as they hurled themselves furiously at the cliffs. Even with the windows shut the wind still found its way in and stirred the curtains, making them flap like frightful ghosts around the big bay window in my room as I lay restless in the four-poster bed. I realised that sleep was not going to come any time soon, and I shuffled across to the desk, fighting against a spell of dizziness, opened the curtains and slumped into the chair so I could watch the storm.

There is something completely thrilling about a storm at sea when observed from the warmth and safety of the indoors. The ocean was in such a state of wrath; it was quite a sight to behold. Heaving and rising up twenty feet into the air, huge foam capped mountains grew from the water and hurled themselves at each other, where they would clash and break apart in showers of spray. Racing towards the cliffs, gaining height and momentum as they went, the mighty waves sped before colliding blindly with the jagged rocks. On a far-off peninsula I could see the beam of a lighthouse sweeping across the sky, warning ships of danger, and I

The Society

once again thought of wreckers and plundered cargo. I wondered if I should try and re-work the scene of the wreck from my book; to do so while sitting here with the storm raging on would surely lend the work something extra.

I was just about to put pen to paper when I spotted a figure down below, dangerously close to the edge of the cliffs, standing with arms spread out, garments flapping in the wind, as if ready to jump...

I leapt from my seat and threw my coat over my pyjamas. Still in my slippers, I raced down the stairs and across the guest lounge. I glanced wildly out of the huge windows; the figure was thankfully still there.

Please don't let them jump, please don't let them jump.

I sprinted to the door in the corner and to my relief found it was not locked. I threw myself out onto the lawn. My feet were soaked within seconds as I flew across the sodden grass. The wind whipped my hair around my face and clawed at my skin, and all I could taste was salt from the sea. The figure still had its arms raised, preparing to take a swan dive off the cliff and be smashed to pieces against the rocks below.

"Wait! Don't!" I cried, but the words were swallowed by the storm.

I doubled my efforts, charging across the grass, losing my slippers and stubbing my toe on a rock. My bare feet squelched in the mud, and I slipped and skidded along the wet ground.

"No, please don't!" I yelled, I was almost there, and this time they heard me and turned. It was Sonny. "For God's sake don't!"

I struggled to my feet again, being hit by another sickening wave of dizziness, and charged towards him. I threw myself at him, grabbed him round the waist, and hauled him away from the edge. As I pulled him I slipped again and we both fell into the mud.

For a moment I just lay there on the wet ground, soaking wet and panting, sensing that the moment of immediate danger had passed.

"What the hell were you thinking?" I asked when I had caught my breath.

Sonny was getting to his feet now.

"Sometimes I think it might be the only way out for me," he said angrily.

I pushed myself up, feeling the mud seeping in between my toes.

I noticed his face as he turned to me; his lip was bloody and one of his eyes was swollen almost shut. I felt a wave of pity.

"Who did that to you?"

"What does it matter?"

I recalled a comment Ethel had made the first night we had met, something about being glad Sonny's face had healed up. So, this was a regular thing? I pulled my coat tight about myself, realising I was shivering violently. He had turned away from me now and was ploughing on through the storm towards the back door. I hurried after him, my sodden pyjamas flapping around my legs and my bare feet so numb I could barely feel them.

"Can't let Dante find out about this," I heard him muttering to himself as we passed through the door and into the blissful warmth of the lounge. "Supposed to have cured me. If they found out they might even make me go back to stage one…"

Stage one? What was he talking about?

We left splashes of mud and wet footprints all the way up the spiral staircase as we climbed to the top

The Society

of the tower. Really all I wanted was to return to my room, have a hot bath, and change out of my wet clothes, but I didn't want to leave Sonny alone, so I followed him up. The whole way he was muttering angrily under his breath, chastising himself for being so stupid.

"Sometimes I can't actually believe it," he snapped once we were in the studio, the rain lashing down on the domed roof. I couldn't tell if he was talking to me or to himself. "I must be incurable. Completely incurable."

"But Sonny, nobody is incurable."

"I've watched countless people join us and go on to have outstanding careers, but it never happens for me," he was looking frustrated now, raking his hands through his hair and pacing back and forth. "Ten years I've been here now and I'm just as fucked up as when I arrived. Ten years and what have I achieved?"

"But from what I've heard you've achieved quite a lot," I reasoned. "You were so proud when you told me about all the celebrities who are fans of your work."

"What, those people?" he gestured to the glass cabinet where he displayed his photographs, a mean look flaring in his eyes. "It's all just a load of shit, a lie!"

I was taken by surprise when in a sudden fit of anger he picked up one of the paintings and hurled it at the cabinet. I jumped up from my chair as the glass shattered, scattering sharp shards across the floor and leaving the collection of photographs in disarray. My eyes darted to the trap door as I considered making a bolt for it. Perhaps I could find Dante and let him deal with this.

"Oh sure, Dante says The Society has 'special plans' for me," he ranted, "just wait until the enlightenment, he's always telling me that, but they never come to anything, do they? It's all just flattery, flattery and lies, and they think I don't know!"

He had picked up another picture now, and he slammed it hard against the edge of a table so the board broke in two. It was really quite frightening to watch.

"Do you want me to go and get Dante?" I asked, not knowing what else to do.

"Oh yes, because that would be a huge help. Go get Dante so he can lie to me some more, tell me I'm good, that I'm bound for great things. He's a great one for compliments, but then he can turn in the very next breath and then you find yourself decked out on the floor with a black eye."

"He did that to you?"

"I deserved it," he said resolutely, "I always deserve it. I'm stupid and weak. Weak! Weak! Weak!"

I watched in horror as with each utterance of the word weak he gave himself a hard slap across the face.

"Sonny, stop it!" I cried in alarm.

I dashed forward and tried to restrain him, grabbing hold of his wrists to stop him from hurting himself further. He made a half-hearted attempt to pull away but I could sense his fit of rage had run its course. His shoulders slumped and he crumpled to the ground. I went down with him and took him in my arms as he started to sob against my shoulder.

"It's all happening again," he cried, "it was the same with Dante."

"What's all happening again?"

"Nothing, it doesn't matter. Please don't tell Dante or Kerrigan about this," he pleaded.

"All right, I won't if you don't want me to."

I hadn't even noticed that I was stroking his hair.

The Society

Misdeeds! My mind leapt back to Dante and the pendulum and I pulled my hand away, gently pushing Sonny away from me. He sat back and turned his head to look out to sea. The storm was subsiding and the moon was visible again.

"I'm sorry I was so horrible today," he apologised. "I've really not made the best first impression, have I?"

"It's all right," I assured him, then in an attempt to try and cheer him up, I added, "I think you might be my new muse, look how much you've helped me with my writing already just by telling me your stories."

There was a hint of a smile on his face now.

"But Sonny, what I don't understand is, if you feel this isn't working for you, why don't you just leave, try something new?"

"Oh, poor naive Quinn," he gave a sharp little laugh, "don't you know it's not that simple?"

Chapter 14

1965

The next five days at Chyanvean passed quickly, with every day much the same as the last. In the mornings we were woken early and the few of us who were on the course met in the observatory and worked on our projects under the watchful eye of Kerrigan. Sonny remained absent and although I was concerned, I told myself it might be for the best.

My initial momentum with my writing had started to wane and the ideas were not flowing as well as they had. I was disappointed to find myself procrastinating, filling my time with re-drafting the early pages, trying hard not to admit that I was only doing this because the story had ground to a halt. Already the programs' teachings were working their way into my mind as I found myself wondering what misdeeds were causing this new block. It had to be Sonny. That night in the studio as I had held him I had undoubtedly felt something for him and this was exactly the kind of thing that Dante had suggested would hold me back.

In the afternoons we sat in the study room and read writings by William Thomas on the subjects of creativity and avoiding and handling misdeeds. The texts remained as confusing as ever and I could not quite work out what we were supposed to be learning from them, other than a long list of things that we should avoid. During these study afternoons nobody spoke, and I found I was able to observe a distinct difference between those few guests who were on the program and

The Society

the members of the hotel staff who also attended these sessions. Whilst the paying guests seemed engaged and interested in what they were doing, I noticed that the staff always looked distinctly disconnected. The more I observed them around the hotel in general, the more I saw it to be true. With the exception of Magda the receptionist and Paul the young waiter, they all seemed to go about their day looking foggy and robotic. It was no use trying to engage with any of them during our time together. Any attempts I might make to look up from the bewildering texts and make conversation were always immediately shot down by whoever was supervising the study time. Usually this was either Magda or Paul, who seemed to be there purely to watch us and make sure that we were reading. They weren't there to teach and would not entertain any of the questions we had about what we were studying, which most of the time made absolutely no sense. It seemed to me to be the delusional ramblings of a man who was in deep conflict with the world around him. The basis of it appeared to be that a person's creative talents were quashed by the negative effects of society and various misdeeds they might commit, and negating these two things was the key to success. From what I could tell the whole textbook was just this same message, repeated over and over in various guises.

On the sixth morning, Kerrigan came to my room and told me I would not be taking part in the usual routine of supervised work and study, instead I was to stay in my room and wait for Dante who wanted to see me. He appeared shortly afterwards, and when he did he was carrying my typewriter.

"This arrived for you," he said, setting it down on the desk.

There was something a little off about his mannerisms and the way he spoke, there was a sort of coldness creeping into his voice.

"Thank you," I said, "I had my editor send it, I need to start typing out some of this work so I can send it on to him."

"That's not all you asked him to send though, is it?" Dante reached into his jacket pocket and pulled out a small brown pharmaceutical bottle and rattled it at me. "I'm so disappointed."

A stab of guilt shot through me. I wondered why I should feel this, after all, he was the one who had gone through my private mail. It should be me who was annoyed at him, not the other way round. Yet that's not how it went.

"I told you that participants in the program cannot be taking any kind of drugs."

"I know, I'm sorry, it's just I've been suffering so terribly from withdrawal that I thought…"

"It's something you just need to work through," he said, his expression softening. "I know it's hard but it will be worth it. Our methods may seem a little odd, even maybe at times cruel to you, but when it gets hard just think of all of those people in our room of success. You can do it, can't you?"

"Yes," I agreed. I hated the fact that I had let him down, "I can."

"Good," he put a hand on my shoulder. "Now, I can't force you to do any of this, but what we usually find helpful in these situations is to employ a technique called 'stress positions. It's part voluntary punishment, part a way to refocus your mind."

I gave him a worried glance.

"Don't be alarmed, it's not as bad as it sounds," he assured me. "It's a tactic we use to really take the

The Society

subject's mind away from any troubling thoughts, in your case your imagined withdrawal symptoms and whatever else is currently blocking your ability to write."

"All right..." I said uncertainly.

"Paul, come in here please," he called. The young waiter must have been standing outside the door. "Ok Quinn, you are going to stand over there, and face the wall."

I did as I was asked.

"Raise your hands and place both palms against the wall," he instructed, and I complied. "Good, now, you're going to stay like that, and that's all there is to it."

"But how long do I have to stand like this?"

"For as long as it takes," he said.

"And if I don't do it, what happens then?"

"Nothing, you'll only be harming yourself if you give in," his voice was so reasonable, so matter of fact. "I would hate to see that happen though. I can't make you do anything you don't want, but it would make me very sad if you do not take this opportunity to learn."

And so, I was held in that room, in that position, by nothing more than Dante's will. I stayed and I suffered. I could have walked out anytime that I liked, but I didn't.

When Dante eventually came for me I actually fell into his arms and began to sob. Every muscle in my body was aching and I felt lightheaded and dizzy. He let me cry into his chest as he held me like a father comforting his son and said, "I know, I know, the first steps are always the hardest and sometimes one has to be cruel to be kind. But I think you're ready now. We are going to do a cleansing, and I promise after that you will never crave those nasty chemicals ever again."

"Really?" I looked up at him, tears subsiding.

His smile was quite possibly the most radiant thing I had ever seen, it was as if all the lights had been turned back on.

"Of course," he held me at arm's length and looked me up and down. "How you have suffered, but suffer no more Quinn Bergman, come with me!"

He took my hand as if I were a child, and I followed him obediently, feeling weak and feverish with my head spinning. He took me to yet another room that I had never been to which, like the others, was white and clinical and had a bed like you might find in a doctor's surgery as well as a table with a few small, unlabelled bottles and a metronome. He handed me a glass of water.

"Drink," he said when I looked at it suspiciously, "your body needs to be hydrated to properly receive a cleansing."

I swallowed the water and he had me lay on the bed and close my eyes. I obeyed. He set the metronome to a steady beat and began to speak.

"You are about to receive from me a transference of energy, energy so divine, so powerful, that it will renew your body and your soul in ways you cannot even imagine." He paused dramatically before going on. "This energy is a pure creative force, it is the very essence of being human, the power that has been dulled and sapped by society, and by all of your misdeeds. The energy will flow through you and wash away the sludge that has accumulated in your spirit."

Then he placed a thumb on my brow and his right hand on my stomach and asked me to open my eyes. He began to chant in some kind of language that I

The Society

did not understand. It was extraordinary. I began to feel warm and euphoric. A strange tingling sensation spread through my nerves. I saw a kaleidoscope of colours erupting around me. It was as if every cell in my body had been electrified, I could actually feel the power of which he spoke washing over me and enveloping my very soul. All the anxious and paranoid thoughts lifted, the self-doubt was gone, before long I felt so high that I cried tears of pure joy. It was like being touched by an angel.

Dante removed his hands and the tingling sensation slowly subsided but the euphoric high remained. The bright lights and colours still danced all around me and when I looked up at Dante he no longer appeared to be a man but some kind of seraphic creature radiating love and light. For a moment I was utterly convinced that I was standing in the presence of a god.

"You feel better now, don't you?" he asked, and for a few moments I just lay there, bathing in his glory.

"Yes, yes I do," I sighed.

"Now sit up, slowly, don't rush," he handed me another glass and when I drank it, although it was just plain water, it seemed to be the best thing I had ever tasted.

"Now go forth, wonderful things await you. There are no classes for you today, post cleansing is a time for appreciating and experiencing the world. You'll find you see things now in a way you never did."

Chapter 15

2009

Quinn felt foolish. Here he was telling this stranger that after only a week he had been completely taken in by the promises of a delusional madman.

"Sixteen hours I stood against that wall, and I did so entirely by choice," he marvelled. "These 'voluntary punishments' were to become a regular thing whenever it was deemed you had committed an indiscretion, but it was always your own choice whether you wanted to take part. A popular one was making you go a night without sleep to realign your mind with your higher self. Sometimes it was as mundane as being made to copy out William Thomas's list of misdeeds over and over. Once I witnessed a small group of the house staff standing in a circle around a miserable looking kitchen hand while Dante encouraged them to yell insults at the poor fellow.

"The power of that man still amazes me. When Dante smiles on you it's like the whole world lights up, and when you are in his bad books everything is cold. He could make you do anything."

"Cult leaders tend to be master manipulators, and that's what makes them so dangerous," she said. "They're narcissistic, charismatic and unpredictable, and from what I know of Dante Lewin-May he was all of these."

"Yes, he was, and I could see why Sonny idolised him the way he did."

Quinn looked off thoughtfully before continuing.

The Society

"In the weeks that followed, as we headed towards that year's conference, I barely left the house, settling into the comforting routine of writing in the mornings, and studying the texts in the afternoon. It seemed like every waking hour was filled for me and I went to bed exhausted each night. Most evenings after dinner I spent sitting by the fire with Sonny, and by the time the conference came around we had become good friends.

"I also endured the weekly ritual of the disclosure, which I always dreaded, but I put up with it because it meant I could attend a cleansing afterwards- the blissful high it brought fast became the focal point of my week."

"And the cleansing, it was some sort of drug induced high? Something in the water he made you drink I'm assuming."

"In the water, in the tea, in the wine, I think we were being drugged the whole time. Yet even after all these years I still sometimes miss that feeling" he said wistfully. "So many times over the years I have had thoughts about going back and throwing myself on their mercy just to experience those few sublime hours that follow a cleansing again."

"A drug addict craving the high," she observed.

"At first it was the highs that kept me there. Later the draw of the celebrity world they introduced me to, not to mention the threat of blackmail which came once they had enough taped disclosures filled with my darkest secrets. And eventually I suppose I stayed for love."

"Love," she repeated the word curiously. "It can't have been easy building a relationship with Sonny within an organisation who sees homosexuality as a mortal sin."

He was not entirely sure he was ready to talk about this yet, he hadn't even told her about his induction into The Society. About Lesley. About the conference.

"Oh, they had their reasons for turning a blind eye where Sonny and I were concerned," he said slowly. "Terrible, awful reasons…"

The Society

Chapter 16

1965

Over a month had passed since my arrival at Chyanvean, when one day, towards the end of November, I saw a coach pull up at the front of the house. I thought it was a little strange given the time of year, and I paused to watch the guests disembark. Sonny was standing near the reception desk with Astrid and Magda and I asked, "Who are they?" as I watched the odd bunch come filing through the front door.

All of the men were dressed in identical black trousers and white shirts while the women wore black skirts and white blouses. The way they moved was almost robotic as they made their way across the room in two neat lines of men and women, none of them speaking, all with eyes facing forward.

"Workers," Sonny told me.

"Workers?"

"A special faction of our group, Workers are people who have pledged their life to serve. It's no way to live really; they aren't allowed to get married, or have children, I've heard that they have to be sterilised but I'm not quite sure if that's true."

"What?" I exclaimed, it sounded barbaric.

"Oh, they're happy enough," Sonny said dismissively. "They're born to be subservient, all they want is to do The Society's bidding."

"I'm sorry, but what's The Society?"

"It's not my place to explain, I'm sure Dante will fill you in very soon."

The Society

"Papa and Mama are having a party," Astrid grinned at me, "we do it every year to mark the birthday of William Thomas. Lots and lots of fancy people come to visit us, the workers help to set it all up."

At the end of my next disclosure I decided just to ask Dante about The Society. So far I had found no mention of it in any of the texts I had been given to read. It seemed like a good time to make enquiries because he had just expressed how pleased he was with all the progress I was making. He said my channels were so clear now that I was in a great position to accept the flow of energy that he would deliver at my next cleansing. He seemed to be in an exceptionally good mood and had not pushed me so hard that day on issues concerning my sexuality, a favourite subject of his, which was a blessing.

"Ah my dear Quinn," he said once the session was finished, "I feel like you are going to be the next great prodigy to come out of the program. That new book of yours is simply outstanding, and you call it a rough draft! Yes, I'm glad you asked me that question, you are ready for such knowledge and it's probably time I told you of my plan, considering I intend to offer you the opportunity to join us…"

Dante sat back in his chair and smiled at me serenely, "Yes, I think you're worthy, but understand this, if I tell you about The Society you cannot tell anybody at all about its beliefs and practices."

"So, it is some kind of secret organisation?"

"The higher levels are, yes. Obviously, the program and its courses are meant for everyone, but membership to The Society is only open to a certain type of person."

Raven Taylor

He got up and selected a book from the shelf, bringing it back to the table and placing it carefully down. It was a large volume bound in green leather.

"The Society of Old Souls," he tapped the book's cover where the name was embossed in gold on the leather.

"The Society of Old Souls?" I repeated back.

"Yes, or just The Society for short," he confirmed. "Membership to the higher levels is very exclusive, and I can't go into all of the details just now, but I can tell you every one of those people you saw in our room of success has taken the Vows of the Old Souls. I can give you a brief rundown of what The Society is all about, but its secrets are only available to members through careful study of the restricted texts."

He leaned in close as if he were about to impart on me some great and delicious secret.

"You know now from your studies here that William Thomas made it his life's work to seek out ways to heal the soul, and his belief that disorders such as depression are in fact illnesses of the spirit rather than of the physical mind as modern medicine would have you believe. You've experienced yourself the remarkable unblocking of a person's creative channels, the healing and restoring properties of the divine energy when properly administered, and this is what forms the basis of the program."

His voice was low and smooth. Dante was one of those rare individuals who you would be quite content just to listen to for hours on end, no matter what the subject matter was.

"Well, Thomas's discoveries did not end there. In a country that was, at the time, deeply Christian, Thomas went against convention in that he was fascinated by the beliefs that came out of Asia, and of

The Society

ancient pagan religions, spiritual paths that far out date the bible and the modern teachings about heaven or hell. A common belief held among a lot of the ancient civilisations was that of reincarnation, something which really caught Thomas's imagination and seemed to make so much more sense than the fire and brimstone of hell and the purity of heaven."

"Yes, this has been alluded to several times since I've been here; in that grand table in the lounge, the mural on the wall of the staircase going up to Sonny's studio," I commented with interest.

Whether I believed the soul returned to earth over and over did not matter, it was still a fascinating subject.

"Yes, and through his studies of these ancient beliefs he came to recognise that, among the people who came to him for spiritual healing and treatment of mental illness, the host bodies housed souls of varying ages; some brand new, some ancient, and everything in between. The age of the physical body was not important. He could look into the eyes of a child and see looking back at him as a being that has visited the earth many, many times. Do you ever get that feeling from a person, that they are old beyond their years?"

"Yes, sometimes I do…"

"He began to observe that the old souls were generally the ones who suffered the most from mental afflictions, but that they also tend to be great artists."

"Creative genius and madness often go hand in hand," I said quietly.

"Quiet, and he recognised these people for what they really were; the ones whose gifts would ultimately lead humanity into a brilliant and dazzling future. Only the old souls could see the world for what it was; they'd experienced the age-old problems of man time and time again; endured greed, war, cruelty, and oppression, over and over until it weighed them down terribly.

"And so he established The Society to identify, bring together and protect such souls, to give them the tools and the space to express themselves, and to access all of the hidden knowledge they had gained in their many lifetimes. The Society recognises that old souls are the most precious resource mankind has."

He paused and looked at me intently. I was lost in the story, in the way he spoke, in his tone of voice. I listened in rapt silence; my imagination had been well and truly captured.

"And that's how it all began. Of course, we don't want to deny newer souls access to some of the wonderful self-help techniques, and they do make excellent parishioners once they sign up, so we open these services to all in the form of The Program for Better Living. New souls are important and deserve help too, but their needs are very different to the old soul. New souls can bear the monotony of work far better than older ones, and so we also allow them to join us as workers should they wish, providing a support service to The Society. They do all kinds of work for us; act as household staff for high-ranking members, take care of all the tedious admin work at our centres, distribute our published paraphernalia, set up events like the yearly conference. There really are wide and varied career options for them."

"Sonny says they are forced to be sterilised so they can't have children."

Dante let out a hearty laugh, throwing back his head and slapping his knee.

"Sonny and his stories," he said when his laughter had died down. "Not the case at all. True, they

The Society

are not permitted to have children and any who do will have to resign their status as a worker, but that's all. It's no different to say, entering the priesthood.

"All of the hotel staff are workers too. They are quite content to serve, but *you* could never be happy with such a life."

I thought of my time in the bank and how miserable it had made me.

"You are an old soul, Quinn; I knew it the very first time I saw you. As a level ten old soul, the highest level you can reach, I have studied the techniques for spotting old souls and am quite an expert at it. There are far more new souls now than there are old with the population being what it is. Old souls can get quite lost these days among so many new, it can seem to them that the world they are being forced to live in is somehow alien and unsatisfying given it is all geared towards the simpler needs of the new soul."

It all seemed to make a funny sort of sense to me. In that moment I thought I could see why I never quite seemed to fit into the world the way others did, why I found the simple things that brought most people I knew joy so mundane and unfulfilling. He was right. I wasn't like everyone else.

"Now the yearly conference that is coming up is not only a celebration of the birth of our founder, but it is also the time of year when new members are inducted into The Society. Quinn, I have put you forward for membership this year, if you are willing, you will say your vows at this year's conference and be admitted into the most exclusive group in existence."

Chapter 17

1965

Over the next few days I observed the workers going about their tasks. They stripped rooms, scrubbed every inch of the place, brought in fresh flowers, cases of champagne, and new sheets for the beds. Dante showed me the grand ballroom, situated in the family's private wing of the house, which would play host to the event itself. It was a large room with a high ceiling painted midnight blue, and a vast, varnished floor. There were no windows but the walls were covered in floor to ceiling red velvet drapes which lent the place an air of intimacy despite its size. Workers were busy setting up rows of chairs and erecting a stage and a lighting rig at the far end of the hall. I was impressed by the set up, and I wondered how much it was costing to host it. I tried to get a rough guess of how many people we would be expecting by the number of chairs, and by my count I estimated it to be around one hundred and fifty.

The workers went about their business in relative quiet, speaking only when they had to, and wearing grim expressions of determination. They worked long hours from morning until night but did not sleep in the luxury guest rooms. As I watched them depart the main house of an evening I was told by Kerrigan that there was a block of staff accommodation at the far end of the large grounds, hidden from sight by a neat clump of trees. The old stables and servants' quarters, apparently.

The gates at the end of the drive, which usually stood open during the day, remained locked and the sign inviting people in for cream teas had been taken

The Society

down and replaced by one which read 'closed for one week for a private function.' Scrubbed and gleaming, the house proudly prepared to welcome the elite: The Old Souls. It was all very exciting.

The anticipation was plain to see on the faces of my hosts, and all study time and supervised creative sessions were cancelled for the week as we fell into a definite mood of celebration. I had little to do while I waited for the first draft of my book to be returned, with amendments from the publisher, and with everyone under strict orders not to leave the house I found myself spending a lot of time in the observatory simply watching Sonny paint and listening to his endless stories.

"My mother was always terribly overindulgent where I was concerned," he confided in me one day, never taking his eye off the canvas he was working on. "I could do no wrong as far as she was concerned. Even when I was expelled from school she didn't even scold me. Father was utterly furious though. I always feel a little guilty as it was only a month later that they died."

He stood back and tilted his head to the side as he examined the half-finished painting.

"No, too much red in the sky," he said to himself, shaking his head.

"Why were you expelled?" I asked.

"Oh, I was always in trouble at school," he shrugged. "What about you? Were you a troublemaker?"

"No, I was always very well behaved."

"I bet you were," he chuckled, stepping back to the canvas and starting to redo the sky of his landscape.

"Tell me, I really want to know, what did you do?"

"I feel like it's always me doing all the talking," he sighed, "you've told me practically nothing about your past. Here I am always rambling on, telling you everything, while you sit there like a closed book, absorbing it all so you can work it into your little stories."

"I'm sorry," I said feeling embarrassed. "You know my stories never have anything personal in them, I just observe people as inspiration."

"I know that, look at your face Quinn! You need to stop being so defensive," he took another step back and frowned critically at the piece. "All right, if you really want to know I'll tell you, but after that I'm going to put down this paintbrush so I can listen properly and you're going to tell me something about you."

A few seconds passed as he dabbed at the canvas before he said, "They found a copy of a questionable book I had been reading and they took great offence and shipped me home with a letter to my parents about morality."

"What book was it?"

"Against the law," he said and turned to see my reaction.

"By Peter Wildeblood?"

"That's the one," he said, dropping his brush into a pot of water and wiping his hands on an old rag. "One man's true account of being locked up in jail on charges of buggery. Not exactly the kind of literature we were encouraged to read."

"And you were expelled just for that?" I knew the text had been controversial but it seemed a little harsh.

"Not just that; I had brief thing with the head boy that year, nothing serious, just stupid, childish stuff, but enough to raise suspicions. In the end it was him who told the headmaster I was reading inappropriate books,

The Society

and he made up some lie to go along with it about me trying to get into bed with him. I felt terribly hurt and betrayed."

I couldn't seem to look at him and I stared instead out of the window at the lazy grey sea. I was sitting on the floor and he came and sat crossed legged opposite me, saying, "I can only speak so candidly about these things because it's not something I struggle with anymore, thanks to Dante. I don't think you're quite there yet, are you?"

My cheeks were burning and I couldn't answer.

"Your turn now," he said. "You told me your father doesn't speak to you anymore. Why?"

"Well," I began, struggling to find the words, "I suppose it's because I'm such a big disappointment to them."

"Well, that's not very specific, come on, you can tell me."

I looked up at him. He was staring at me earnestly with his beautiful green eyes.

"Our relationship was always a bit rocky," I began. "I spent my whole childhood trying to make him proud but it seemed as if he were indifferent to everything I did. I wanted so much for him to notice me, I'd write stories and give them to him to read. He had fought in the war like most of his generation and liked to tell tales of the heroics he'd witnessed. His time in service was a great source of pride, so I tried to write about soldiers on exciting missions, things I knew he would be interested in- he was my very first source of inspiration. But he never read them and told me I shouldn't be filling my head with fanciful ideas about becoming a writer. Even when I won a competition that the local paper was running, he still wasn't interested.

All he could say was that I'd wasted two shillings on the stamp to send away my entry."

I had only been twelve and the memory still stung. After that I finally gave up trying to get him to read anything I wrote.

"It happens all too often," Sonny said sadly. "I suppose I was one of the lucky ones to have two parents who encouraged my artistic endeavours."

"Well, as you know, I was once engaged to a girl called Emily," I continued. "Both my parents adored Emily; they couldn't have been happier when we announced our plans to marry. My father in particular was over the moon. For the first time in my life he was proud of me. I was working alongside him in the bank, I was marrying a lovely girl, there would be a wedding, grandchildren..."

I trailed off. I had been looking down the whole time, twiddling my fingers nervously in my lap. I glanced up at Sonny who had a sympathetic look on his face.

"It broke his heart when I called the whole thing off. Broke both their hearts actually, but what really killed our relationship was my suicide attempt."

I took a deep breath and swiped at my cheek, wiping away a tear.

"Oh Quinn," Sonny reached out and took my hand.

"I could have just quietly gone about it in private, but instead I had to cause a scene. I don't think I really wanted to die, I just wanted someone to listen, because nobody ever really listened."

"I'm listening now," he said gently.

"Emily got together with my friend George shortly after. It sent me into such a state of despair. I should have been happy for them, but it was George I

The Society

loved, always had, and knowing I couldn't have him nearly killed me. Some kind of psychosis took hold of me. I ended up outside their house one night yelling at the windows to George about how much I needed him and how I couldn't live without him. I had cut my wrists with a razor blade by the time the two of them had rushed out to see what was going on."

Sonny turned my hands over. The scars were very faint, you would never really notice unless you were looking for them. He ran a thumb over the white line of slightly raised flesh on my left wrist. I snatched my hands away.

"George and Emily stood by me," I said, "but that was the end as far as my father was concerned. I was a disgusting gay and worse still I had shouted it in the street for everyone to hear. News travels fast. The people he worked with soon knew what had happened and why. He claims the shame of it all is what killed my mother."

"I'm sorry," he said sincerely, "I really don't know what to say, but you're in the right place now and all of this is going to go away, you'll never be bothered by these kinds of issues again. I'm certain you'll make a real success of yourself and make the old man proud again."

Sonny leaned forward and gave me a hug. I looked up at the domed ceiling and tried to hold back my tears.

"You're going to be fine; I promise."
But what if I wasn't?

Chapter 18

1965

Most of the conference guests arrived a few days before the event, and as Chyanvean welcomed the stream of people and I picked out the faces of well-loved singers, actors and writers, I was so excited that I felt the urge to call George and tell him all about it.

"I actually saw Philip Larkin checking in today, can you believe it!" I said into the receiver. Of course I had been careful not to mention The Society or the real reason for the gathering.

"What, the poet?"

"Yes, and not just him; Anthony Burgess, George Harrison..." I rhymed off the impressive list of celebrities I had so far identified.

"That's crazy," exclaimed George, "you do seem to have landed on your feet Quinn, soon you'll be so in there with your successful peers that you'll forget all about your old friends..."

"You know that would never happen."

"We haven't seen you in a while. I'm almost done with the first run through of your manuscript, we all love it by the way. I was thinking perhaps you could come back to London, even just for a few days and we could go over a few things?"

The suggestion that I leave Chyanvean for London made my stomach clench uncomfortably, and I felt a little stab of panic.

"Not necessary," I insisted, "just post it back to me with the suggestions and I'll start redrafting."

"But surely you could spare us a few days..."

The Society

"George, at this stage I'm quite sure that all the work I have done on healing my mind would be instantly undone if I was to expose myself to the negativity and ugliness that is London," I could feel myself growing inexplicably angry.

"Well, maybe I could come to you? I'd love to see this place that has captured your imagination."

The stab of panic spread from my stomach and squeezed my heart. Quite why I should feel this way I couldn't say, but a visit from George seemed out of the question. I was happy having him at a distance, at the other end of the phone, but to bring him into the world I was now building around myself was too much like letting the outside in, and wasn't the whole point in these walls to keep the real world out? I had disclosed much to Dante about my infatuation with my friend, and we had identified my feelings towards him as a huge block in my creative energy. To have him turning up here would surely be devastating.

"Sorry George, the house isn't accepting guests right now. I'm not sure when it will be again."

The way I snapped at him did not sound like myself at all.

"But Quinn, aren't you a guest?"

Was I? A guest who didn't pay for his keep, who dined every night in the family's private quarters? I found I was no longer sure exactly what my place was here.

"George, you just can't come right now, soon maybe, you and Emily. I'll let you know when the timing is better, right now if you could just send me the manuscript?"

"All right Quinn," George sighed, defeated, "are you sure everything is alright there?"

"Yes, never better."

"Right, then I'll have the manuscript sent out as soon as I'm done with it."

We said our goodbyes and I hung up.

*

Dante told me everyone was required to attend a disclosure ahead of the conference. He explained that there were others among the guests who were trained, and of a high enough level within The Society, to carry out this process. He referred to these people as Inquisitors and he identified them by the dark purple robes they wore. The Inquisitors were all men and did not appear to count among their number any of the celebrities. I was informed that there were inquisitors based all across the country as everyone, including workers, were required to attend disclosure once a week. I later asked Sonny if the inquisitors could also perform cleansing.

"No, the ability to do that only comes when you reach the absolute highest level of study. It's what we all strive for, but so far there are only a handful of people authorised to administer a cleansing," Sonny informed me, "we call them keepers of the divine energy."

"But if there's so few of them, how does everyone manage to get a weekly cleansing?"

"They don't," he looked at me as if I were mad. "Regular parishioners only need a cleansing once a year, workers don't get them at all. It's only sick people like you and I that need one every week."

In my next disclosure, I told Dante about my phone call to George and expressed my concerns over his determination to visit.

"I see," said Dante, his eyes never leaving the pendulum. "I really was hoping there would be another way. I know the history the two of you share and how

The Society

much you value his friendship, but this person is a huge toxic influence. I fear that while this man is still in your life you will continue to experience blocks. I suspect there's still lingering feelings for him, isn't there?"

There was no point in lying, the pendulum would always give me away, so I admitted that yes, there was.

"I see all of these blocks when you attend your cleansing, like little dams stopping you from getting the full benefit of the energy. It's difficult, I know, but sometimes we just have to cut people out of our lives in order to move on. George belongs to the past; a miserable, painful past, and he has no place in the bright new future you are building."

"But he's my editor and we're working on the new book just now."

I watched the pendulum start to swing in wide, erratic arcs, seemingly in response to my anguish over this suggestion.

"Just look how much stress this is causing," said Dante, nodding at the wildly swinging pendulum. "I wouldn't worry about your working relationship too much. Just look at the people we have here with us this week, the connections The Society has. Don't you think you should be aiming a little higher than George and his tiny publishing firm? Once you've said your vows and you're one of us, we will look after you, we'll make sure you are signed up with one of the big literary houses, with people who have the money and the expertise to really get your work out there again, and make all your dreams come true."

What he said, if it was true, did make sense. My current publisher was a lightweight, a small -time operation in comparison to some of the larger companies. Their marketing budget was always small, their authors had never won any awards, and most remained relatively unknown. A change could be what my career needed, but could I really cut one of my oldest friends out of my life? The pendulum had calmed somewhat but was still swaying.

"See, you're feeling better by simply *thinking* about cutting ties and moving on. There's still a little doubt but that's only natural."

I watched the pendulum. Did I really need George anymore? Wouldn't it be best to move on?

"Think about it," Dante said, "only you can make this decision. It is entirely your choice. You are free to walk away from The Society, quit the program, and go back to your old life. Nobody is forcing you to say your vows and join us, perhaps The Society is not for you…"

"No," I said quickly, "I don't need to think about it, I want to join The Society."

"Ah," said Dante with a grin as the pendulum settled into a smooth clockwise spin, "at last, truth and clarity of the mind."

The Society

Chapter 19

1965

On the morning of the day before the conference, a final guest arrived. We were all summoned to the foyer; myself, Sonny, Dante, Kerrigan, Astrid, and all of the other guests. Strangely, there had been no effort yet on Dante's part to actually introduce me to any of the other attendees. I noticed that the guests mainly kept to themselves, staying in their rooms or reading William Thomas's texts quietly in the library, studying and reflecting in the birthplace of their founder. To members of The Society, Chyanvean was a sort of mecca, and this was the very serious business of their yearly pilgrimage. This was a spiritual event for them as well as a social one.

The Workers had laid out a red carpet which ran up the front steps of the house, across the foyer, and up the grand staircase. We were all lined up in two rows at either side of the carpet, forming an aisle down which our final guest would walk. There was no talk as we waited, just a tangible sense of expectation hanging in the air. Soon the two workers who were stationed at either side of the entrance, pulled open the doors and there, waiting at the start of the red carpet, was a silver Rolls Royce. A woman, identifiable as a worker by her dress, got out of the front passenger seat and held open the rear door. I wasn't sure what to expect, but out stepped a well-dressed man in a fine pinstripe suit. He was tall and slim with neat grey hair and high cheekbones, and he was carrying a silver head cane. I noticed he was also wearing white gloves.

The Society

"That's James-Anthony," Sonny whispered in my ear. "They say he wears those gloves because the flow of divine energy is so strong in him that it transfers to everyone he touches."

"Shut up Sonny!" Dante hissed, and I saw him give the artist a sharp elbow in the ribs. Sonny looked annoyed and took a deliberate sidestep away from Dante and closer to me.

I watched as James-Anthony raised a gloved hand and waved at the guests, grinning broadly at them. Everyone began to clap as he strode down the carpet, swinging the cane which was clearly all for show rather than being a walking aid. The clapping continued as he made his way down the aisle. As I looked around me I saw the adoring expressions on the faces of the parishioners. It struck me as curious that these people, who were themselves used to walking red carpets, being the centre of attention, and followed by fawning fans, were now the ones who appeared completely star struck. He passed by us all without speaking a word, just smiling, nodding, and waving. Dante and Kerrigan had stepped out of line and were now standing side by side at the foot of the stairs.

"Welcome home my old friend," Dante said, and the pair shook hands.

"Welcome," echoed Kerrigan, and when he took her hand and kissed it I swear she looked like she was going to faint.

"Dear guests, let us all welcome back to his spiritual home, our Grand High Master of Souls!"

Grand High Master of Souls?

A loud cheer erupted, and the applause intensified, but still James-Anthony did not speak. He simply stood for a few moments, bathing in their affection, then he turned and allowed Dante to lead him up the sweeping staircase.

After that the crowd began to disperse as a hush fell over the place again. I spent the remainder of the day in the study room with some books I had found in the library, trying to find any reference to grand high masters, keepers of the divine energy, and inquisitors, but with these being public works there was nothing but the usual self-help tricks and techniques. I guessed that once I was made a member tomorrow I would start to get access to the materials that were reserved for old souls.

The afternoon gave me suitable amounts of free time to work myself up into a state of anxiety about the following day. Nobody had told me what to expect, and I began to feel very apprehensive and on edge. I tried to talk to Sonny about it but he would tell me nothing, insisting I would just have to wait until tomorrow. To make matters worse, that evening neither Sonny nor I were permitted to join the family for dinner as we usually did and were made to sit among the other guests in the public dining room. Sonny was most put out by this. Even Astrid was left in Sonny's care for the evening, and so it ended up just being the three of us sitting at a table together while all around us the rich and famous dined but did not speak to us.

"It's because he'll be dining with James-Anthony of course," Sonny said as we sat listening to the murmur of civilised chatter mingled in with the birdsong from the speakers. "The likes of us aren't good enough to eat with the Grand High Master."

"I'm sorry that having dinner with me and Astrid is such a chore for you," I said jokingly, smiling at the little girl who had been looking very sombre since we sat

The Society

down. "Well, the pair of you are great company this evening, I must say!"

"Oh, it's not that, it's just, well, look at these people," Sonny's eyes swept the room.

"Yes, what about them?"

"I just sometimes feel so resentful towards them," he confessed. "I mean take Francis Bacon over there."

"Who?"

"Him, the one with the messy hair and the bad suit," he nodded towards a man a few tables away from us.

"I've heard of him, he's an artist too, isn't he?"

Sonny snorted, "I suppose so. I don't know if you've ever seen his work, it's completely deranged, and yet somehow because of The Society he sells, and because he sells he gets away with things he shouldn't. See that fellow sitting next to him?"

I nodded, trying not to make it obvious that we were looking at them.

"That's George Dyer, everybody knows they are lovers. Yet everyone pretends it's not the case and they turn a blind eye because he makes huge donations to The Society. Do you think he has to talk about all the sordid details of their affair to his inquisitor? Of course, he doesn't! He buys his way out of it. The whole thing is revolting and completely wrong, William Thomas said so, it's one of the worst misdeeds, yet they're allowed to get away with it because he has so much money and his paintings are in galleries all over the world. Also, he claims the program cured the pair of them of their alcoholism yet look at him there, knocking back the port at quite an alarming rate. He's clearly not properly applying the teachings."

It seemed to me that Sonny was jealous.

"And here they are, the lot of them, for no other reason than to have a big party, and to grovel at the feet of James-Anthony. Then afterwards, off they'll go back to their successful lives where they can pretty much do as they please, while us mere mortals are stuck here under constant scrutiny."

"It's really not that bad, I think it's wonderful that The Society has helped all of these people get where they are."

"Well, you would, wouldn't you?" he snapped. "You're going to be one of them. You'll get to leave one day and live your life. You'll have all the fame and success, and we'll see you back here once a year, maybe with your lover who officially isn't a lover, while some of us remain stuck here being constantly interrogated, punished, and never getting any better."

"Stop it, Sonny!" The small, stern voice interrupted his ranting. Astrid's tone was far too serious for such a small child. "Papa and Mama look after you very well, why would you want to leave us?"

"Oh, I don't, my love, not really," he gave her a smile, but the frustration on his face was plain to see. "I'd just like a little of what they have, that's all. Seeing them and what they've all achieved is just a reminder of what a failure I am. The only old soul for whom William Thomas's teachings does no good. Sometimes I just want to say fuck The Society and fuck William Thomas."

He laughed nervously, looking around to make sure no one had heard him, and took a large gulp of his wine. Astrid was staring at him with an angry look on her face.

"It's a misdeed to speak negatively about our founder and The Society," she scolded, "you know all transgressions have to be reported, and you don't want to end up in the hole again."

The Society

I stared at her, so completely astounded by the adult way she spoke that it didn't even cross my mind to ask what 'the hole' was. What was even more astonishing was that Sonny actually looked terrified of her.

"You don't need to tell them," He reasoned, "I'm just being silly, I don't really mean it, I love being here and I love William Thomas and your parents and James-Anthony and all these other old souls. And I love you. This is my little family and I'm so grateful for every one of you."

"That's better," she gave a curt nod and went back to her meal.

"Anyway," he said, changing the subject, "you must be excited about tomorrow? Saying your vows, being inducted into The Society?"

"Actually I'm a little nervous, I don't tend to fare too well at big functions."

Parties. Social gatherings. They had always been things I had shied away from, always making excuses not to attend. I felt that I was not good at making conversation, I was awkward and shy, a complete introvert if truth be told, and yet I felt that some of the techniques and teachings that I had been studying of late would be a great benefit to me come tomorrow.

"I wouldn't worry about any of that," Sonny said, "Dante won't let anything go wrong on your induction day, given he found you, you're his prodigy. You have no idea how excited Date is to have discovered you. He's never really recruited anyone of any real value, lots of excited new souls mainly, fodder for the workforce, general parishioners, but no one he can shout about."

"But what about all of these people?"

Raven Taylor

"Discovered and recruited by James-Anthony. Not actually Dante's own converts. They come here to be inducted, and for the odd course when the big city gets too much, but that's all really. When they do come Dante makes them sign the guest book and pose for photos. James-Anthony is based at our centre in London, the majority of their instruction took place there."

"So, they didn't actually study here?"

"Some of them did, in the early days, before James-Anthony took off for London, and most have done *some* courses here. The capital's a lot more convenient for most, this place is a bit out of the way. There's a little bit of rivalry between Dante and James-Anthony. Dante's still determined for Chyanvean to be more successful than London, that's why he's always putting adverts in magazines and trying to sell the magic of the location. It's also why he dotes on you so much and lets you stay here for free; you're the only of note who's ever answered one of his ads and chose to come here full time. He's desperate to make a success of you so he can at last say *one* of his own recruits reached the elite ranks."

The elite ranks. I liked the sound of that.

The Society

Raven Taylor
Chapter 20

1965

"It's your big day Quinn," Sonny grinned, patting me on the back. It was morning and he had been sent up to my room to fetch me. "I'm so glad that you're joining us, though it does make me a little sad as it means you will probably soon be leaving to go off and make a big success of yourself."

It was an odd thought. I had given little consideration to how long my stay might last once the conference was over. My flat in London, the life I had left behind there, seemed a distant memory, shrouded in fog and unhappy feelings. I wondered where I would go.

"Today your soul should be as clean as possible," Sonny told me as we wandered downstairs. The house seemed quieter than it had all week; there were no guests sitting in the lounge as we crossed it. "You are to attend disclosure followed directly by cleansing, but not with Dante this time, with the Master himself!"

Sonny looked excited. I paused next to the carved table, suddenly feeling anxious and afraid. I had built a sort of trust with Dante and his pendulum over the last month or so, and though disclosure was always difficult I had grown accustomed to sharing my innermost secrets with him. He was no longer a stranger; in fact, I considered him to be a friend and a faithful advisor. To have to start divulging things about my life and my misdeeds to someone I had never even met was an alarming prospect. There was a small voice in the back of my mind, which I had been gagging since I first

The Society

agreed to take part in all of this, which broke free now and told me I was losing my mind, and that I should leave, run away from this place while I still could.

"Sonny," I paused, my throat suddenly feeling constricted, a symptom which used to precede the panic attacks I would sometimes have as an adolescent, "Is all of this real? I mean The Society, old souls, new souls, cleansing, misdeeds. Is it really responsible for the success of all of these people, or is it just some kind of game, a fetish; rich people playing at rituals for their own amusement?"

His expression was grave as he regarded me. I suddenly felt like I couldn't breathe, as if there was an enormous weight crushing my chest.

"Oh, it's real Quinn," he assured me, "such doubts and questions will be tolerated at this early stage, but understand this, once you sign that contract you must be fully open and accepting of anything they might tell you, and you must never question The Society."

I had started to sweat and tremble. My head was spinning and my heart was pounding.

"It's a small price to pay for the knowledge and the power you will be granted," Sonny went on, before stopping as he noticed my distress.

I had to pull out one of the high-backed chairs from the table and sit down.

"Are you alright?"

"I'll be fine in a minute," I said, pulling at my shirt collar with a shaking hand.

"You don't look very good…" Sonny pulled out the next chair and sat facing me. "Can I do anything?"

I shook my head. I tried to remember what I used to do to handle such attacks. I focused on my breathing and tried to get my ragged gasps back under control, counting in for five and out for five. Eventually my breathing evened out again and my heart started to slow.

"What was that?" Sonny asked, frowning at me.

"A panic attack," I said, "I used to get them when I was younger, but not for years."

"Oh dear," he looked genuinely concerned. "Tell James-Anthony about it in disclosure, I'm sure he'll be able to identify the cause."

"I think I'm ok now," I said. "Can I ask you something?"

"Of course."

"If you were me, would you go through with this today? Do you ever have any regrets about joining?"

"Yes, I would and no, absolutely none. The Society is the best thing that ever happened to me, but at the end of the day it's your choice. Though I will say this; don't enter The Society lightly, it's a lifelong commitment, the vows are taken very seriously. You're either in, and you fully embrace it, setting aside all doubts, or you go and pack your bags and leave us to our celebrations." He stood up and extended his hand to me. "So, are you coming?"

I took his hand and went with him.

"Try not to worry," he said encouragingly, "I'll be there cheering you on the whole way."

The first step of the induction was a physical cleansing, which I likened to some sort of baptism. I was taken to a pleasant suite of rooms which I had not been shown before. It was like some kind of Victorian health spa; we passed a steam room, and I was led into a large space with frosted windows, bare yellow sandstone walls, and a rough grey flagstone floor. There was a wooden sun lounger in one corner with fluffy white towels and robes lying on it, and in another was a

The Society

beautiful, huge, square plunge bath, which was sunken into the floor and tiled with the most exquisite blue and white Mediterranean style tiles. There were countless green house plants along the edges of the room, and the whole place was pleasantly warm and humid, almost tropical.

Dante was waiting there for me, and he told me that the plunge bath was an original feature of the house, installed by William Thomas for use in his various treatments and therapies. Today he was impeccably dressed in a white suit over a white turtleneck sweater. I was my usual shabby self, but that didn't matter, as I was told to remove my garments and get into the water. Feeling terribly self-conscious I did as I was told, shocked to find that the water in the plunge bath was freezing cold.

"Right in," Dante commanded, "the cold will purify you. Your head as well, right under."

I submerged myself in the icy water and emerged gasping, feeling like all of the breath had been knocked out of me. Dante beckoned for me to come forward and I climbed up the little steps, now shivering violently, and was received into a white robe which Dante wrapped around me.

"Well done my son, your journey has now begun."

I was then taken through an arched door into what looked like a small dressing room which was painted in a deep red, had a chair and a dressing table with a mirror above it, and another long mirror on the wall. Dante handed me a shot glass with a dark liquid in it.

"Brandy," he said, "drink it, it will warm you up."

Raven Taylor

He left the room, closing the door behind him and leaving me alone. I sat down on the wooden chair and threw back the brandy, feeling the burning sensation it produced spreading through my chest.

I had just about regained the feeling in my cold body when two workers, one male and one female, entered the room without knocking. One of them was carrying a black bag.

"We have come to tidy you up so you look presentable for the Grand High Master," the woman was plain and straight faced as she opened the bag and began to lay out a line of tools on the table; scissors, clippers, nail files, tweezers.

"Yes, everyone must look their best when they meet his majesty," the young man who accompanied her said with a sneer. His companion shot him a warning look. "The likes of us could never hope for a personal audience with *him*, just a lifetime of being a slave."

I heard the slap as she struck him across the face, and I stared at them in shock.

"Never speak ill of the Grand High Master. It's an honour and a privilege to serve The Society. I'll see that you're punished for such insolence."

"I'm sorry," he muttered. There was a red mark on his cheek where she had hit him.

"There's really no need for that…" I protested, alarmed.

She had picked up a pair of scissors, and the way she held them while glaring at me made me think I'd better shut my mouth. She started trimming my hair, and the young man took my hand and began filing my nails. When they were done trimming and plucking and combing, the young man brought me in a new suit, and then they left me alone to get dressed. The suite was white, like Dante's, and fitted me perfectly. There was

The Society

even a pair of shiny white shoes to go along with it. I examined my appearance in the full-length mirror. I was no longer my shabby self; I couldn't remember having ever looked so good. The clothes felt expensive and were of far better quality than anything I had ever owned.

I was then escorted by the workers to the disclosure room where both Dante and James-Anthony (also in a white suit) were waiting for me.

"You're looking very sharp," Dante nodded in approval, "I don't think I've formally introduced you yet. This is James-Anthony, Grand High Master of Souls."

On closer inspection I guessed James-Anthony to be older than I had first thought, probably late fifties, but he had that same charismatic air about him that Dante had; that funny energy radiated off the pair of them.

"This is Quinn Bergman of course, the one I have been telling you about."

We shook hands, and then we all sat down around the table. With the pleasantries over it was straight to business. Dante handed James-Anthony my folder, which was now growing rather large with the notes he had transcribed from the recordings of our sessions. James-Anthony reviewed all the areas of trauma we had identified, all of the misdeeds I had been guilty of committing and asked what we had been doing to address them. He then took out his pendulum and started to push me harder than Dante ever had on every single digression that I had ever committed. It was the toughest interrogation I have ever endured, and soon my head was spinning. James-Anthony was cold and persistent, and there was not a hint of kindness or compassion when he questioned me over matters of childhood, family, relationships and, of course, my sexuality.

"Not an uncommon problem in old souls, often found in creative types, difficult to treat, but not impossible. We have had great success in remedying such blocks in The Society."

"You speak as if my being gay were some kind of disease."

"In a way it is. Like any perceived mental health problem, it is actually a disorder of the soul. It causes much unhappiness. Were it not for your condition, you would now be happily married to your Emily rather than being in the tortured state you are in now. Your life would be much easier, would it not, if you could fall in love with a woman?"

My life would be much easier if I was just allowed to fall in love with who I want.

James-Anthony glared at me as the pendulum started to swing erratically.

"Your thoughts are committing misdeeds," he said, narrowing his eyes at me. "This really is something you need to work on if you want to progress and do well within The Society, or you will become stuck and never obtain those higher levels of knowledge, ability and enlightenment."

"Like Sonny?" At the mention of him the pendulum went into a frenzied side to side swing.

"Dante, you might want to keep those two apart," he said, still staring at me.

In all I was quizzed for around two hours, and once we were done I felt so mentally drained that I couldn't even think straight. That was, however, remedied by the cleansing which followed right after. It too was delivered by The Grand High Master himself. It was carried out in the same way as usual, but the hit I

The Society
received dwarfed anything I had ever experienced with Dante, and resulted in the incredible high that would carry me through the whole night.

Chapter 21

1965

The guests were all gathered in the ballroom, sat in the rows of chairs the workers had laid out. I sat in the front row with Dante, Kerrigan, Sonny, and Astrid. Every guest in the place was dressed in white; the men in white suits and the women in lavish white dresses, subtly accented with the odd glittering jewel. The room was filled with excited chatter, and as I looked at the famous faces around me they all appeared to be in a similar state of euphoria to myself; wide-eyed with large pupils that never seemed to quite focus. On entry everyone had been handed a glass of champagne, and the whole place had the air of a high-end award ceremony. Once everyone was settled in their seats, and the main doors had been closed, Dante left his chair and took a stand behind the lectern on the stage. Behind him, two giant, crimson banners had been hung, each emblazoned with the golden bird logo. Between them, an overhead projector cast the word 'the arts above all' onto a white background. Lights had been perfectly rigged to illuminate the stage with a spot picking out the lectern and the speaker.

"My dear, dear friends," Dante spoke into the microphone, "I am humbled that my family home is once again able to play host to the annual conference of The Society of Old Souls. It's such a pleasure to see so many old friends, and to welcome some new ones."

He paused and there was a small round of applause from the audience. Taking my cue from them, I joined in.

The Society

"Now I know you didn't come all this way to listen to me rambling on, so without further ado, I give you our glorious leader, The Grand High Master of Souls, Mr. James-Anthony Broadbent!"

With that the room erupted. People clapped. They cheered. They whooped. They got to their feet, and when I looked around I saw that some of them were so overwhelmed they had tears of joy running down their faces as they clasped their hands and cried like frenzied teenagers at a Beatles concert. For a time James-Anthony simply stood there grinning, nodding, and waving at them as he basked in the glory of the adoring crowd. I had heard of similar reactions among parishioners to certain American evangelists; holy men who would take to the stage and reduce their congregation to a quivering mass simply with their presence. James-Anthony had this effect on the crowd, and God help me if I didn't feel it too; the sensation that the room was somehow blessed.

"Thank you, thank you all for such a wonderful and enthusiastic welcome," he said when the noise finally started to die down. Dante had vacated the stage and James-Anthony took his place at the lectern. "Welcome one and all, to this, our annual celebration of our founder, William Thomas, a name, which when spoken transcends all languages, all barriers and all lifetimes, and inspires every one of us to be the best we can be."

A ripple of cheers and applause swept around the room.

"This year has been huge for The Society," he boomed. " Let me show you just what we have achieved this year."

He paused and the room waited in rapt silence.

Raven Taylor

"In the past twelve months we have opened three new Centres for Better Living, bringing the total up to thirty, meaning we are halfway to our target of having one in every major city in the country."

The slide on the projector changed to display these statistics and everybody clapped.

"And in those centres, we have enrolled a further five hundred new participants onto the program. That's five hundred new parishioners whose lives have been changed forever. Five hundred people who now have the tools to live a better life, who are now committed to helping humanity thrive. Take a moment to think about that. That's a momentous achievement that every one of us can be proud of."

Once again the slide changed and his pause was filled with applause.

"Seventy-five graduates of The Program have this year decided to dedicate themselves to The Society full time by choosing to sign up for our workforce. We all know how important our workers are, so let's take a moment to show our appreciation for these devoted individuals without whom none of this would be possible."

As the enthusiastic cheers rang out I glanced to the edges of the room at the smartly turned-out waiters. Their faces remained neutral as we all clapped for them and their colleagues.

"The speech is always taped," Sonny said to me amid the resounding noise, "and the workers and regular parishioners all get to listen to it afterwards, copies are sent out to all the centres."

"The Program has this year rehabilitated over one hundred drug addicts, provided a place to stay for countless homeless people, and sent out aid workers to

The Society

assist in famine struck Indonesia and the war-torn Republic of the Congo."

Hollers and whoops of support echoed.

"And all of this before I even get to our contributions to the thing that matters most of all, the very reason we exist. These are all small matters in the bigger picture, our little ways of giving something back to those lesser beings, because we all know that the most important thing of all is."

Behind him the slogan appeared again: the arts above all.

"On top of all we have invested in the program and in our centres, we have donated over two thousand pounds this year to theatres, art schools, libraries and galleries. And this is all down to you and your generous contributions. I am proud, so proud of every single one of you and I thank you from the bottom of my heart. We are at the forefront of a new age of enlightenment! We are the bright beacon of peace that will end all wars! We will heal the sick, help the needy, and elevate creative genius, putting it back at the head civilisation, where it should be. We are the ones who will lead humanity out of this dark age and open their eyes to all the wonders and the beauty the world has to offer!"

Another huge roar came from the crowd, and their enthusiasm was so infectious that I found myself getting completely carried away.

"And we want to build on our success and make this our biggest year yet!"

Everyone was on their feet again; screaming, weeping, cheering uncontrollably.

"You all have positions of influence. Each one of you is loved and admired for your work. You can help us reach more people, share our vision of a world free from drugs and oppression, filled instead with beauty created by artists like yourselves. Show them that they can be free from the shackles they have been put in. It's time for our group to stop hiding in the shadows. Time to tell the world that you are old souls!" He raised a fist in the air and asked, "What are you?"

"Old Souls!" we chanted back, mimicking his gesture.

"That's right, and we are on the brink of something big. We now have only five years until the greatest event in the history of The Society, the event that William Thomas has foretold will change the world forever; the long-awaited enlightenment. Five years may seem like a long time, but it's not, and we must be prepared, this means getting our message out, recruiting as many new parishioners and workers as we can, and I'd like for us to have identified and brought under our protection, every old soul in the country by the time this date arrives."

This time there was an awed silence. I desperately wanted to know what this big event was.

"So that's my request for you all this year; recruit, recruit, recruit!" There was another cheer. "And as always, your donations are vital in keeping our work going, and will only become more so over this important time, so dig deep whenever you can, The Society needs you."

Donations. Contributions. George's voice in my head warned 'nobody gives anything away for free, Quinn.'

"Ladies and Gentlemen, we are in the midst of a war," he warned, "and we must never stop fighting, we must seek to bring an end to those who would crush us. But never doubt that this is a war we can, and will, win. Those we fight against have no vision and no clarity. They are weak and spineless. We already have them

The Society

retreating; with every old soul we save, every worker we recruit, every parishioner whose eyes we open, we force our enemies to step back. They have had us in chains for too long, but no more! We are rising, our ranks are swelling with each passing day. People are waking up in great numbers. Enlightenment is almost upon us, and in the end, it will be the old souls who triumph, and it will be to the benefit of every man, woman and child on this planet!"

The applause and cheers were immense and lasted many minutes. They rolled and echoed around the ballroom like a savage war cry and when it eventually calmed down James-Anthony spoke again.

"I'm pleased to announce that today we have some members with us who have shown huge dedication and commitment, the type of which will truly get us where we need to be. These individuals have studied and worked and are now ready to progress to stage six."

"What's stage six?" I whispered to Sonny.

"Shh, you'll learn about the stages later," he hissed.

"This is a very significant achievement worthy of great celebration, as these individuals are now ready to learn the details of enlightenment, knowledge which is not available to those on the lower rungs of the ladder."

Three people were called to the stage: fellow writer Lesley Holmes, the artist Francis Bacon, and actress Stephanie Barnes. Each approached the lectern in turn and stooped to sign some paperwork. Then James-Anthony would announce them again by name, shouting, "Lesley Holmes, stage six old soul!" and everyone would cheer, and he would pin some sort of medal on them before kissing them on the forehead.

Each and every one of them appeared to swoon at his touch.

"And now," he said once the newly recognised stage sixes had returned to their seats, "I am glad to say we have some new initiates to welcome into our family. Can I have Amelia Baxter, Maxwell Archer, and Quinn Bergman on the stage?"

"Come on, make me proud," Dante said, standing up to escort me to the stage.

"We bid you new initiates not to enter our family with a faint heart, or doubts in your mind," James-Anthony addressed us. "Those who join us with their spiritual channels open and ready to receive the great gifts we will impart on them shall never again feel fear, desperation, pain or sickness. Secrets will be revealed to you that will bring an end to all of the suffering that a human being is born with and give you the power to achieve the highest possible success in your life. But be aware, you are about to enter into a contract that will see you bound to our cause not just for this life, but for all those that follow. This is a serious commitment, for you take on the burden of being at the forefront of a war that has been raging for centuries, and you will be the ones who will lead the world into the light. But never doubt, great rewards await all those who take the Vows of the Old Souls. Anyone not ready for this affirmation should go now, leave with our blessing and good wishes, but understand that it would be better to die and start again than remain an old soul living in the dark of ignorance."

There was an ominous pause and I glanced nervously at my fellow initiates. Nobody moved.

"As you wish. Now let us proceed with the vows."

It seemed like I was watching everything through a thick haze, like this wasn't happening to me. I

The Society

had the most unusual sensation of being outside my body as I waited while the other two said their vows and signed their names. I barely heard a word of what was being said, James-Anthony's voice had become a smooth, indistinct drone as he instructed the initiates on what to say, their response a distant hum, and the applause after each one rolled over me like a restless tide. For a horrible moment I thought I was going to pass out as I looked at the sea of faces, and then I realised it was my turn, I was being summoned, and I walked in a trance over to James-Anthony and the lectern.

"Now it is time for you to make your commitment," he told me seriously. "Hand over your heart and repeat after me. I, Quinn Bergman, through free choice and of my own accord, do enter into the sacred Society of Old Souls."

I repeated the line back, still feeling strangely detached from the moment. He continued, and I found myself echoing each affirmation.

"I swear that I will dedicate this life, and all those that follow, to living by the rules of The Society.

"I will always value creativity above all and understand it is my duty to share my art with the world.

"I renounce the evils of a suppressive government and will seek to always defend The Society from its enemies.

"I swear that I will guard The Society's secrets with my life and never speak ill of this most glorious organisation.

"I understand that if I break my vows to The Society my soul will be in jeopardy, for this is a crime that will follow me into all future lives."

Once the vows were finished, I was led to the lectern to sign my contract. I was not given time to review the document's numerous pages, but I was feeling reckless and drunk in the overwhelming atmosphere and did not want to appear hesitant or afraid in front of so many of my peers, and so I signed my name. James-Anthony added his signature as witness, and we stepped out from behind the lectern.

"Quinn Bergman, you are now a sworn member of The Society of Old Souls!"

The Society

Chapter 22

2009

"You signed your name, just like that, without reading it?" She gave him a sceptical look.

Quinn's expression was vague as he gazed off into the distance, a tiny smile tugging at the corner of his mouth, lost in his thoughts. Clearly even now, after everything that had happened, that particular night was still a happy memory for him.

"I've seen copies of society contracts," she told him. "Among other things you signed away your right to choose your own medical care should you fall ill, agreeing that The Society would take sole responsibility for your treatment. That's actually quite a terrifying prospect, and it's happened before. I've heard some horror stories in recent years of parishioners being denied proper medical care."

"I know that, and that wasn't all I had agreed to. In signing that paper I had also agreed that I would give thirty percent of any and all earnings that I made to The Society, and that I would pay a fee of two hundred pounds to begin my stage one studies. George was right, nothing is free."

"And once you're hooked, they suck you dry, financially, don't they?"

"Yes, that's how it's become the huge machine it is today, it has more money than it can ever spend, and thanks to being granted religious status it now doesn't need to pay any tax, despite the fact that it's run like a big corporation."

The Society

She knew this. There are centres across the world now. In every city you went to you could find a Centre for Better living where you could go and pay to receive miracle cures for addiction and mental illness and ultimately end up being recruited. Plaques with the bird logo could be seen on many arts venues. Whenever there was a natural or manmade disaster, among the humanitarian aid workers pitching in on the news you could generally spot a high visibility vest or two with their emblem.

"The Society relies on members' desire to progress through the 'stages. There are ten in total, each promising new and more dazzling levels of power and success, until you eventually reach ultimate enlightenment. Each stage comes at a cost, which gets progressively larger as you proceed. Many get stuck on the bottom rungs purely because only the very wealthy can actually afford to climb higher."

"Another classic cult tactic," she sighed.

"That's how it can afford the huge spectacle that is the annual conference too," Quinn continued. "After James-Anthony was done addressing us that night there was a big celebration. There was an endless supply of champagne, a band playing, and huge fireworks display on the cliffs. Everyone got into the party spirit, and all of the people who I looked up to and admired were no longer ignoring me. Now that I was a member I was their equal, someone they could engage with. Drink flowed, probably more drugs too, who knows what they were giving us, but I felt elated. I chatted with Philip Larkin, Lesley Holmes, and Giles Gilbert. Literary giants who I greatly admired throughout my career. I even talked with John Lennon!"

Raven Taylor

That far away expression crept back over his face, and his smile grew wider. For a moment she just watched as he fell silent and seemed completely consumed in his own internal reminiscence. It was the first time since they had begun this interview that he had actually looked happy. It was good, she thought, that he at least had *some* pleasant memories of his time in The Society.

"I slept with Sonny that night," he said abruptly and then immediately looked embarrassed.

"Sorry?"

"Yes, in my four-poster bed. Both of us were drunk and high and crazy. I thought I could get away with it, thought that maybe now I was a member perhaps the same allowances that were apparently given to Francis Bacon might now be offered to me.

"I remember the thought struck me that I had never had sex with someone I actually cared for. What a sad thing that was. It bothered me. I wanted to put it right. And this time it was so far removed from all of those horrible, sordid encounters I had had behind Emily's back. Yet I was still plagued the next morning by that same sense of guilt. When the high had worn off and I woke up with Sonny in my bed I felt panicked and angry with myself. This was one of the main things that I was supposed to be working on, the biggest misdeed that I could possibly commit. I had been inducted into The Society mere hours ago and here I was already breaking the rules!"

He was twisting his hands anxiously in his lap now and looking distinctly uncomfortable.

"You don't have to talk about this if you don't want to," she said kindly.

"But I have to," he insisted. "Sonny had similar misgivings. There we were, two adults, absolutely

The Society

terrified of what Dante would do to us when the pendulum betrayed us and he found out. I feared being expelled from The Society, crawling back to London having thrown away the promise of a glittering new career. Sonny feared the physical violence he knew he would suffer. I knew Dante hit him, even that morning I could see he was covered in bruises. He told me he got them because Astrid told on for saying negative things during our dinner."

"That's something The Society has become well known for in recent years. Physical abuse and torture of its lower members."

"I'd eventually fall victim to it too. It starts to feel like you're trapped in an abusive relationship; you want to leave but something always stops you."

"Dante was very clever and very manipulative. I have found out a few things about him during my research that you might be interested in."

"Oh?"

"For instance, he was a trained hypnotist. Even more interestingly, before he partnered up with James-Anthony and became involved in The Society, he was a talented stage performer. He used to put on a sort of illusionist show, but not the rabbit in a hat kind, it was more psychological manipulation. He'd plant subliminal keywords in the minds of the audience and have them do his bidding. He could quite literally get people to do anything he wanted."

Quinn was surprised by this new information, he had had no idea, but it certainly went a long way towards explaining how Dante was able to exercise such control over people.

"Yes, Dante was performing that kind of 'magic' long before he ever heard of William Thomas. There's also a curious account I came across from a young man who claims to have been present at a bank robbery, during which he claims he witnessed Dante, also a customer waiting in line that day, talk one of the armed robbers into shooting his partner in the leg, and the man did it, so the story goes, with very little prompting, he just followed Dante's suggestion, like he couldn't help himself."

"Is that true?"

"Who can say, but if it is, it just demonstrates how dangerous this man is, how he has an uncanny ability to get into people's heads."

The Society

Chapter 23

1965

"No, it can't be!" I exclaimed, staring at the letter in disbelief.

Across the breakfast table, Dante was grinning at me. "I think I know what that is," he said with a wink.

"But New Horizons is one of the biggest publishers in the country!"

"And let me guess, they want you?" Dante's eyes were twinkling.

"So, they say!" I gasped. "I just can't believe it, I really can't. Lesley Holmes is with them and she won the Geoffrey Faber Memorial prize for fiction this year. Her last book is currently getting made into a Hollywood movie!"

"Perhaps she put in a good word for you, it looked like you two were getting on well at the conference."

"But it's all happened so fast..."

"That's the power of The Society," he smiled.

"This is marvelous news!" Kerrigan beamed. "Congratulations Quinn, I couldn't be happier for you."

"Yes, well done," Sonny said a little sourly.

New Horizons had an excellent reputation and was a much larger player in the literary world than George's firm, Blue Elephant, and I knew they could really do my new novel justice. That did not mean that parting ways with George and Blue Elephant was easy, far from it. Dante was there to supervise when I made that final phone call to George telling him I was breaking my contract with him (New Horizons were so eager to

The Society

have me on their books that they had agreed to a generous, advance and to take care of any money owed to Blue Elephant for breaking my contract). Dante insisted that it was only proper that I call George myself and tell him ahead of the official documents which would soon be arriving at his office.

"It will be a good time just to make a clean break," he told me, "Tell him you have moved on and you no longer need his friendship, or his publishing services."

He coached me on what I should say ahead of the call, we even rehearsed it, going over it so many times that words lost all meaning to me. That, Dante said, was the intention, he did not want me getting emotional. I was to completely detach myself from my old friend or else further 'blocks' were sure to follow.

"Well," said George, sadly, "I'm disappointed to be losing you as a client, but well done all the same. I won't even try to pretend that we can offer you as much as New Horizons can. I'm pleased for you, honestly, as your friend I'm delighted to see you moving up in the world."

The first part of my news he was handling rather well, exactly as a friend should. The next part he was not so willing to accept.

"I'm assuming you'll have to come to London at some point to sign your contracts with New Horizon, why don't we all meet up then, me and you and Emily?" he suggested "We miss you and we haven't seen you for ages."

"I'm sorry George, but that's the other thing; I've been doing a lot of work on my emotional wellbeing while I've been here, and it's really helped me to identify the negative things which were causing my unhappiness and holding me back. George, I'm afraid you are one of them, Emily too. So long as the two of you are in my life I am never going to be well. I'm going to have to disconnect from you, this phone call will be our last communication…"

"What? That's absurd! We've been friends for years! What the hell is going on in that place? Who are these people that say Emily and I are bad for you and that you can't see us anymore?" He was shouting into the phone now, clearly very angry and frustrated.

"I'm sorry George, but you have been identified as a negative influence and I have to disconnect."

"What is this? Listen to the way you're talking, you don't even sound like yourself, who speaks like that anyway? Please, let's just meet up, talk this over, I don't think you're in your right mind."

"I'm sorry but I can't do that, this is just the way it has to be I'm afraid," I said, my voice entirely flat and without emotion.

"I'll come down there, I swear, I know where you are, and I won't be told I can't see you. I'm going to get to the bottom of this Quinn, you don't just throw away years of friendship like that without good reason."

"I'm going to hang up now George, don't try to contact me again and don't waste your time coming down here because I won't see you. Same goes for Emily. Goodbye George."

"Quinn, this is insane, listen to me…"

I hung up.

"Nicely done Quinn," said Dante, patting me on the back, "I couldn't have done it better myself, now let's go and get you a drink."

But that was not the end of it. I should have known that George would not simply let this go.

The Society

Two days later I was in the lounge having coffee with Sonny, watching a handyman trying to hang his latest work above the fireplace. It was a huge piece painted on heavy board; a colourful panorama of Chyanvean itself and the landscape around it. Neither of us had attended disclosure since the conference, so Dante was not yet aware of our transgression. I wasn't feeling too concerned about the whole thing as I had already convinced myself that I could beat the pendulum. I planned simply to steer the conversation in another direction, I had plenty of other past digressions I could bring up that would be sure to satisfy him and keep me from dwelling on this particular one. Sonny, however, was not so confident, and remained entirely on edge about the whole thing. While I might have thought he would have tried to keep his distance from me, he insisted on following me around and telling me this was all my fault, that he had been doing just fine until I came here. I should be the one to confess and admit to it all being my doing and take as much of the blame as I could, he said. I tried to tell him he should just do the same as me and not say anything, that Date and his pendulum surely relied at least in part on the mindset of the person under examination. My logic was if you convinced yourself you had done nothing wrong, nothing worthy of disclosing, then you wouldn't give yourself away. He insisted it did not work like that, and whilst on the pendulum it was impossible to have any secrets.

We were arguing about this very point in whispered tones when we heard a commotion coming from the reception area. We both fell quiet and listened.

"No Sir, he's not receiving visitors, as I have just explained," came the voice of Magda, raised in exasperation, "we have strict orders not to permit anyone to see him without the permission of the owners."

"All right then, let me speak to the fucking owners then!" I had never heard George swear before. Actually, I could never recall ever even hearing him raise his voice, but it was definitely him, shouting at Magda.

"Mind your language Sir!" Magda cried indignantly.

"Right, this is a hotel, isn't it? Do you accept guests? I'd like to book a room."

I had crossed the guest lounge now and was lingering in the doorway to the foyer, watching the scene unfold, Sonny was right behind me. Seeing George standing there caused a painful twinge in my heart. Dear, handsome George looked absolutely furious as he glared at Magda, who was struggling to keep her composure.

"I'm sorry sir, but I don't have a room that you can have."

"Well, I know that's not true, is it? At this time of year? A place this size? The board outside says that you have vacancies."

She shrugged, "I'm afraid I can't help you."

"Fine, then I'll find him myself!" George marched across the foyer yelling, "Quinn! Quinn! I know you're here, and I'm not leaving until I've spoken with you."

"Sir!" Magda dashed from behind the desk and grabbed at George's arm, "You are making a scene and disturbing the guests, if you don't leave I will call the police."

George shook her off. "Go ahead, call them, maybe they will help me get to the bottom of what kind of operation you're running here."

The Society

George threw open the door to the bar and Magda, still protesting, followed him in. As they disappeared I could still hear him yelling my name. Sonny put a hand on my shoulder and said, "be strong Quinn, these things are sent to test us."

George came barrelling out of the bar and back into the foyer, Magda trying desperately to calm him down and get him to leave. I realised it was no good hiding here, I would have to confront him.

"I'll need to talk to him, tell him to go," I said.

"I'm right behind you," Sonny said as we stepped out into the foyer.

"I'm here, George," I called out, and George stopped dead.

"Quinn, thank God!" He hurried towards me, looking relieved, but I held out my palm to him in a gesture that told him not to come any closer. He hesitated.

"George, we talked about this," I said calmly. Thomas Williams taught that a good parishioner could keep his calm under any circumstance, and that composure must always be maintained. "I told you that I don't want you in my life anymore."

"But Quinn, I just wanted to see if you were all right, on the phone the other day, that wasn't you."

"I'm quite well, as you can see, now leave and please respect my wishes when I say that I no longer want to see you."

"You should listen to him," Sonny stepped up beside me, and his hand settled on my shoulder again, "he's decided to disconnect from you."

"Disconnect? Listen to yourself, nobody in the real-world talks like that, who the hell are you anyway? Are you the owner?"

Raven Taylor

"No, not the owner, just someone concerned for Quinn's wellbeing, someone who cares a great deal for him, in ways you never could..."

"I'm his oldest friend!" he yelled. "Quinn, I just need a few minutes of your time, that's all, we need to talk."

By now Dante had appeared from his private quarters, brought down by all the noise we were making.

"George, I assume," he said evenly, "you're making quite a racket down here and disrupting the peace in my beautiful hotel."

"I only want to talk to my friend but your people won't let me," George snapped angrily.

"My people? Why, Quinn is right here, no one is stopping you, but he's told you quite plainly that he doesn't wish to speak to you. Now kindly leave."

"I'm not going anywhere. I want to know what the hell is going on here that has turned him so completely against his friends. This is not the Quinn I know, what have you done to him, what have you been telling him?" George demanded.

"You're quite right, this is not the Quinn you know. This Quinn is getting better, he knows his own mind, and he knows which negative influence he does not need in his life anymore." Dante's tone remained smooth and charming as approached George calmly and tried to guide him towards the door.

"Get your hands off me!" George shouted as he swatted at Dante, who stopped where he was, folded his arms, and stared at George. "Quinn, this isn't you," he appealed to me again, looking distraught.

"It's no wonder he seems a different person," Dante reasoned, "the Quinn you knew was miserable, needy, low in self-esteem, and you preferred him like

The Society

that didn't you? Sure, we all know you had no intention of returning the love he felt for you, but having him trailing after you, so besotted and downtrodden, you liked the power that gave you, didn't you? You're angry because thanks to us he is finally learning to value himself and to stand up for himself."

"That is absolutely not how it was! Tell him Quinn!"

But I couldn't.

"We've helped Quinn to identify the problem areas in his life," Dante continued, still speaking as if this were nothing more than a casual chat. "He has restored his sense of self-worth, he knows he can do better than to keep pining after you, and that he will be better off if you are out of his life."

George dashed forward and grabbed my hand, looking at me with a desperate expression of concern.

"Quinn, look at this place, listen to these people, something is very wrong here. Come back to London with me," he pleaded.

"Not so," said Dante patiently, "everything here is *right*. You should look at yourself, you are the only one here who has raised his voice. You are agitated, angry, and not in control of your own emotions whilst the rest of us have remained calm. Now I will ask you one more time, please leave, or we will do as the lovely Magda suggested and call the police and have you arrested for breach of the peace."

"Quinn, please…" he tried one last time.

"Go away George, I don't need you anymore."

"Fine, I'm going" George backed away towards the door, looking hurt. "But this is not over, I'm going to find out who the hell you people are and get to the bottom of what this is all about."

And with that, George left. I had not even realised I had been holding my breath until all of the air escaped me in a long sigh.

"Quinn, I'm so sorry," said Dante as he strode across the room towards me, "but well done! You handled that beautifully, I can see the techniques for better communication are really starting to help you. Look at how calm you remained in the face of such hostility, it really was a wonder to behold, I'm so proud."

It was funny how praise from Dante could instantly lift my spirits.

"And hasn't this just demonstrated what we knew all along; that your friend there really is a terribly negative and out of control individual. No power over his emotions whatsoever. We all remained perfectly calm and rational, he was the only one who felt the need to shout and project his anger. He is obviously very jealous that you are doing so well without him."

"I suppose you have a point."

"Sonny, can you submit a report to The Grand High Master about this incident? I was hoping it wouldn't come to this, I thought I might be wrong, but I'm afraid we are going to have to add George to the list."

"The list?"

"Don't worry about that now, you'll learn about it all in good time."

*

"I can sort of see what you saw in him," Sonny admitted that evening as we were having our usual after dinner chat by the fire. "He's incredibly handsome and so passionate. But if Dante thinks there's something not right about him, then it must be true, he's never wrong about these things."

The Society

It had been an exhausting day. My nerves were frayed and stretched after the encounter. Cutting George out of my life, despite it being for the best, had left me with a hollow feeling in my stomach. I couldn't get the image of his anguished face out of my mind. I had not hurt him this much since the night of my suicide attempt.

"You've never really talked much about him to me," Sonny observed.

"George is one of the most compassionate people I know," I said. "It's incredible that he stood by me for so long knowing how I really felt."

"He drove you to attempt suicide," Sonny reminded me.

"I know, don't worry, I'm not going back on my decision. I understand that it was bad for me to keep holding onto our friendship, letting go was definitely the best thing to do," I believed what I was saying, but it didn't make it any easier.

"Was there ever a time when you thought you might have a future with him, as more than friends I mean?"

"I would try to convince myself that he could love me. I'd dream up scenarios in my head where he would tell me he was living a lie and couldn't deny it any longer. I remained ever hopeful that one day he would say he wanted to be with me, that he loved me. I think I always knew deep down it was never going to happen, but just allowing myself to have that little bit of hope lit a warm fire in my heart and kept me going through some bad times. I think that's why I held off telling him for so long, because as long as he didn't know he couldn't reject me and I could keep that tiny bit of hope burning."

"I know exactly what you mean," Sonny said slowly. "It was the same with me and Dante. When I first came here I was infatuated with him. I would tell myself that his marriage to Kerrigan was only for show, a mask to hide who he really was. If he didn't have feelings for me then why had he taken me in? Who was I to him?"

He stared off into the flames. I was not entirely surprised. He had hinted before that he had once felt something for Dante.

"In those days things were a bit more loose. Dante and James-Anthony hadn't properly been through all the texts and they were still really just laying the foundations for a program for better living. The Society came before the program. Back then we didn't have such a great understanding of William Thomas's teachings, neither of them had fully committed to it and at first they just treated The Society as an exclusive club for rich people, an excuse for parties with weird rituals and lots of play acting. There were drugs, drink, orgies, you wouldn't believe the things that went on back then."

This surprised me. Somehow I couldn't picture Dante, who took the teachings about misdeeds so seriously, behaving in this way.

"Thank goodness they gained a better understanding of it all and we were able to embark on the right path and set ourselves straight, otherwise god knows where we would be today."

I wondered why he was telling me this.

"Anyway, so you see how back then I, like you, could indulge myself with a little bit of hope. Anything was possible in those days. But that's all long in the past now."

I tried to look at him but he wouldn't meet my eyes.

The Society

"Except it's not, is it?" He mused. We were sitting side by side on the sofa and I was taken completely off guard when he took my hand. "Because it's happening all over again…"

Raven Taylor
Chapter 24

1965

After George's visit I was prescribed a course of Detoxification Therapy. It was another of the programs' wellness treatments but it felt more like torture. It was a process that I was assured would rid my body of any remaining toxins that still lingered from my time in London, my use of prescription drugs, and from George's visit. I was required to spend a full six hours a day sitting in the steam room in the Victorian spa. It quickly became unbearable as my organs began to work overtime to keep up with the excessive sweating; my heart raced and felt like it would burst out of my chest, I felt dizzy and lightheaded, and my lungs ached from inhaling the steam. I was only allowed one meal of boiled rice a day. As if that wasn't bad enough, once an hour I was required to leave the steam room and submerge myself in the icy cold water of the plunge bath. The shock of going from one extreme temperature to another was excruciating. This went on every day for two weeks.

During my time with The Society I would be prescribed this treatment a further two times. This first time, though highly unpleasant, I found I was able to endure it and convinced myself that I did feel a little better each day as I gradually reduced the toxins in my system. The second time was following an unavoidable trip to London, and as I was already ill to begin with, this course was pure hell. The third time was after I stupidly gave in and took some pain killers after having

The Society

some dental work done and had to purge their lingering presence from my body.

I did not see any sign of Sonny at all during my first round of detoxification therapy, and I began to wonder if he had talked to Dante about what had happened between us. Was he being punished? I worked myself into such a panic over this possibility that I found I had to tell Dante what had happened in our next disclosure. I was afraid that if I was a bad parishioner and tried to hide my misdeeds, then things might end up even worse for Sonny.

I was fresh out of a stint in the sauna when we sat down to talk, and my brain was still a little foggy, but I was feeling oddly relaxed as I watched the pendulum spinning. Dante made me go over every little thing in detail, while the tape recorder made sure my confessions were preserved. I think it was his intention to shame me as much as possible, to make me feel sordid by analysing the whole thing. It worked too, and by the end of it I was so filled with guilt that I wanted to punish *myself,* never mind waiting for Dante's sentencing. Yet no punishment came.

"Being open about this was the correct thing to do. I'm very glad that you trust me enough to be able to talk about such things, because hiding things would only have caused the worst kind of blocks in your energy."

"I've committed a grave misdeed, as a sworn member of The Society, I'm assuming there must be some repercussions."

Date tucked away the pendulum indicating that the disclosure part of our chat was over.

Raven Taylor

"My dear friend, didn't I tell you we weren't in the business of punishing people? Our aim is only to help."

I was puzzled. I thought back to Sonny's bruises. He had been beaten simply for saying something negative about The Society. I looked at Dante who was smiling at me with a look that could only be described as a mixture of compassion and pity. In those moments, when he seemed to be offering me some kind of absolution for my transgression, I could not bring myself to believe that he had beat Sonny. Was Sonny lying? Was he making up stories for attention? Perhaps it was as Kerrigan said, he was difficult, unresponsive to the program, troubled and plagued by psychological problems. I had, after all, caught him trying to jump off a cliff…

"I can't say I'm not deeply disappointed," Dante sighed, "but you see, in forcing you to talk so openly I've already helped you. You see how negatively the shame of this has been affecting your thinking, and now that you've let it out you feel better. By talking it through you recognise what a horrible act you committed, and I'm confident you won't let me down again, will you?"

"No," I was overwhelmed by his kindness. I felt pure love for him as he looked upon me with his air of patience and forgiveness, and I had to blink back the tears that were threatening to spill from my eyes.

"Well, then," he said gently, "why would there be any need for punishment? Let's just write it off as you get carried away by the events of the conference. You've made me proud. Go now, it's time for you to eat."

I had fully expected that I would leave that room with at least a black eye, but instead I left feeling exhilarated. I always felt that way when I had done

The Society

something right in Dante's book. Even my plain boiled rice tasted good that evening.

At the end of the two weeks I was declared free of toxins, and the steam room regime came to an end. On finishing my treatment Dante surprised me by telling me my new editor at New Horizons would like to meet with me to go over the manuscript, and that he thought it was time I take a trip to London. To begin with I was apprehensive about returning to my home, but I was delighted when Dante told me he thought I was well enough and far enough along in my studies that leaving for the city would not set my wellbeing back.

"Just for a short visit of course, I wouldn't be recommending you move back permanently just yet."

"Actually, I was thinking of putting my old flat up for sale and this might be a good opportunity to arrange that. I can't see myself ever living in London again."

He seemed very pleased to hear this and even told me that my stay at Chyanvean could be made more permanent for a modest rent, if that's what I wanted.

"I have a couple of things which might make your trip a little more enjoyable, too" he told me. "I thought we might get Paul to drive you in my Rolls Royce rather than you going in your own car. When he's not serving dinner or pouring drinks he often acts as my chauffeur and personal assistant. Also, I know you hit it off with the lovely Lesley Holmes at the conference so I've told her you'll be in the city. I thought that now you are colleagues it might be nice for you to take her out to dinner, all expenses paid by The Society."

"That's very kind," I said. It would be nice to talk to someone else who was an old soul and maybe get a fresh perspective on The Society from someone who was not closeted away in Chyanvean.

"Yes, and I thought perhaps you might take Sonny."

"Sonny?" I felt my heart flip a little. Why would he suggest such a thing? Was it some kind of test?

"Yes. He's been hanging about here for far too long; a change of scene might do him some good. Besides, I've pulled a few strings with a gallery in Chelsea and managed to get him some space to exhibit some of his paintings. I've sent some of his best pieces ahead and had some workers set it all up. All he needs to do is turn up at the opening. I've even asked some contacts to show face and maybe bid on a few pieces."

"That's very good of you."

"Well, I have to try and boost his confidence somehow, he's been very low these last two weeks, barely left his studio, and he hasn't been eating properly."

This dispelled the last bit of nagging doubt I had that Sonny's recent absence was on account of him being punished in some way.

"He doesn't apply William Thomas's teachings the way he's been taught and so things get on top of him. Not like you; you've already proved you know how to handle things correctly and look at how well *you're* doing. You haven't spent your time moping and beating yourself up over it."

Interesting choice of words.

"It's settled then!" he said, grinning. "And Quinn, by all means go back to your old house and arrange to have some of your things sent here, start making plans for a sale, but let me get you a hotel to stay in. If you stay in your old home I'm worried that certain negative people may make an appearance."

The Society

"Yes, no doubt," I agreed.

It was two days later that we left for London in Dante's fancy car. As well as Paul, who was driving, Dante had also sent another of the hotel's staff, a burly man who usually worked in the kitchen called Aleksanda. Dante told us he was there for 'extra help with whatever we might need,' though to me it felt more like the pair of them were there to keep an eye on us. As we drove through the Cornish countryside I wondered how time could have passed so quickly since my arrival at Chyanvean. It did not seem possible that I could have been cloistered up there like a hermit for almost three months. Christmas was approaching but there had been no mention of it at the house; no decorations, no cards, and I assumed that The Society did not celebrate it. That in itself did not bother me, I had always found Christmas to be an especially stressful time of year.

It was as if the hotel existed on its own timeline that ran independent to the rest of the world, and the feeling was a little unsettling. One thing was for certain though, as I left Chyanvean on that crisp winter morning, I was a different man to the one I had been when I arrived. I felt refreshed and stronger, with greater clarity of mind. Gone was the heavy, depressing cloud under which I had arrived.

There was a small, well stocked, drinks cabinet in the car and within half an hour of leaving Sonny had insisted on opening the champagne.

"This reminds me of our senior prom," he said as he handed me an overflowing crystal glass. "The father of one of the boys in my year sent his car to take a group of us. We weren't used to drinking and we got horribly drunk in the back on the way there. We were staggering about the place by the time we arrived at the venue and guess what, they wouldn't let us in! They said they weren't going to have us disgracing the school and told the driver to take us home."

"I'm not surprised."

"That's not all though," his eyes were shining. "What happened on the way home was worse. We were furious at being denied entry to the party but determined to have a good time anyway. That's when Frederick, one of the boys, revealed that he had brought along a bag of coke from his father's stash."

Sonny laughed wildly and downed his champagne before re-filling the glass again.

"So, when the driver stopped for petrol we were all high as kites and Charles, the one whose father owned the car, jumped into the front seat and away we went, leaving the driver yelling after us and waving his fist."

Sonny spluttered as he tried to contain his laughter. I didn't really see the funny side.

"You could have killed someone, or yourselves," I said sternly.

"Don't be such a bore!" he elbowed me. "Nobody was hurt. Other than the car, that was a right off…"

He exploded with laughter again, and when he saw I wasn't joining in he folded his arms moodily and looked out the window.

"I suppose you realise Dante is trying to set you up," he said after he had finished his second glass of champagne in silence.

"What do you mean, set me up?" I asked.

"Lesley. The beautiful writer. Candle lit dinner for two."

"Don't be ridiculous, we're peers, that's all, contracted to the same publisher. I've no interest in her in that way."

The Society

"Well, *I* know that," he rolled his eyes, "but nevertheless, that's what's happening. If Dante can marry you off then he can at last brag that he has cured you. I know, he tried it with me too. You'd be best just to go along with it, you'll have an easier life, you don't want to end up like me."

"You're being absurd."

"Am I? You've been a member of The Society for five minutes and you think you know it all. I've been a member for half my life," he said with a hint of bitterness. "Let me tell you how it was for me; listen and take heed."

Sonny folded his hands in his lap and looked very serious.

"When I was first taken in by Dante he tried to give me the world; he arranged exhibitions for me, gave me a safe place to work, and for a while I was tipped to be the next big thing in the art world. I attended my weekly disclosures and overcame so many of my blocks; drug addiction, alcoholism, mental health problems, all cured by the program. But there was a problem that I just couldn't seem to overcome."

"You're feelings for Dante?"

"Exactly," he confirmed. "My sexuality was viewed as just another condition that could be treated, and if they can marry you off it looks like the program has cured you and they can parade you round as a success story.

"They'll hand pick someone for you from The Society who you have things in common with. They picked me out a charming girl- Charlotte her name was- she had been a member of The Society for two years and was at stage two. I had been a member for six months and was still at stage one. Charlotte was intelligent, beautiful, and a talented sculptor. We had so much in common and we could talk for hours, we got on so well and quickly became best friends. But I refused to marry her because as you know I could not love her in that way."

"Why are you telling me I should just go along with it then? You didn't."

"Yes, and look at me," he said in an exasperated tone. "That's why my career has stalled, that's why I've never reached the dizzy heights of stage ten. If I'd stuck with the methods then perhaps I wouldn't have spent nine years stuck on stage two!"

This was a lot to take in. My mind was in two places. Part of me thought that if this were true then yes, I would go along with it; it would please Dante and I could no doubt have a happy life. Perhaps there would even be a chance for reconciliation with my father.

Then there was the little voice that crept into my thoughts and asked me, *why go back to Chyanvean at all? Just take Sonny and go to your old flat and live your life.* But by this point I was already conditioned to police my own thoughts. The program teaches a technique called 'thought stop' which involves the immediate shut down of any notions that could be considered improper. So I immediately shot that idea down and scolded myself for committing a misdeed of the mind.

"Don't even think about messing this up Quinn," he said, suddenly sounding angry. "Don't give up like I did, I won't allow it, I care too much about you to see that happen. The program works if you stick with it. If you don't go through with it they have their methods they'll use to try and cure you, and they're much worse than getting married, believe me. I won't condemn you to the things I've had to endure when you could have the world…"

The Society

He turned and looked out the window at the passing scenery. It looked as though he was holding back tears. I thought about the night on the cliffs, about the bruises on his body.

Are things really that bad for him?

Chapter 25

1965

The hotel we were staying in was in Knightsbridge and was very fancy. I noticed immediately that the place had the same kind of vibe to it as Chyanvean, from the piped in bird song in the foyer, to the stiff, expressionless faces of the staff and the smell of lavender. I was left with no doubt that this place was owned and run by The Society, just like Chyanvean. But while Chyanvean had a sort of old-world charm, this place was modern and the height of luxury. With its sleek plastic furniture and futuristic feel it was everything I hated about 1960s design. To an unsuspecting guest it would simply seem to be a very high-end hotel. I could certainly see how James-Anthony had far more success in recruiting people while based here than Dante had tucked all the way down at the tip of the country. I even spotted one of Sonny's paintings hanging in the foyer, and a door marked with a plaque which read 'Department of Study and Well Being.'

After unpacking, our first task was to visit my old flat, which was a most peculiar experience. Although I had only been gone a little under three months, it had become an alien world to me, and suddenly this place, which had always made me feel safe and comfortable, seemed terribly uninviting, even hostile. The ceilings seemed incredibly low, and they pressed down above my head. The rooms were small and claustrophobic and cluttered with my collection of pointless possessions. The lack of light let in by the small windows looking out onto a grey world was oppressive, and the constant

The Society

noise of traffic and people in the street below was maddening. We had left our two minders downstairs in the car, much to my relief, as I was beginning to find their constant, silent presence a bit unnerving.

"God, how did I ever live here?" A thin layer of dust had settled over everything in my absence and there was a faint musty smell of abandonment in the air. "And to think this is considered desirable in London and it cost me a fortune!"

"It's so small and depressing," Sonny said with a disapproving wrinkling of his nose.

"It's just awful," I said, "and all of this stuff…" I picked up a small ceramic elephant off the bookcase. "It's all just tat. I don't need any of it. I came here thinking I might want some of these things sent to Chyanvean, but now they don't even seem like my things anymore, this isn't my house, it belongs to someone else."

"It does, to the old you."

Sonny was close by me now, looking at me intently and I let the ceramic elephant fall from my hand where it broke in half on the hard floor. All I wanted to do at that moment was…*No!* I corrected myself, *don't allow your thoughts to commit misdeeds!*

The thought stop method saved me again. It would take me years and years to stop policing my own mind in this way.

"I don't want any of this," I said briskly, stepping away from him, "other than my clothes, none of this is of any use, I'll have a house clearance firm come and take the lot, there's no point in dragging artifacts from an old life around with me."

"Not even this?" Sonny had picked up a framed photograph from the mantle. It showed myself and George on the day my first book was released, smiling broadly, arms around each other's shoulders, and me clasping a hardback version of my work.

"Especially not that," I took the picture from him and threw it on the ground next to the broken elephant where the glass shattered.

"I have to tell you something about George," Sonny said, poking the broken picture with the toe of his shoe.

"What?"

"He's on the list."

I had completely forgotten about that. I had meant to ask at the time, what list Dante was having George placed on, but it had slipped my mind.

"What's the list?"

"It's a list of people who are a threat to The Society, dangerous people."

"Oh, come on, I might be better off without him in my life but George isn't a threat to anyone," I scoffed.

"He's a non-being."

I looked at him questioningly. I had no idea what he was talking about.

"A non-being is a person born without a soul," he said seriously. "The population is skyrocketing at a rate never seen before, so not only are the numbers of new souls going through the roof, it's now gotten so bad that demand can't keep up and so some people end up being born with no soul at all."

"Ok, but why are they a threat?"

"Because they are like black holes. Simply being in the same room as one can sap your very life force."

Funny, but it seemed plausible. I had already been conditioned to believe in reincarnation, new souls and old souls, so this didn't seem too far a stretch. I shivered as I looked down at George's empty eyes staring up at me from behind the broken glass.

The Society

*

I consulted an estate agent who was confident that the flat would sell quickly and made the necessary arrangements with a house clearance firm to have the contents removed and sold off. Sonny had gone to the gallery where his exhibition was being held, accompanied by Paul. They had taken the car so I was left to be escorted by Aleksanda to the offices of New Horizons Publishing in Bond Street by means of the tube. I tried to make some idle chat with my unwanted companion, but he seemed reluctant to talk with me and so I gave up.

The hustle and bustle of Bond Street was quite a contrast to the tranquility of Chyanvean. I started to feel quite excited as we walked, passing serious looking men in business suits and glamorous ladies in expensive dresses all rushing about their day. Everyone seemed to be in a hurry; all of them dashing to get to the next appointment that could make or break their big business deal or skipping off to meet their lovers for lunch. The rush of the deal I was about to sign had captured me and swept me up so I felt like one of them; someone important on my way to deal with essential business.

At the offices I met with David Summers who was the director of the company and he told me he had received glowing reports about my work from my new editor, who had said it was one of the best books she had been given to work on in years. They all had high hopes for its success and there was even mention of film rights; David telling me that the company was well connected with a few of the big studios in London. Next, I spent the afternoon with my new editor, Gloria, a lady in her fifties with greying hair and a sparkle that appeared in her eyes as we talked through my work and she highlighted some areas I should consider working on. She had been very thorough, and her suggestions were highly insightful. I was struck by how professional and creative she was in comparison to the staff I was used to working with at George's firm. In fact everything about this place, from its modern offices to the countless posters for well-known books on the walls, made Blue Elephant look positively amateurish in comparison. Finally, we went over contracts and legalities, including the documents their legal team had drawn up to allow them to buy me out of my contract with George's firm.

From there I returned to the hotel with Aleksandra so I could get ready for dinner with Lesley, after which we would both be attending Sonny's opening. I was anxious given what Sonny had suggested about this being a set up, but I tried to tell myself that he didn't know that for a fact, that we were just peers meeting for a friendly chat.

This hotel was larger than Chyanvean and of course London is never 'off season' so it was rather busy. I observed that they had decorated for Christmas, unlike Chyanvean, probably to fit in and keep up the appearance of being just a normal hotel. I watched the staff with interest as they all went about their duties in a quiet and efficient way, just as the workers at the house did, barely speaking, smiles on their faces which seemed forced and frozen in place. Like little drones, worker bees in a colony, they buzzed about on autopilot; clearing tables, serving drinks, directing people to their tables. Then I noticed one young girl clearing tables who did not have the frozen smile on her face, in fact she actually looked close to tears. As she moved in the direction of the bar where I sat, waiting for Lesley to arrive, I saw the tears begin to slide down her cheeks and I offered her my handkerchief. She looked around with an almost fearful expression to make sure no one was watching, then took it and dabbed at the corners of her eyes.

"Thank you, Sir," she said quietly, not looking me in the eye. She spoke with an eastern European accent.

"Are you alright?" I asked her.

"Just feeling a little tired and homesick. I have not been in this country long and I miss my family. They say I have a new family here now and I should try to just forget about them, but it's hard, my sister and I, we were so close. I'm afraid I won't ever see her again…"

At that moment the grinning concierge came striding towards me with Lesley in tow. The young girl jumped and quickly handed me back my handkerchief and picked up her stack of plates.

"Come now Roksana," the concierge addressed the young worker, "stop bothering our guests with your troubles."

"Oh, it's really all right…" I started to say, but he had swept his arm around her and was guiding her away.

"This must stop," I heard him saying as they departed, "where is your smile? Remember our true mission, to save the world, that's all that matters, not your family, not your home, you're part of something much more important than all of that now."

"That girl looks absolutely petrified," I observed.

"Oh don't worry about it," said Lesley, "they are all the same at first; young, away from home for the first time. The enormity of what they have signed up for sometimes takes little getting used to. She'll be ok. Now let's start again without such a rude interruption. Good evening, Quinn my dear, it's lovely to see you again."

Raven Taylor

She leaned in and kissed me on both cheeks. She smelled vaguely of roses. I felt quite awkward.

"Good evening, Lesley, I'm glad we could find the time to meet up."

Our literary careers dominated the conversation during dinner; how we got into writing, the successes we had had (she had considerably more than I did), our major influences. She spoke in glowing terms of New Horizons as a publisher and expressed her delight that they had agreed to take me on. She really was very easy to get along with, we had a lot in common, and I wondered again if it would be so bad just to settle down with her and rely on The Society to help me make it work. Really it would make my life so much easier; wife, nice house in the countryside, two literary geniuses working side by side on our latest masterpieces, retiring in the evenings to discuss our work and bounce ideas off each other. Wouldn't it be nice, and so easy, just to live a normal life?

But will it be easy? Living a lie? You'd be happy to use her like that?

"Quinn?" Lesley was laughing. "It looks like you are miles away."

"Sorry, my mind was wandering," we had just finished dessert and were sipping black coffee.

"I know what it's like, as writers our minds are never far from our plots, and our beloved characters, and once we start thinking about our work it's so easy to get lost."

"Yes, you're quite right."

"Well," she said, putting down her coffee cup and looking serious, "I think there's a subject on both of our minds that we should just get out in the open before we go off to the gallery."

"Ah, they've told you too?" I said, relieved.

The Society

"That The Society thinks we would make a fine match for marriage, yes."

"And what are your thoughts?" the conversion was taking an uncomfortable turn; I wasn't even sure how to proceed with discussing this with a woman I had really only just met.

"It's not uncommon for this to happen in The Society, I've seen it before. Don't look so worried, it's not like they'll force us to do it right away, we'll have time, a long engagement. I think I know why they are so keen to match us up, in almost every case of arranged marriage I've heard of in The Society, it's been done with a view to putting an end to one of the parties' misdeeds."

Does she know?

I felt my chest tightening and my breath shortening like it had the morning of my induction. I couldn't have another panic attack, not now, it was something I had been working on dealing with using William Thomas's methods. It was just a case of mind over matter.

"Yes, I'm afraid that my flaw is that I have always been terribly promiscuous. I can't help myself. I just love sex and I seem to just go through life having an endless string of meaningless affairs. It's so easy when you're in The Society and always mixing with the elite, so many beautiful and talented people. The Society takes a very dim view of such behaviour. I would imagine that's why they're trying to marry me off, to force me to settle down."

I felt my heart rate slowing. She was talking about herself. I sipped my coffee and tried to hide the shake in my hands.

"I'm constantly having to go on the pendulum and disclose my misdeeds, all the intimate details of my many sexual encounters, is becoming so taxing and humiliating that I wonder if it is indeed time to settle down. I have no doubt you would make a fine husband and could help cure me of my misdeeds."

I'm sure I'd be the perfect match for a woman with such a libido! Ha!

"Look at the time," I said, "we really should get going."

When we got out of the car at the gallery there was already a small crowd gathered inside; trendy looking individuals clutching long stemmed champagne glasses, laughing and critiquing the paintings among themselves. Many of the faces I recognised from the conference.

I entered with Lesley on my arm. She nodded and greeted people by name while I cast my eyes around for Sonny. I saw him towards the back of the room and he hurried over to greet us. Lesley excused herself as she had spotted someone she wanted to talk to.

"Welcome, Quinn!" Sonny took a glass of champagne from a tray being carried by a passing worker and handed it to me.

"This all looks fantastic," I said, glancing around at the display of his work.

"Doesn't it?" he said, beaming, "the lighting and everything is just perfect, the pictures look divine, and I've already sold two! There's also someone here from the press wanting to do a little story."

"That's excellent news!"

"I know! And I have just met the most wonderful young lady who came along today because she says she already owns one of my paintings. She received it as a gift but didn't know much about it so she couldn't believe it when she saw the advert for the exhibition. Hold on and I'll find her…"

The Society

Sonny bustled off, and I amused myself by studying a large seascape with a colourful sailing ship cutting through the middle of it.

"I found her," Sonny tapped me on the shoulder, and when I turned around I felt the air catch in my throat.

"Emily?" I squeaked, a cold sense of horror washing over me.

"Quinn," she said in a small, uncertain voice, "I had hoped you would be here."

"Is George with you?" my eyes darted wildly around the room, searching for any sign of my old friend.

"No, it's just me," she confirmed.

Sonny was now wearing a dark scowl as he said angrily, "how dare you trick me like that! Why didn't you tell me who you were?"

"You need to leave Emily, now," I told her.

"Leave? But why? I just want to talk to you Quinn, can't we just have a few minutes alone? Why have you cut off contact with us? What have we done wrong?"

My heart ached. I had known Emily since we were ten years old, we had grown up together, I had loved her dearly...I still loved her...

"Maybe you should give the girl a few minutes," Sonny whispered in my ear, "just explain to her that she's part of a painful past that you are trying to leave behind. Let her down gently but be firm. There's a little office through that door at the back, you can use that."

I sighed, "come on, Emily," I said, guiding her through the small crowd to the office.

"Oh, my dear, dear Quinn," she cried once we were alone. She tried to throw herself at me and hug me, but I stiffened and pushed her away.

"Sit down Emily."

"Quinn, I don't understand…"

"Just sit, please."

She took a chair at the desk and I sat across from her.

"What's going on Quinn? You look different, sort of distant."

"Listen Emily, things have changed, they couldn't keep going on the way they were with you and me and George. It was insane. I've moved on now, like I told George, I've got new friends, my career is taking off, I'm happy now."

"But must all of this be entirely at the expense of your old friends?" she pleaded, "Who are those people who have gotten under your skin so much in such a short period of time? George asked about in the village where you've been staying after you threw him out of the hotel. They didn't have anything good to say about the people in that house, or what goes on there. Half of them refused to even talk to us about it. Quinn, most of them looked terrified at the very mention of that place."

"George has been going around snooping and asking questions? How is this any of this his business?" I was angry.

"We're worried. The locals say that place is run by a cult."

Her use of the word cult left me feeling incredibly offended. How dare she use such language about the people who had helped me so much, about people who just wanted to make the world a better place. I rubbed my temples. I could feel a headache coming on.

The Society

"That's simply not true," I insisted, "these people are wonderful, they have helped me and so many others to turn our lives around. You know as well as anybody the state I was in before I left, how much I was suffering, and now I'm doing great, and you and George can do nothing but criticise!"

"This isn't you. George was right. What have they done to you Quinn?" Emily started to sob in despair.

"Done to me? Why they've lifted the influence you and George had over me, you were holding me back, I can't be around you anymore," I really was starting to feel quite unwell. My head was pounding and I felt like a fever was suddenly coming over me. "I wish you no personal harm Emily, I just want to be left alone to get on with my life. But beware of George, get away from him if you can, he's bad news, believe me..."

"Listen to yourself!" she exclaimed, "You sound like a raving lunatic..."

"Can't you just be happy for me? I'm doing well, I'm even going to be married." I was calm on the outside but angry and frustrated in my head. My hands had started to shake and beads of sweat were forming on my brow.

"Now we both know that's definitely not you," she insisted.

"Oh, isn't it? Maybe it was just being with you that drove me to do the things I did, because it's true, I've met someone, and we *will* be married."

She shook her head, looking hurt before she challenged me, "So there's nothing going on with that man out there, the artist? I was watching you; I saw the way you look at him, exactly the way you used to look at George."

"I have no idea what you're talking about."

"Come on Quinn, I know you too well, you can lie to yourself but I can see what's going on, it's obvious. Maybe that's the draw for you then, is that why they have such a hold over you? You've developed another of your stupid infatuations that make you crazy, haven't you?"

"How dare you!" I jumped up from my chair, and immediately felt dizzy and lightheaded. It was the most unusual sensation; it was not like my usual attacks of panic or anxiety; it felt like the energy was draining out of me, my body was growing heavy and my movements felt sluggish as if I was soaked in treacle, the weight of it clinging to me, clogging up my mind and soul. Then it struck me, what was happening.

"You're one of them too," I gasped. Her presence was abhorrent to me; she was a thing to be feared; I could not be in the room with her anymore. "It's not just George, it's you too..."

What I had been told about none-beings began to make sense; Emily was quite literally sucking the energy from me, sapping my creative force, and that's why I was feeling so ill. I stared wildly at the door. She was blocking my path to it. The thought of even brushing by her was unthinkable.

"You're a non-being," I said, sinking back into the chair and wrapping my arms around my head to block out her negative influence.

"Quinn, are you alright?" she sounded alarmed and she rushed around the table.

When she put her hands on me I actually screamed as her touch sent an uncontrollable convulsion down my body.

"Get off me!" I yelled in horror.

The Society

My yells drew attention to us and Sonny burst into the room with Lesley close behind him.

"Come on, you need to leave," Sonny cajoled her towards the door.

"Does he even know his mother died or do you confiscate all his mail?" She tried in a last desperate attempt to get me to listen.

Sonny paused and she pushed her way back into the room.

"Your father wrote to you," she said, slamming her hand on the desk, "It was just after George visited. She had a stroke. We didn't think for a second you'd ignore such news. By the look on your face as I'd say you had no idea. They kept that from you, didn't they? You weren't even at your own mother's funeral Quinn, let that sink in."

My mother was dead. It did not provoke any real emotion in me.

"We don't have funerals, we don't believe in grieving the dead, it's just a transition to the next life, nothing more." I was repeating lines from a text I had read on how to allow oneself to get emotional or upset by death could cause terrible blocks. Death was a thing to be treated with indifference.

"I don't believe this. You're sick Quinn, you're a victim and you need help," she called over her shoulder as Sonny shoved her out the door. "We won't give up on you, I promise!"

Sonny followed her out and slammed the door shut behind them.

"Oh, Quinn, my dear," Lesley said dramatically, "you look awful, an attack like that from a non-being can be quite unpleasant, you probably haven't been taught how to fend off spiritual attacks yet have you? Are you alright?"

"I really don't know..." I did feel like I had just been attacked, and the ill, heavy, feverish feeling remained.

"It's all right, she's gone now," Sonny came back into the room. "What a spiteful, vindictive, negative person. I can't believe I didn't spot her for what she was, I'm so, so sorry."

The pair of them were fussing over me, patting me on the back and asking if I was ok. I had my head on the desk and couldn't even lift it.

"We need to get him back to Chyanvean, he needs Dante," Sonny said.

"That won't be necessary," Lesley insisted. "He can come back to the hotel; we have everything we need there to help him.

"No, he needs divine energy."

"Yes, we have a keeper at the hotel, he can receive the energy there, you know that."

It was as if I was watching the whole exchange through a thick fog, powerless to give any of my own input.

"Your keepers aren't as good as Dante, and he should be in a familiar place."

"Nonsense," Lesley argued, "what are you going to do? Abandon your show and have him travel all the way back to Cornwall when he's sick? We can take care of him perfectly well here in the city."

"No, you're not taking him away from me, he belongs in Chyanvean, not in London where there are non-beings lurking around every corner. I don't know why we came here; everything is so much better in Chyanvean with our little family."

The Society

I glanced up and saw Lesley's eyes narrow, "I know all about you Sonny Newton, still holding onto your perversions, still stuck at stage two while Dante keeps you in that hotel like an overgrown house cat."

"I stay there because that's what The Society needs me to do, I've got a big part to play in the enlightenment."

"I'm sorry to interrupt but I don't feel good…" but they continued on as if I wasn't there.

"Oh yes," she laughed, "the enlightenment. But you don't even know what's going to happen then do you? Not allowed that knowledge at stage two, are you? You learn all about it at stage six though, and I'm a stage six now, which means I'm pretty confident it's not going to be all that wonderful for you. I wouldn't pin too much hope on those promises Dante has made to you. As for Quinn, he and I are to be married."

"Do you think I don't know that, you stupid woman!" Sonny exclaimed. "I told Quinn about it myself."

"Then why don't you just go back to Dante and wait out the next five years of your miserable life until you can fulfill your grand purpose."

Sonny was shaking with rage. "Oh, you'll get married, I'm sure, but you'll never really have him, because Quinn will always belong to me and for now, I'm taking him back to Chyanvean!"

Chapter 26

1965

I think I truly fell in love with Sonny on that car journey back to Cornwall. A person's emotions can be funny sometimes. You might expect the moment of love to strike in some romantic setting; walking along a beach at sunset, an early morning kiss as the summer sun falls through the window, after a pleasant evening spent together dining and drinking. But for me it came in the most unlikely of settings; in the back of a Rolls Royce with me feeling violently ill.

It's always been the small, seemingly insignificant things that really stir my passion, sometimes waking in me emotions so intense that they threaten to completely consume me. It's never the obvious things like kissing, holding hands or sex that incite in me feelings of love. Rather it is the subtle little things, such as the time George helped me do up my tie before I was due to speak to a small gathering at a book club, or when John Burns who was in my year at school lifted me off the ground in celebration when I scored a goal for my school's football team.

I think perhaps I had conditioned myself to look for love in the little things over the years, given the things that usually get a person's pulse raising were entirely forbidden and out of reach for me.

And so it was with that car journey. I remember little of it other than the brief snatches when I was actually awake. By this time I was in the grip of a terrible fever, burning up and shaking from head to toe, sweating profusely, drifting in and out of consciousness, a complete mess. I lay across the back seat with my head in Sonny's lap, and he stroked my hair, brushing it back out of my eyes, talking to me softly and telling me I would fine, and it was those small gestures, the sense that he really did care about me, and the concerned look on his face, that did it. How could I marry Lesley now? I loved Sonny. Yet how could I not?

When I closed my eyes and drifted away I had feverish dreams that switched between me and Sonny being happy together, away from Chyanvean and the world in a remote cottage in the Cornish countryside, to me living in my old flat with Lesley, with all of London clamouring madly outside and a baby crying in the back somewhere while I went slowly out of my mind. I was in a state of delirium by the time we reached Cornwall, and I think I told Sonny I loved him, though I couldn't be sure, it might have just been part of another dream. I don't remember him saying it back.

What was the true cause of my sudden illness I couldn't say, but I was soon to learn of The Society's views of medical professionals and medical treatment in general. What I needed was a doctor, but that's not what I got.

Much like the journey back to Chyanvean, I remember little of the next few days other than brief snatches. I was prescribed another course of detoxification therapy and workers came to drag me in my delirious state to the steam room every morning where I would be dumped and left to drift in and out of consciousness for hours. Now and then I remember Kerrigan appearing to force water down my parched throat. Dante would come and deliver cleansing which did not seem to produce the same euphoric feeling it usually did, but instead gave me intense and twisted nightmares. At least once a day he would take me to the disclosure room and urge me to confess all of my misdeeds, as I struggled to remain sitting up. I have absolutely no idea what I told him during those sessions. Christmas and the new year came and went without me even noticing. Eventually I began to feel better, and when I was not in the steam room, disclosure or cleansing, I was encouraged to sit up in bed and read William Thomas's writings on recovering from spiritual attacks.

I remember at one point asking for Sonny, but I was told he could not come.

I don't know how long I went on in that state, but at last my fever broke, and I became more lucid, my temperature went down and I was able to walk to the steam room without leaning on whoever was escorting me.

"I think you're over the worst of it," Kerrigan finally said one morning as she sat on the edge of my bed, "and I have some news for you. Well, two pieces of news actually. Firstly, this letter arrived from your new publisher."

The letter, addressed to myself, had been opened. Perhaps they were concerned that George and Emily would try to get in touch? Yes, that must be the reason they're screening my mail– to protect me.

"They have a proposed release date for your new book, February 31st, so you had better get back to work! Though I'm not sure joining the group work sessions is quite appropriate until you fully recover. Myself or Dante will sit with you for a few hours a day and supervise while you work, making sure you're staying on track and getting things done."

The Society

"Right." The 28th of February did seem a little tight to me, but I suppose if I put in enough hours then it should be possible.

"The next thing is that Dante thinks it's time we started some work on past life regression. He thinks there may be misdeeds from precious lives that contribute to your illness. It's very important to be able to connect with your former lives. Isn't that exciting?"

I agreed that it would be very interesting.

"We have some books here that you should study on the subject. Now that you're feeling a bit better we need to get you back on track with your stage one studies, you've fallen behind a bit. We're going to reduce the steam room hours to four hours a day in the morning, then you'll have five hours of writing time in the afternoon, followed by five hours of study. You can start back on three meals a day now too which is good news. We'll confine your activities to this room for now though, apart from the detoxification of course!"

To me that seemed like a heavy schedule. It would leave little time for anything else other than sleep, but if that was what must be done…

And that was my routine for a while.

There was a young worker who would come to my room to tidy up and bring me my meals each day. I wondered if Sonny was also unwell, and if he was, this worker could also be tending to him too. I decided to risk asking her the first time we were left alone together. At first she just ignored me and continued with her cleaning, so when she came to clear my lunch things aways from my desk I grabbed her by the wrist.

"You have to tell me if you've seen him since we returned from London."

"Please let me go," she pleaded, a terrified look on her face.

"You don't need to be frightened," I assured her, "just tell me if you've also been taking food to him, is he in his room, sick, like me?"

"No."

"No, he's not sick or no you haven't seen him?"

"I haven't seen him."

"Since when?"

"Since you came back from London."

"Not at all?"

"I told you, no!"

"What about your colleagues, has anyone mentioned tending to him?"

"Nobody has been serving him, it would have been on the list of chores!" She pulled hard and I released my grip.

"I don't suppose you know where he might be?"

"How should I know? But I will give you some advice, sir," she glanced fearfully at the door as if someone might be listening, "don't talk about him anymore. People often disappear from here, and it's generally accepted that when someone leaves, you don't mention them ever again, you go on as if they never existed." She made as if to leave.

"Wait, what do you mean?" I called after her. "Who else has disappeared?"

*

As soon as I was feeling strong enough, I decided I would have to go and look for Sonny myself.

As I entered Sonny's studio I was hit by how bright the sun was as it shined through the glass domed roof. The ambience there never ceased to amaze me; no matter what the weather, that very special Cornish light was harnessed by all of the glass and amplified,

The Society

naturally beautiful whatever the mood of the day. I wish I could say the same for the room itself. The place had been trashed. Everything was in disarray; furniture was overturned, canvases slashed, sculptures broken, paint splattered everywhere.

What the hell had happened here?

I surveyed the mess in disbelief. If Sonny had been sent away then he had not been happy about it. Then something caught my eye; a book, one of the texts of our founder, across the front of which someone had scrawled the word 'lies.'

I jumped when I heard the door open and spun around, my heart pounding in my chest.

"Mr. Bergman?" Said a small voice. Astrid was standing in the doorway. "I thought perhaps Sonny was back."

"No, it's only me."

"Oh well," she sighed.

"Come on, I'm not sure your parents would be too happy if they knew we were here. I'm supposed to be resting, not wandering about."

"You and Sonny were bad when you went to London," she said as we made our way down the stairs. "You associated with non-beings and Sonny ran away from your girlfriend and didn't let her help you. Papa says he has an unhealthy obsession with you and that's bad. That's why you got sick. Getting sick is punishment enough, Papa says. He also says as you're just new it's not really your fault. Sonny should know better though, so Sonny had to be punished."

"Punished?"

"Yes," she sighed again. "Sonny is *always* getting punished. I hardly ever am though because I obey the rules."

Raven Taylor

We were now in the foyer and to my horror I saw Dante emerge from the door that led to the family's private quarters. I froze. I had been caught in the act.

"Ah Quinn, it's good to see you up and about on your own, you must be feeling a good deal better I take it?"

Dante smiled and I felt relieved. I had been expecting him to be angry that I had left my room.

"Thank you, I'm getting there I think."

"Splendid! I'm so glad to hear this, I was hoping you'd be well enough soon to start taking part in some past life regression work."

"Yes, I've been reading about it and I'm very curious. I have to ask you something though, and I hope I'm not speaking out of line, but where is Sonny?"

Dante frowned and glanced toward the door to the tower and then at Astrid with an accusing look, before his winning smile sprang to his face and he said, "Why, he went back to London of course, his exhibition still has three weeks to run, he's needed there to oversee things."

It did make sense, I reasoned, and Dante's smile was confident and sincere as he looked me straight in the eyes.

"So, he's not been sent away to be punished?"

"Why would you ever think that?" he laughed. The smile stayed in place, but his blue eyes frosted over as he glanced at Astrid again, "has someone been putting ideas into your head?"

He reached out and took Astrid's hand, pulling the little girl away from me so she stood at his side. She looked up at me with an anxious expression.

"Or perhaps something happened in London that I don't know about," the smile was gone now and his cold eyes bored holes in me. "Have you been holding back in disclosures?"

"No, nothing like that, it's just that I went up to the studio and it's a mess. It looks like something must have really upset him for him to do that to his work and his space."

"Yes, well, you know what he's like. Prone to dramatic outbursts," some of the warmth returned to his gaze. "He did get a little bit angry when I suggested he should have let the hotel in London tend to you rather than abandoning his show which I put so much effort into organising. We won't be seeing him for a while anyway, he'll be staying in London for the foreseeable future. I've arranged for him to teach some art classes at the hotel you stayed in and host a couple more exhibitions. I really felt it was time he tried to be a bit more independent. Regrettably, I've had to be honest and admit that perhaps we were stifling him a little. Some time away is what he needs now."

I felt my heart sink.

Raven Taylor

The Society

Raven Taylor
PART TWO

The Society

Chapter 27

1966

It would be a whole year before I saw Sonny again. In that time I had become so entrenched in The Society and its brainwashing that I no longer questioned anything I was told and obeyed every rule like a perfect parishioner. But there was someone in the house whose innocence and curiosity refused to be blinded, and she often saw what myself and the visiting guests refused to.

"I wonder if Sonny will be allowed out to join us for the conference this year."

Astrid would often sit with me while I wrote, and just as she used to copy Sonny while he painted, she had taken to scribbling childish stories in a little notebook. Her choice of words struck me as odd because she had not said 'home' but 'out.'

"What do you mean?" I glanced up at her.

"I hope Papa lets him out to join us, I don't ever remember there being a party without Sonny. He's like my brother and I think he's been punished enough. When Magda was punished it wasn't for nearly as long as this."

"I'm sure your father will let him come back from London for the conference," I assured her, watching her reaction.

She put down her pencil and looked at me curiously. "Can I tell you a secret?"

"Of course."

"But you have to promise not to tell anyone, it might be a misdeed and I don't want to get into trouble."

"I promise I won't tell anyone."

The Society

"Sonny got back from London *ages* ago. They think I don't know, but I do."

"So, he's here, in the house?"

"Yes," she picked up her pencil again and added, "I think I might like to be a writer one day."

I got up from my desk and went over to where she was sitting in the armchair by the fire. I crouched down so I could be at her level.

"Astrid, where is he?" She ignored me and stared at her page with an intense look of concentration. I reached out and took the pen from her hand. "This is important Astrid, where's Sonny?"

"In the hole," she told me.

The hole. I had heard that term once before from this same little girl, as we had sat for dinner and she had scolded Sonny for criticising William Thomas.

"What's the hole?"

"It's where people go to be punished," she said, "but only when they've done something really, really bad. Some things, like thinking the wrong thing, or little misdeeds can be fixed with disclosure and cleansing or other punishments which aren't as bad. For worse things people get sent to the hole."

"What kind of things?"

"Saying bad things publicly about The Society, trying to run away, not following instructions of people of higher rank. I've never done anything like that. I'm good."

I felt a chill run down my spine. My stage one studies had been very clear on The Society's rules but said nothing about what happened if you tried to leave. Was I being held a prisoner here without even knowing it?

"Is that what Sonny did? Try to run away?"

"It wasn't the first time. I do wish he'd learn!" she sighed dramatically. "I don't even know why he would want to leave, it's lovely here. You won't try to leave, will you?"

"Oh no, of course not."

"I'm glad," she smiled.

"Astrid, do you know where the hole is?" I ventured.

"In the basement."

"How do I get there?"

"There's a trapdoor at the bottom of the stairs to the tower."

What the hell is going on in this place?

I gave Astrid her pen back and resolved to go looking for the place once the household had retired for the evening.

Chyanvean at night, when it is sleeping, is a creepy place. In the darkness the house seems to brood and sigh, as if troubled by the things it has seen over the years. The quietness amplifies the sound of the sea and you can hear the waves heaving in the cove down below throughout the whole place, and sometimes it sounds like the voices of the dead speaking from their watery graves.

I found the trapdoor easily enough. The small space behind the door to the tower before the stairs began was only about a couple of square feet, and all I had to do was to pull back the Persian rug and there it was. The wood of the trapdoor looked old and thick, its surface scarred with years of footfall, with a heavy brass ring set towards the top edge next to a keyhole with an ornate metal surround. I tugged at the ring but of course it was locked. I wondered where the keys might be, but quickly realised any attempts to locate them would be futile. But then I remembered the skeleton key. I had

The Society

never had cause to use it and it had been in my drawer since the night Sonny gave it to me. His words from that evening echoed in my head.

You'll probably never need it, but keep it close, just in case...

I hurried quickly back to my room to retrieve it. In the guest lounge the fire had burned down to glowing embers and the room had been claimed by shadows. As I dashed across it in my stocking feet I fancied that they crept out from their places in the corners, from under the chairs and table, and began to chase after me, sinister shadow mouths open and echoing with the wail of the sea.

Once back at the tower I slipped the key into the lock and was glad when it turned smoothly and released the mechanism. I heaved open the heavy door and was met immediately by a glare of clinical, white light and a white staircase. The brightness was jarring in contrast to the dim shadows of the world above. As I descended into the glare I pulled the trap door shut above my head.

At the bottom was a long corridor, again all in white and lit with fluorescent strip lights. I paused, my heart pounding and my mouth dry, listening to the sound of the bowels of Chyanvean as it groaned and echoed, projecting the sound of the high tide that filled the caverns and caves below its foundations. It was an eerie effect and I wanted to turn around and run back to my bed like a frightened child.

As I began to make my way down the corridor, the clinical surroundings gave me the feeling I was traversing some kind of hospital. The corridor went on for about 200 yards before turning off abruptly to the left. This new section of corridor had eleven doors, all numbered, five on each side with a final one set into the dead end ahead.

"Sonny?" I called cautiously, my voice echoing off the walls. I listened for a reply but none came.

It was freezing down here and I shivered and rubbed my arms, wishing I had put on my dressing gown. I pushed the first door, number one, and it swung open. The room beyond was much like a prison cell; small, square and white with a metal framed bed, a desk and a toilet. I made my way down the corridor, opening each door in turn and finding them all of identical layout but presently unoccupied.

Finally, there was only the door at the end, and now that I was close to it I could read the plaque which said, 'Rehabilitation Room.' Feeling a bit sick, I twisted the handle and pushed it open, and that was where I found them.

The room beyond was much larger than the cells and was again painted all in white. On the wall facing me hung a portrait of a serious looking William Thomas, watching over the scene in the room with stern grey eyes. There was a hospital bed against one wall with leather restraints and bookshelves filled with Society textbooks. There were several white plastic tables with matching plastic chairs. Around one of the tables sat a small group of six people all dressed in white scrubs. They were all paired up and were doing card sorts with each other, trying to figure out their misdeeds.

I was already familiar with card sorts. I'd been made to do them on many occasions. It was a technique for identifying personality types and predicting the types of misdeeds a person may be prone to. It can be performed alone or with a partner. Each card has a statement on it, for example 'I enjoy the company of animals' and the subject would respond to each

The Society

statement by categorising it as 'strongly agree,' 'somewhat agree,' 'somewhat disagree', 'disagree', or 'strongly disagree'. At the end of the sort the subject would have five piles of cards, and the results of where each statement had landed would then be analysed. So, if your 'strongly agree' pile contained many cards with things like 'I am nervous about voicing my opinion' you might be considered to be lacking in confidence, and that would be an area you would then have to work on, and so on.

Four of the people in the room I did not recognise, but I was able to pick out Sonny and the young girl who had brought my meals when I was sick the previous year.

They were all so absorbed in those little stacks of cards that they hadn't heard me enter. For a moment all I could do was stand and stare at the bizarre scene.

Why are they doing this down here in the middle of the night?

There was a man of around fifty with a stern look of grim determination on his face and a black eye, reading out questions on the card to a sobbing woman with a wild shock of grey hair who seemed to have broken down and was incapable of answering. When she failed to respond her partner would slam his hand on the table and ask her again and again "I sometimes have thoughts about committing incest". Next to them was a middle-aged man, who looked like he was in some kind of trance, being quizzed by a woman whose eyes were red and puffy and who looked like she hadn't slept in weeks. Finally there was Sonny and the young girl who attended me in my sickness. All of them appeared to have bruises and minor injuries, and they looked malnourished, their faces gaunt and their skin pale and sickly.

"What the hell is this?" I finally managed to say, and they all stopped what they were doing and looked at me. The grey-haired woman stopped sobbing and abruptly began to scream while pressing her hands to her ears. Her stern-faced partner slapped her and the sharp sound echoed around the room.

"Who are you?" he demanded, turning his attention to me, and I observed that he actually looked angry that I had dared disturb them. The woman put her head on the table and resumed her sobbing.

"Quinn, what are you doing here?" Sonny stood up and came towards me, he had an angry purple bruise on his temple and what appeared to be the impression of finger marks on his left arm. He had lost a lot of weight and looked quite unwell. I was lost for words.

"You can't be here," he said urgently, "Dante will be furious when he finds out you're interrupting our rehabilitation."

"What are you talking about? This is insane. Dante said you were in London getting help from James-Anthony."

"That didn't work out," he said bitterly, "I found a way to mess things up as usual. I only lasted a few months."

"And you've been down here the rest of the time?" I asked, horrified.

"Yes, and I'll stay down here until I'm well enough to leave, we all will."

"This is madness," I protested, "come on, I'm getting you out."

I was aware of the others, watching us intently.

"Be strong, don't fuck this up or we'll all suffer," warned the stern-faced man.

The Society

"Yes," said Sonny, "we have to stick to the treatment plan. Quinn, I'll show you out."

Sonny grabbed my arm and guided me back through the door.

"You must have been down here for about eight months," I said when we were alone in the corridor.

"Really? It doesn't seem that long."

"This isn't right. This is nonsense. I'm going to leave. I'm done with all of this."

"You can't leave," Sonny warned, "they won't let you."

"Rubbish! They can't stop me; I'll just walk out the front door and never come back."

"If you do, they will do everything they can to ruin your life and your career. Think of all the things you have told them during disclosure, it's all on record. They'll follow you. They'll tell the world your secrets. They won't leave you alone. Once you've said your vows and signed a contract there's no leaving. Once you are in, the only way you can hope to have a decent life is to keep playing the game and stick to the rules."

"Sonny come on, come with me, we'll take my car and go, right now."

I grabbed his hand and pulled but he resisted.

"I can't. I just can't. This is my home. They are my family."

"You have me now."

He shook his head.

"I'm leaving," I insisted, "and I'll come back with the police if I have to and tell them how Dante is keeping people locked in his basement."

"It would do no good if you did," he said, "there's not one person down here who wouldn't simply tell them they are here by choice, not force, including me."

"But I can't leave you here knowing what's going on!" I reached out and touched the bruise on his face. "Look what they are doing to you!"

"I deserve it," he said miserably. "What a privilege it was to have one on one time with James-Anthony, few people get that, but it was wasted on me. It's all your fault anyway! I was doing well until you came along and made me fall in love with you."

I stopped. I was sure I must have misheard him. Sonny loved me. Despite the dire circumstances we were in I felt my heart leap.

"I shouldn't have said that," he said, looking shocked, as he glanced nervously back at the door. It was now open and the stern faced mine was watching us. But he *had* said it, and that was enough for me and I felt elated. Nobody had ever actually been *in love with* me. All my life I had felt this way about people who could never return the sentiment until now, and I was overwhelmed with joy and a new sense of hope. I hadn't realised how lonely and empty I had been this last year, and now it was as if all the warmth had come back into the world. I remembered way back in the beginning, and the first time I had dined with the family…

"You asked me a question once and I never gave you an answer," I said. "Well, here it is: I don't think I've ever felt alive, not really, not until this moment."

I could tell by his face that he knew what I was talking about. Through the obvious fear he couldn't hold back the hint of a smile. The stern looking man was glaring at us with an expression of anger while in the room behind him his partner had returned her head to her hands and was sobbing again. "You'll get us all punished!" He warned.

The Society

"And in the car back from London, you told me you loved me," Sonny said. "I wanted to say it back, but you were delirious, and I convinced myself it was just the fever talking and that you couldn't possibly mean it."

"It's true. I do love you, and I don't give a damn what these people think!"

I shot a defiant stare at the stern looking man who seemed to be shaking with rage, his fists clenched by his sides. Sonny's confession had strengthened my resolve and convinced me that we could do this, that we had to get out of here.

"This is all nonsense, all of it," I said. "If you love me just come with me, please."

He looked conflicted and completely exhausted. "I can't," he said.

I shook him hard, "Don't you see what's happening? It's all lies! Come with me and we'll be together, live a quiet life somewhere out of the way."

"But what about Lesley? Dante tells me you'll be marrying her soon," he said doubtfully.

"To hell with Lesley and Dante!" I shouted, "I love *you* and that's all that matters!" I tugged on his arm. "Come on Sonny!"

He glanced around nervously at the others again, and then I saw that hint of a smile trying to break through his fear and confusion again as he said, "All right, let's do it."

"Go and pack a bag," I instructed him once we were in the foyer, "just essentials, be quick, and meet me back here."

But then a thought struck me, and I suddenly saw the plan falling apart in front of my eyes.

"The gates," I said quietly, "they'll be locked."

"Don't worry, I know the code, I figured it out ages ago, it's Astrid's date of birth."

"Right, good. Let's get going, hurry up."

"I don't think I can do this…" he had started to shake and he looked terrified.

"Yes, you can," I took his face in my hands and kissed him. "You have me now and it's all going to be alright. I love you; you can do this."

"I love you too Quinn." Those words gave me all the strength I needed.

In less than fifteen minutes we were back in the foyer. Sonny had changed out of the white scrubs and was carrying a large overnight bag. I had thrown my clothes into my suitcase along with my notebooks containing my latest unfinished work. I was eager to get going but Sonny was dragging his feet, lingering in the foyer, staring around at the place with a sad expression on his face.

"This has been my home for so long. Dante and Kerrigan have been like parents to me since I lost my own. I would have liked to have said goodbye, to thank them for all they've done for me. Running away like this just seems so wrong…" he trailed off.

"This really isn't the time to get sentimental," I urged, "and we aren't 'running away', we're two adults for Christ's sake, we aren't children or criminals in jail! This is just a house, a hotel."

"Yet what kind of life will we have without The Society?"

"A good one. Now come on, we don't have time for this."

I grabbed him and shoved him in the direction of the front door. Using the skeleton key, I unlocked the heavy doors and pulled them open, pushing Sonny ahead of me and out into the cold night air, before

The Society

closing them behind us. My car was parked opposite the hotel entrance, next to Dante's silver Rolls Royce, and we threw our bags on the back seat. There was a mounting sense of urgency growing in me; despite my attempts to rationalise things it really did feel like we were running away. I opened the driver's door and was just about to get in when I heard Sonny let out a panicked "Oh no", and when I looked at him he was staring with wide eyes at the house.

Chyanvean loomed black and ominous against the clear starry sky, watching us accusingly. What had once appeared magnificent and inspiring tonight seemed threatening and sinister. It was a monster which had swallowed us and we had been trapped in its putrid belly ever since while it slowly digested us, stripping us of our ability to think freely, of our identity, absorbing us so that we had become nothing more than another part of the twisted innards that kept it ticking. In my haste I had not closed the front doors properly and one of them had flapped open so that the cavernous entrance became a hungry mouth desperate to swallow us again.

It feeds on people, I thought manically, *and once it has its meal it doesn't want to let go!*

But then I saw what had made Sonny look so afraid. The place was in darkness but for one window in which a light had snapped on. Somehow we had disturbed it and the house was waking up and now had us fixed with a single bright eye.

"Dante's up," Sonny said, "let's go back inside before he sees us out here, that is if he hasn't already."

"No, stop it, just get in the car," I had to dash around the front of the vehicle and grab him as he had already started in the direction of the front door.

This is insane! Calm down! You are not running away, just leaving!

Raven Taylor

There seemed to be no strength left in him to resist as I hauled him back to the car and pushed him into the passenger seat. It might not have been so easy in the past, but the months spent in the basement had left him weak and underweight.

Once in the driver's seat it all started to go wrong. I should have known the bloody thing wouldn't start. It had been sitting idle for months and the battery was dead. What had I expected? I slammed my fists on the wheel and cursed. I pressed my foot to the accelerator and turned the key again. The car responded with a weak splutter as the engine turned over and died again.

"Come on! Come on!"

I glanced back at the house as I desperately tried the ignition over and over. Another light had come on now; the one in the foyer.

"It's too late," whimpered Sonny.

Light was spilling out of the open front door, and a long shadow fell down the front steps. Dante appeared as a black silhouette in the entrance way. I turned the key again and barely even got a splutter this time.

"I'm an idiot," I cursed, "I should have known!"

"He's coming," Sonny cried, now shaking from head to foot, "he's going to kill me for leaving the basement."

"Look at me," I urged, "I'm not going to let anything happen to you, he's just a man, we don't need to be afraid of him, let's just stay calm and handle this rationally."

Dante's slippered feet crunched in the gravel of the driveway as he approached. He was wearing a heavy crimson velvet robe with his initials sewn into the front in gold, his silk pyjamas flapped around his legs as he walked. I opened the door and stepped out of the car.

The Society

"Quinn?" Dante sounded surprised. "What on earth are you doing? The front door alarm went off and I thought we had an intruder."

"I was thinking it was time I was leaving," I said, trying to sound calm, "It's been an illuminating experience and all, but I'm not sure it's working out, I'm not sure I'm entirely compatible with the beliefs of The Society."

Dante had stopped a few feet away from me and he chuckled. His face was in shadow and it was difficult to make out his expression.

"How odd that you should feel the need to sneak away at night without telling anyone," he said, sounding disappointed. "I would have thought you would have at least owed us a goodbye after all we've done for you. Perhaps you should come back inside, have a good night's sleep and in the morning, if you really want to be on your way, I'll help you jump start the car."

I faltered. Now I just felt completely ridiculous. There had never been any reason to assume Dante would try and stop me leaving. I was again struck by how reasonable this man seemed. It was altogether possible that the people in the hole were indeed there by consent, that they opted into this as just another part of the program, it certainly didn't seem that Dante was holding anyone against their will.

"Who's that you've got with you there?" he asked, noticing Sonny in the passenger seat for the first time. "I might have guessed," he sighed, shaking his head, "come on out Sonny, you aren't going anywhere tonight."

Dante approached the car and pulled open the door. Sonny got out and Dante placed a reassuring hand on his shoulder.

"It was all Quinn's idea," he said in a shaky voice, "he talked me into it. It's all his fault, it's always his fault, you know I was doing better, everything was fine until he came along and got into my head."

"Shhh, I know, it's all right," Dante put his arms around Sonny and Sonny started to sob. "Haven't I been like a father to you? Tried to help you? Loved you like a son?"

"Yes," Sonny croaked.

"Well then," he said softly. There had always been something about Dante's voice when he spoke in a certain tone that instantly made people feel at ease, which removed all worries and woes from a person's head. "I think perhaps we'd better all go inside; it seems we have some things that need talking over."

The Society

Chapter 28

2009

People in emotional distress had always made her feel somewhat uncomfortable. Showing empathy and offering comfort to an upset person had never really come naturally to her. She had been brought up to believe that shows of emotion were weak, but the nature of her job on this investigation had unfortunately brought her into contact with a lot of people whose stories were filled with tragedy. Inevitably, they all reached this stage eventually, when they would crack and the enormity of their recollections would overwhelm them. She was impressed that Quinn had made it this far, but now his pain had gotten the better of him, and he was now red faced, sniffling and teary eyed.

"I'm sorry," he sniffed, "it's just that I can't believe I went back inside, just like that. If I'd only just insisted on leaving! I should have just got him out of there that night no matter what it took. We could have walked into the village, anything! I think if we'd even managed to spend just one night away from The Society's influence it could have all been different."

"Please don't blame yourself," she handed him the box of tissues from her desk. Fortunately she had dealt with so many people like this that she had learned to at least fain sympathy. She knew the right things to say, the right way to act, even if inside she believed such displays of emotion were the ultimate sign of weakness.

He took a tissue from the box and blew his nose, cursing himself for becoming so overwhelmed. At least she seemed to understand. She smiled at him kindly and said, "it's as you said earlier, abusive relationships can be very difficult to leave…"

"I can't stop thinking about those people in the basement," his nose was all stuffed up and his words came out muffled and sloppy.

"Do you think you could tell me a little more about what happens to people in the hole? Were you ever sent down there?"

Quinn dried his eyes; the tears had mercifully subsided.

"Yes, I had spells down there," he confirmed, "but mine were brief and infrequent. Much of what I know comes from what Sonny and others at the house told me. One of the staff confided in me once about what she had been through. She vanished soon afterwards, of course, as they always did if they spoke out of turn."

She nodded and her pen scurried across her notepad.

"It's the ultimate way to break a person. Down there you are deprived of sleep, you never know what time of day it is as those fluorescent lights are never turned off. You have to work constantly on certain drills designed to help parishioners who have lost their way. Sometimes it was hours spent working with a partner on card sorts. One of the more odd ones was having Dante come down and yell very random commands at you which you must obey and repeat over and over. For example he would shout at you 'pick up that pen' and then he'd yell at you to put it down again and repeat that same command over and over. You'd be made to adopt stress positions and hold them for excruciating periods of time. We even played children's party games which were always given a sadistic twist. The whole thing was designed to push a person to the limits, physically and mentally."

"And you all just did what you were told?"

"There were always cameras watching. If you were caught slacking off from a task the whole group was punished. Everyone who was down there would be beaten or have food withheld so it got to the point where everyone was policing each other too."

"It just beggars belief that someone could be so sadistic, these methods of torture all seem very modern for something written in Victorian times."

"Well, that's just the thing. I'm convinced a lot of this was conceived by Dante and James-Anthony, not William Thomas. I think when Thomas started out his intentions were good. He was just exploring new ways to help people with mental illness and to encourage people to connect with their creative side. But then he started to get into the whole reincarnation thing and appears to have been driven to madness by his grief over his wife's illness and the barbaric way in which the medical professionals of the time treated her. I think he was just an eccentric man trying to deal with what he saw as injustices."

"And of course, when the man himself was alive there was not so much rigid structure to The Society."

"No, as Sonny told me, it was more abstract back then. It was James-Anthony and Dante who resurrected the whole thing and made it what it is today. It's impossible to say what parts really can be credited to William Thomas and what parts the pair of them just made up as they went along."

"That's interesting," she said, "because of course they are often known to break their own rules or rewrite them to suit their current agenda."

The Society

"Yes, they'll change things when it suits them, and it suited them to do that for us. I thought it was just kindness, compassion on Dante's side. Of course now I know what their real agenda was and why they were so desperate not to lose Sonny."

Chapter 29

1966

"Why don't you go up to your room? I need to have a little word with Quinn," Dante said to an exhausted looking Sonny once we were inside. "I'll come up and see you soon, all right?"

I watched as Sonny slouched away.

Dante took me to the family's private living room. It was not a room I had ever been in before, but like the rest of the place it was beautifully decorated with red textured paper patterned with gold vines which climbed up to the high ceiling, and heavy velvet drapes at the large windows. In front of one of the widows was a stunning antique rocking horse which had been lovingly restored so that its mahogany body gleamed and its mane and tail shone. Above the fireplace was a skilfully rendered romance style painting of little Astrid in a red dress with a white rabbit sitting at her feet. On another wall hung a portrait of William Thomas. He was dressed in a smart black three-piece suit and was leaning on a walking cane. He had stern grey eyes, bushy grey mutton chops, and wore a top hat. He looked a formidable man; proud and determined. There were also a few of Sonny's paintings dotted around; his whimsical, psychedelic style looking out of place amid the elegant period decor of the room.

Dante gestured for me to sit on the red Italian silk sofa while he went to the drinks cabinet and poured two large measures of brandy. I sunk back into the comfortable upholstery, my brain feeling confused and foggy. Dante sat down opposite me, crossing his long legs and smiling. He took a slow sip of his brandy and looked at me intently.

"Now then my friend," he said evenly, "what's this all about?"

"We could start with the fact that you have people locked in your basement," I challenged.

"I'm hardly keeping them there," he laughed. His demeanour was calm; nothing about my discovery seemed to have rattled him at all. "It's part of their treatment, they are there entirely by choice, because it is their desire to get well and be able to rejoin the group. I don't deny that rehabilitation is tough, designed to mentally and physically push a person, but it's really no different to being put through, say, a military boot camp. Notice that they did not try to leave when you left the door open tonight. Tell me Quinn, did any of them beg you to take them away, to let them out?"

"Well, no," I admitted, "but what about Sonny? He wanted to leave."

"I'm assuming you had to talk to him about it?"

"I suppose so, but still..."

"How many times do I have to tell you about Sonny's stubbornness and his inability to work with us? It's because of his constant resistance that he doesn't get the benefit of the program the way so many others do."

"Well then he's clearly not compatible with it, and if that's the case, why keep doing this to him? Why not just let him leave?"

"Sonny is important to us in more ways than you might think," I noticed Dante's gaze had drifted to the portrait of William Thomas, and he continued to stare thoughtfully at our founder as he spoke. "I love him as if were a member of the family, but there's more than that. When the time comes he will have a job to do, a job that is vital for the future of The Society, and so for that reason alone we simply cannot lose him. But alas I can't tell you all the details, as much as I would like to, because that information is restricted to those who have reached stage six."

He was looking at me again. I was beginning to feel very tired and sluggish. I glanced at my glass and wondered vaguely if he had put something in it.

"But I want to talk about *you* my dear Quinn. It seems you are harbouring desires to leave us, and while it would disappoint me greatly to see you throw away everything you have worked so hard for, ultimately it is your decision."

"I don't want to seem ungrateful," I said honestly, "I really do appreciate everything you have done for me. Much of what I have learned over this last year about handling my mental health, growing my self-confidence, improving my communication skills, and keeping my creativity flowing has been invaluable. I can't thank you enough for that. I know I wouldn't be where I am today without your help, without The Society's contacts, but I just think maybe I've come as far as I can."

"You're ready just to lose it all then?"

"But why should leaving The Society mean I'll lose it all?"

"Oh, but that's exactly what it means," a sly grin had spread across Dante's face, and he swirled the remainder of his drink slowly in his glass. The ice cubes chinked against the crystal and he watched me like a hungry cat toying with an injured bird. "We can take it all away as easily as we gave it to you, never forget that. And then there's the matter of your file; hours and hours of taped and transcribed confessions. I know the very deepest, darkest recesses of your mind Quinn Bergman,

The Society

and if you leave The Society I can't guarantee that they will remain confidential. They could fall into the wrong hands. Wouldn't your readers love to know all about what a deviant pervert you really are? Just think of it; your family, friends, fans, everyone; all party to every misdeed that has ever even entered your head…"

"So that's how it is? Blackmail? I stay here and live a lie or you'll expose me?"

"Blackmail is such a harsh word," he swallowed the rest of the brandy, and leaned forward in his chair. The sly expression had gone and he was now looking at me with what appeared to be genuine concern. "You still don't understand that everything The Society does is for the benefit of its members. I care about you. I don't want to see you fail. I want you to be happy."

"And yet it doesn't seem like enough…I have a career, a beautiful place to live, people who care about me, but there is always something missing…"

"And the pursuit of that missing piece is the true driving force behind tonight's incident is it not?"

"Yes, I suppose it is…" I rested my head back on the soft cushions of the sofa, my eyes starting to close and my body heavy with tiredness. My grip loosened on my now empty glass and Dante, seeing I was about to drop it, stood up and moved it to the table.

"Stay with me just a little longer," he said, giving me a light shake, "this is important."

I lifted my head and sat forward, trying to wake up and pay attention.

"Let's get to the point," he said, "I know everything about you so I'm not sure why you are being so evasive when it comes to this. The fact is, you love Sonny. I know you do. I also know that Sonny loves you and I'm not sure the program is ever going to cure either of you. I've been wondering for a while how to tackle this, and I think I have a plan that can work to everyone's advantage."

"What are you trying to say Dante?" I was so tired that his words were barely registering, and he seemed to be rambling. I wished he would just get to the point.

"The Society needs Sonny, his part in the enlightenment will be vital, and I think you could be the key to keeping him on side. We can overlook certain misdeeds, make allowances when the stakes are this high," he looked thoughtful as he finished the rest of his drink. "I think perhaps that you have a purpose too, I think maybe you were sent to us because Sonny needs someone."

"I don't understand," my head was now thumping.

"This is what you are going to do," he said curtly, "you will marry Lesley, as planned."

I groaned. "So, what was the point of what you just said?"

"I'm not finished. Try to pay attention. The pair of you have been dragging your heels over the whole marriage subject for nearly a year now. If truth be known, she doesn't relish the idea of giving up her lifestyle in London. She's really not keen on settling down, and in truth I think she suspects there's something going on between you and Sonny. So, I'm proposing you marry her and it becomes the perfect cover for you both. You'll stay here because this is where you need to be to work, she will be away most of the time in London. The Society will be off her back about her sleeping around and you, my friend, will also have the perfect cover that will allow you to have the relationship you want with Sonny."

The Society

He looked rather pleased with himself as he waited for my response. His proposal did not make me as happy as you might have imagined. I couldn't fathom his motives. If he was so into The Society and the teachings of William Thomas, why would he allow this to happen?

"Now I'm not pretending I condone such behaviour," he went on, as if reading my thoughts, "but some things are more important. I think if you both attend disclosure and confess your misdeeds regularly, and we keep you on the right regime of treatment, then you shouldn't suffer too much of a setback."

I stared at him in disbelief.

"And it's not as if it will be forever, there'll be plenty of time to set things right after he's done what we need of him. We only need to keep this up until the enlightenment, it's four years, but I think we can do it." He seemed to be talking to himself, thinking out loud.

Four years? And what happens after that?

Chapter 30

2009

"We're getting there, aren't we?" she asked, trying to contain her eagerness, "to what happened in 1970?"

"Yes, I suppose we are," he confirmed, with a hint of reluctance in his voice. "When I told Sonny what Dante had proposed he was delighted. For him there could be nothing better, he could stay with his family and The Society and still have me. Now that I knew Dante would seemingly stop at nothing to keep Sonny I had insisted on some demands of my own being honoured in our agreement. I made him promise that no-one was to hit Sonny or punish him again, and if they did, I would make sure we were both gone long before the enlightenment."

"And you went through with your marriage to Lesley, didn't you?"

"I did everything they asked," Quinn looked pained as he gazed off out of the window. "I married Lesley in the new year, I studied and passed my stage one exam. I kept writing and donating massive chunks of my earnings to them. In the years that followed there *were* some good times. Things with Lesley were exactly as Dante said they would be. We remained dear friends but nothing more, and she knew exactly what she was getting into, and went along with it willingly. It was good for our imagination within The Society; to be seen by regular parishioners across the country in the media as the darling couple of the literary world, and outspoken members of The Society. We were

The Society

photographed together on the red carpet at Leicester Square at the premier of the film adaptation of one of my novels, and attending award ceremonies, things like that. Yet outside of these occasional public appearances we led very separate lives; she in her place in London with her string of casual affairs, me closeted away in Chyanvean, writing and finding great joy in my blossoming relationship with Sonny. For a while I was actually happy."

She pulled a newspaper article from her file and slid it across the table to him. It was a photograph from The Evening Standard showing Quinn and Lesley Bergman, arm in arm, on the red carpet at the premier he had mentioned. She watched as Quinn gave a small smile at the memory.

"And there, behind us," he tapped the two blurry figures in the background, "Paul and Aleksandra, because of course I was never let out without an escort from The Society. They had to make their presence well and truly felt at all times in case I got any ideas about taking Sonny and running."

She left the press cutting lying between them and continued with her questions.

"And Dante stayed true to his word, he did not let on to anyone that your marriage was a sham?"

"Yes, Dante kept his word on that, but not so much on his other promises. After a while things began to slip back into their old ways."

"The beatings and punishments continued?"

"All just part of being a member of The Society," he laughed nervously.

"Yet you stayed, you didn't make good on your threat to leave?"

"Stop judging me!" Quinn jumped up from his chair and raked his fingers through his hair. "Now it was no longer just the promise of a fabulous career, or the threat of exposing my secrets that stopped me leaving, it was Sonny. What I had with him there seemed to make it all worthwhile. I told myself, we should feel privileged. After all, in those days it would have been extremely difficult for us to have any kind of relationship at all in the outside world. It was still a crime back then. At least, I told myself, we were relatively well shielded from judgement at Chyanvean, having only Dante to contend with and not the whole world.

"Seems pathetic now, how I clung to the tiny snippets of time we had together, which weren't much. Though Dante permitted our relationship to continue, he did not like it, and he made that very clear. I felt like we were always watching our backs. If I accidentally sat too close to Sonny while in the guest lounge or forgot myself and tried to take his hand in public, Dante would quite literally scream at us, and sometimes one of us would be sent to the hole as punishment, the other would be beaten. But the time we did get to spend together, when no one was watching, was wonderful, and as the years passed my love for him continued to grow. Funny, isn't it, how such things no longer seemed to cause a block in my creative flow?"

She nodded in agreement.

"But no matter how much he hated permitting such things, it was worth it for Dante, not only because it kept Sonny from running away, but he also loved the absolute power he now had over us. Few things mattered more to Dante than power, except perhaps money."

The Society

She opened the file again, saying, "and you knew that if you left, this is the type of thing you would be up against."

She laid a second article on the desk next to the first.

"I suppose I can understand why you would have no desire to go from this," she tapped the red-carpet picture with a long fingernail, "to this." She tapped the second piece.

Quinn had been standing by the window, but now he turned around to see what she was referring to. The second clipping showed a grainy black and white picture of himself and Sonny, lying in bed together, side by side, asleep. He remembered this. It was from a flyer which they had distributed to all of the residents in a small village where he had tried to settle not long after leaving The Society. The headline read 'The pervert in your midst: are your children safe with this sexual deviant around?.'

"Yes," Quinn moaned, sinking back into his chair, "and it was much worse than that. They hounded me relentlessly when I first left. They'd put leaflets through the doors of all my neighbours wherever I was living, send pictures and tape recordings to the newspapers."

She began to pull out more material from her file; newspaper clippings, leaflets, posters, lining them up until they covered the desk. Words such as 'pervert,' 'deviant,' 'dangerous,' 'immoral' leapt out from the colourful collection.

"The whole place was bugged in the latter years, once Dante's paranoia really started to set in," he told her. "It seems that we were being watched every second, not just during disclosure; spied on, photographed, recorded. I can assure you that far more compromising pictures than these were circulated to my family and friends. And that's the root of it all, that's how they get people to stay, and they're still doing it to this day, to other helpless people who've dared to escape! That's the worst part of it, they're still getting away with it!"

He banged his fist on the desk in fury.

"Maybe not for much longer," she tried to reassure him, "if we can get enough people like yourself to come forward and testify to the abuses that have taken place, then we think we can get the police to open an investigation into The Society. That's why this is so important. We've been campaigning for years for someone to look into it, but now, finally, people are coming forward and people are starting to pay attention."

She could see that the array of articles and pictures were upsetting him so she gathered them all up and slipped them back into the file.

"And that's why you disappeared for so long isn't it? You've been hiding all this time."

"Yes. For a while I thought I would never escape them, that they'd never leave me alone. They were most persistent in their reign of intimidation. I think it was because I knew too much and they were worried I would speak out, like I'm doing now, so they had to try and continue to break me and make me feel afraid and under attack. They wanted to make sure I was constantly reminded of their power, and so they launched a very successful smear campaign. The Society was, at this point, viewed quite favourably for its community work, for its programs to help aspiring creatives and its work around addiction. I was just a bitter ex member; a sexual deviant, an aggrieved and dangerous man who was out to discredit them. They absolutely could not have me seen as in any way credible, because *I knew!*"

The Society

"You knew what happened at the enlightenment," she finished for him.

"Yes," his voice began to crack and a tear formed in the corner of his eye. She watched him intently and tapped her pen on the desk. What exactly he knew, she felt sure she would soon be finding out. "But I didn't say anything. Nobody would have listened."

"I'm listening," she said.

"I had been living at Chyanvean for five years," he continued, seeming to regain his composure. "I may not have been a prisoner in the physical sense, but I was a prisoner nonetheless, my own mind being the jail cell. I wrote my books, I donated my earnings to The Society, I lived in relative solitude in the house. Knowledge of events of the outside world were strictly rationed; there were no televisions and no newspapers, and so the world went by without us. There were moments of fear and pain, but the punishments were all for our own good, of course, and every now and then there would be times of sheer bliss that would make all of the bad times- the beatings, the sleep deprivation, the isolation- seem worth it. Several times throughout those five years Dante left the house, taking Kerrigan and Astrid with him, for family vacations to exotic places. He left Magda in charge of running the hotel in his absence. During these times we could relax a little bit too and didn't feel like we were constantly being scrutinised, and those few weeks of freedom allowed us to temporarily feel like relatively normal human beings."

She listened carefully, taking notes and trying not to interrupt with her questions, though she desperately wanted to hurry him on.

"But it was not a life, it never was. We were so cut off from everything, and Dante was growing increasingly more unstable and power hungry. More and more often Sonny was taken away for 'special instruction' which would last for hours at a time. He was told this was to prepare him for his part in the enlightenment. Yet none of it ever gave him any clue as to what it was he was going to have to do. He told me this special training was just hours and hours of past life regression exercises and reading lots of texts about reincarnation.

"He seemed to find the whole thing liberating. He often wondered out loud if he and I could find each other again in future lives and under less difficult circumstances. He said there was nothing left to fear in life now he knew for certain that you could always start again, that you would always be given another chance. I think he was still looking for a way out…"

"He was suicidal again?"

"It worried me," Quinn admitted. "As for me, I was being pushed to work harder than usual as Dante wanted me to reach stage six by the end of the year, for he was eager for me to be able to attend the enlightenment."

"We're getting there now," she tried to keep the eagerness from her voice, but her excitement was growing. This is what she had invited him here for. This was what she needed to know. It was vital she discovered what happened on that notorious night. It was all she could do to hold herself back from telling him just to get there, to tell her about the enlightenment and skip the rest. But this was his story and she would have to be patient.

He looked at her and said abruptly, "It was a month before the big event that I was kidnapped."

The Society

Chapter 31

1970

I was crossing the foyer, on my way to dinner, when a man stopped me. He was massive; broad chested and muscular with huge arms like tree trunks and he towered over me. I recognised him as one of the guests who was just passing through. He was not here to attend a course, but I had noticed him in the bar the last couple of nights.

"Excuse me," he said, catching me by the arm. He spoke with a soft Californian accent. "Are you the owner of that black car out there, the Magnette?"

I frowned. I hardly ever had the need to use my car anymore, because if I ever went anywhere it was usually with someone else from The Society, in Dante's Rolls Royce. I did, however, go out and start it most days to try and keep the battery alive, just in case, and he must have seen me doing this.

"Yes," I confirmed. "Why? What is it?"

"I'm really sorry, man," he said, nervously running his fingers through his hair, "but there's been a slight accident. It's nothing bad but I might have given it a bit of a bump while I was trying to park, you should come and take a look."

I sighed, frustrated. I had just sat my stage five exam and I was drained and hungry and did not want to be late for dinner.

"I'm sure it's fine," I said, "just leave your details at reception, we'll sort it out later."

"I'd rather you came and had a look just now or I'll be feeling guilty all night."

The Society

"Oh, all right then."

I followed him out to the car park, muttering in annoyance under my breath and wondering how on earth he had managed to hit me in such a large space with so few vehicles. Didn't they teach people to drive properly in America?

"For God's sake, how did you manage that?" I exclaimed on seeing my crumpled front wing.

"I don't know man, it's these English cars with their shifters, can't seem to get used to them."

His own vehicle, a rental, was on the road, engine still idling, with its taillight broken and a big dent in the rear bumper.

"The hire company is going to charge me a fortune for this," he grumbled to himself.

I approached my car and crouched down so I could inspect the damage. I ran my hand over the ruined wing and felt an inexplicable tug of sadness. I had owned this vehicle for a long time. I remembered going to look at it, taking my father with me for advice as he knew a lot more about cars than I did. It was one of the rare moments when we had really connected as father and son. This vehicle had taken me on so many happy adventures; picnics in the country with Emily, long lazy drives down to the seaside at Brighton. The sudden nostalgic connection to a lifelong gone made me feel momentarily quite wistful. Then I felt him grab me, his hand clamped a handkerchief over my nose and mouth, and it all went black.

I felt sick. Somewhere in my troubled dreams I had been down in the hole with Sonny, watching Dante laughing as he struck him across the face and started dragging him away. I tried to help but somehow I could barely move, my legs were like lead and refused to respond. All I could do was watch helplessly as Dante hauled him off down the corridor, laughing maniacally all the while.

"Sonny, Sonny," I muttered as I started to come around.

The ground seemed to be moving under me, rocking and making my nausea worse. I tried to open my eyes but it felt as if they had been glued together.

"Sonny!" I cried urgently, sitting bolt upright, at last being able to open my eyes.

"So, you're awake," a voice penetrated the fog that clouded my mind.

It took a few moments for my vision to start to clear and my senses to return and I had to lie down again as I was hit by a wave of dizziness. As I slumped back into reality I realised I was in a car, lying on the back seat. I could see enough of the driver from where I was to recognise him as the American who had hit my car.

"What the hell is going on?" I muttered through parched lips.

I tried to sit up again, but the dizziness overwhelmed me and I collapsed back down.

"Careful, you should probably lie down for a bit until you recover," the driver glanced at me in the rear-view mirror. "My name's Dwight, by the way."

"You drugged me!" I said incredulously.

"I had to."

"You can't do this!" Panic was setting in and I started to tug on the door handles. "Stop the car, let me out! Who are you? Where are you taking me?"

Oh, the thoughts that were going through my head! I was convinced he must be some kind of madman, that this was going to end with me dead in a ditch somewhere. I stared wildly out of the window seeing a dark, quiet country road and no other traffic.

After all the madness I have endured over these last five years is this really how it ends?

Was he somehow something to do with The Society? Was this another punishment? What if he was going to kill me? Had I messed this life up so badly that they thought the only solution was for me to start again?

"Let me out! Let me out!" I sat up again and started to bang on the window. "I'll be a better parishioner, I promise, I'll leave Chyanvean, I'll never see Sonny again, let me disclose all my misdeeds and I'll take whatever punishment you have; I just don't want to die."

"Calm down," Dwight said calmly, "I'm not going to hurt you, I'm not from The Society. I'm here to help, to save you from those people."

"No," I insisted, "I don't need help."

Was it perhaps a test? Was this maybe part of the stage five exam to test my loyalty? If I protested and refused to be 'rescued' then would I pass?

"This is kidnapping, you can't do this," I persisted, "you have forcibly removed me from my home and from my family against my will, take me back, now!"

"Can't do that," he said, still sounding entirely unfazed, "I've been paid to do a job and I intend to do it."

"No," I yelled, once again rattling the door handle. "Stop this car!"

"You protest and yell all you want, it's not going to happen," he said calmly.

"Please," I begged, "take me back, I can't leave Sonny."

"Sorry," he shrugged his large shoulders, "I only have orders to collect you, no one else."

I had a pounding headache and I had to lie down again. I felt so terrible. I pleaded repeatedly for him to turn back and at least let me get Sonny. He soon became agitated at my constant whimpering and begging and turned on the radio.

"You know I've done this so many times now it no longer even bothers me," he told me. "The first few times I snatched a target I was terrified, convinced someone would see me and something would go wrong. It's like second nature now though."

"You've kidnapped people before?"

"Saved," he corrected me in his quiet Californian voice. "We call this an intervention. We've had somewhat of an epidemic of these cults back home in recent years. Weird Jesus freaks and the likes promising our young people salvation, love, and spiritual enlightenment. I almost lost a daughter to one myself. That's what started it. I promised myself if I could ever stop a family, or friends, going through what I went through with her, then I would do it. So that's what I do now, I help people get their loved ones back. I have techniques for fixing what has been done to your brain. Just as the mind can be manipulated and reformed by evil people to suit their intentions, so too can it be deprogrammed. That's what I am, I'm a deprogrammer."

"I don't need deprogramming" I insisted, exhausted and sick now, "I'm not in a cult or anything like that. You're wasting your time. I love my life in The Society."

The Society

"They all say that at first," he chuckled. "Your view is so blinkered that you choose only to see the good and not the bad. You'll thank us all later; I promise you that."

I slept for a bit again after that as we drove on through the darkness, and it was pitch black when we reached our destination.

When I awoke the car had pulled up, Dwight had turned off the engine, and we appeared to still be in the remote countryside. It was very dark and the wind had picked up, I could hear it howling around the car, and I began to panic again. My earlier theory about him being crazed murderer could still be true. I sat up and watched him get out of the car. Ahead of us I could see yellow light spilling out of the window of a small dwelling, and as my eyes adjusted I was able to pick out the outline of a cottage, surrounded by the skeletal silhouettes of trees which were bending and groaning in the wind. I could not see any other signs of civilisation besides the cottage. What a wild and remote place this was.

Dwight walked around the car and opened the rear passenger door.

"Come on," he beckoned, "out with you. And don't bother trying to run, there's nowhere to go."

I was still feeling groggy, and I was unsteady on my feet as I got out of the car. As I tried to take a few steps forward I staggered and fell. Dwight picked me off the ground and helped me towards the cottage. As we approached a figure appeared at the lighted window, and seconds later the door had been thrown open and I saw two people in the doorway. Soft yellow light tumbled out across the grass, and as Dwight guided me closer the two waiting figures came into focus, and I saw George and Emily.

"No! No! No!" I renewed my protests, digging my heels into the ground and trying to fight him off. "These are none-beings, bad people, I'll get sick again! What the hell are you trying to do to me?"

I could see a third figure jostling for position behind them, but I couldn't quite make out who that was. I should have been relieved to see the familiar faces of my two friends, but I wasn't, all I could feel was a sick revulsion. My mind had been completely corrupted against them. Emily dashed forward, and hurried down the path, her dress billowing around her, so that she looked like a banshee hurtling towards me. She threw herself at me and wrapped her arms around my neck, kissing my cheek and causing me to shudder in horror at her touch.

"Oh Quinn," she signed in my ear.

I shoved her away and stumbled back.

"Get away from me!" I spat. "Don't touch me!"

Emily's face fell and she looked devastated. George had come out now, and he put his hands on Emily's shoulders and looked at me sadly. The third figure was emerging now too, and I was horrified to see that it was my father.

What the hell is he doing here? We haven't spoken in years!

"Son?" My father's face was haggard and drawn, and he had aged terribly since we had last spoken.

"I can't believe you would stoop so low as to have this thug kidnap me. You couldn't just leave me, could you? Couldn't stand the thought of me being happy! And you, George, you didn't want me, but you can't bear to not have me under your thumb. As for you, Dad, you're the worst of all. What made you want to come? You turned your back on me. You couldn't stand

The Society

the idea of having a gay son, could you? Well, let me tell you, they let me live how I like in The Society. I've been in a relationship with a man in that house for the last four years and they've been far more tolerant than you ever were!"

"None of that matters now, son," there were tears in my father's eyes. The years certainly had taken their toll on him.

"He's not himself, as you can see," Dwight told them, continuing to hold onto me so I did not fall over. "This isn't your Quinn, but he will be soon, I promise you."

I started to struggle and he tightened his grip on me. I struggled harder, became a wild, crazed thing, thrashing and kicking and cursing them. George came forward and grabbed my other arm and together they hauled me through the front door. Emily and my father followed behind us, closing the door and locking it once we were all inside. I was dragged into a small, very rustic living room with a bare flagstone floor and white stone walls. A fire was blazing brightly in the hearth, throwing its intense heat out into the room. Dwight threw me roughly down into an armchair.

"Just stay there," he commanded, "the doors are locked anyway and you can shout all you want but there's no one around for miles." He turned to George, Emily, and my father. "This was a good place you picked, perfect for our needs."

"So, what happens now?" asked George.

I glanced at Emily who was nervously tugging at her gold necklace. My Father was wearing a pained grimace. George's eyebrows were knitted together in concern. Dwight looked entirely relaxed.

"We deprogram him," said Dwight. "Just as the brain can be programmed to think a certain way, so it can be deprogrammed. It's not as difficult as you might imagine. The real person is still in there somewhere, buried under a mask of lies, and the lies of these groups tend to be incredibly flimsy. They rely on the victim always being around others who have been indoctrinated. They rarely stand up to logical questioning once the victim has been removed from the source."

In the meantime I was staring around the room, wondering who this place belonged to, when I spotted a camera on a tripod in the corner.

"I'll need to ask the three of you to leave us alone," Dwight addressed the spectators, "it's already late, and we could be on this all night, it might be best if you at least try and get a bit of sleep."

"If you think so," George said uncertainly.

"It's how I work. I've learned it's best not to have any distractions."

I watched as they filed out, glancing at me anxiously as they left, and closed the door behind them. Dwight went to the camera and started to make adjustments.

"I like to document all of my sessions," he explained, pushing a button; a red light started to blink on the camera.

"Look, this is nonsense," I insisted, getting up from my chair. "I don't know you. You've drugged me, snatched me, taken me from my home without consent, and you are now holding me against my will, all on the request of people who, for all you know, could want to cause me harm. They could be anyone."

"But they aren't," he said confidently. "I don't go around grabbing people just because people tell me to.

The Society

I've been in contact with George and Emily and your father for months. I've conducted thorough research in that time, spoke to people who know you, looked into those people you've been staying with, and there is no doubt in my mind that this is genuine and an intervention is required."

"Right, is there a phone here, I want to call the police, see what they have to say about this."

"Sit down Quinn," he said calmly, "all I want to do is talk. You're not going anywhere."

"Stop blocking the door you maniac!" I yelled, rushing towards him.

He easily stopped me by grabbing my shoulders.

"Why bother?" he said. "The doors are all locked, you can't get out, and there is no phone. Now either sit down, or I'll make you sit down."

He shoved me.

"So, I'm being held prisoner here?"

"If that's how you want to look at it," he advanced and pushed me back down into the chair.

"How long do you plan on keeping me here?"

"That all depends, my friend, on your willingness to talk."

"So that's why you brought me here, to talk?"

"And to listen. Often the best way to deprogram a person is simply to reason with them. I'm going to go through all of this logically with you, and at some point, something will strike a chord, you'll have what I like to call a light bulb moment, and you'll realise that The Society of Old souls is just a load of bullshit."

Hearing an outsider criticise the system that I believed had worked so well for me lit a rage deep in my heart.

Raven Taylor

"How dare you! Do you even know what they've done for me? Gave me a career, a home, restored my mental health, allowed me to live my life with the person I love in safety, which I could never have done on the outside."

"Well, let's look at all of these points individually, shall we?"

He was pacing back and forwards in front of me as he spoke, I wished I had the strength to overpower him.

"Do you place so little value on your own talent that you believe them solely responsible for your success as a writer? It couldn't possibly be that your work is outstanding, you're only where you are because of them, not your own merit. How sad and empty your triumphs must be if you really believe that."

"I was washed up when I met them. Finished. They turned it all around."

"You're still young. You were even younger when this all began. Far too young to be 'washed up.' You were unwell, it wasn't them, or that place that fixed that, it was you. Your talent never left, you don't lose an ability like the one you have, it's always there, and you would have gone on to great things without them on your own merit."

I stared at him. It was nice that he thought me talented, but even if that was the case, I would never have had the breaks I had had without The Society's contacts.

"Now, your mental health. Do you really believe they have fixed your issues? I can tell you now that they haven't, they've just replaced them with a whole other set of problems. What I see is someone who is controlled and not in possession of his own mind. Someone who feels guilty almost all of the time, who over analyses

The Society

every thought he has, who lives in fear of the outside world. You must see that this is not healthy."

I shook my head. He was making no sense to me.

"And you mention a relationship with someone you love. I assume you are referring to the artist whom I observed you with at the house?"

"Yes, Sonny."

Dwight picked up a heavy looking cardboard filing box off the table in the corner and dumped it with thud on the flagstones. I could see that it was filled with books and papers, and it had written on the side 'the Society.'

"I told you my research was thorough," he said. "You see, you only see what they allow you to see. I see it from all angles. So, quite tolerant of your lifestyle choices, are they?" He was now rummaging through the box and pulling out a book, a textbook which I had never seen before entitled 'The Sexual Disfunction program.' "They welcome homosexuals? They don't judge? Two people in a gay relationship can be safe with them?"

"Dante allowed Sonny and I to live as a couple when we were at the house."

"Really? I wonder what your definition of living as a couple is. We'll get to that in a minute." He pulled up a wooden chair and sat down right in front of me. He placed the open textbook in my hands and pointed out a passage. "Read that out loud for me."

"Anyone who engages in sexual relations with a person of the same sex is committing the gravest of misdeeds. The condition of homosexuality is a dangerous perversion, and yet it is treatable. There are methods in place, as detailed in the sexual disfunction program, which can help a person overcome such an affliction. Pursuit of the eradication of such destructive tendencies should be rigorous and firm. Though it may appear to hurt the individual in the short term, remember that, ultimately, they are being helped. Homosexuality is a major block to a person's energy flow and spiritual progression. Any person harbouring such perversions can never hope to attain true spiritual enlightenment."

"How does that make you feel?"

"It might make me angry if I had ever been made to study this course, but I've never seen it before in my life."

"No, maybe not," he agreed, taking the book back. "The Society tends to treat its elite more favourably than its workers and its low-level parishioners. Just because you weren't subjected to this doesn't mean others aren't. Any ideas what some of the suggested treatments in this book are? It's not pleasant as I'm sure you can imagine. They prescribe rape you know?"

"Come on this is absolute madness, nothing like that ever went on at Chyanvean," I said, outraged.

"Yet there it is, in the words of your group's founder. Don't doubt that it does happen. I've spoken to people who have attended some of these more extreme courses at different places. People turn to them in desperation because they genuinely think they can be helped. Some of the accounts I've heard…"

"You should shut up now, this is all just vicious lies," but I was beginning to waver. Hadn't Sonny alluded to going through some terrible things during his time in The Society, things he would never talk about even with me.

"But I forget, Dante is a saint, so who cares if some people further down the line are using these vile writings as an excuse to abuse people. Dante was

The Society

tolerant, wasn't he, let you live how you wanted, in a proper relationship."

"Yes, he did," I said adamantly.

"So, I suppose I didn't really witness him storm across the room and yell at you the other day because he saw you forget yourself and kissed Sonny in the bar?"

"He just doesn't want it to be public, that's reasonable."

"It's exactly like being allowed to live a proper relationship then. I suppose he never kisses his wife in public?"

I tried to find words to argue but I couldn't.

"And tell me Quinn, do you feel guilty every time you have sex with your partner? Do you have to confess to your misdeeds? To be humiliated by talking about things that should be private."

"Yes, but that's just to stop blocks from forming. If you don't disclose your energy won't flow and the cleansing won't work."

"Of course. But it's a normal relationship, so I assume Dante has to disclose everything he does with his wife?"

"That's different."

"Exactly my point," he said, smiling. "If Dante cares so much then I'm sure he told you that homosexual acts in this country were decriminalised three years ago?"

"W-what?" I stuttered, shocked.

"Thought not," he said with smug satisfaction, "and let's take a quick look at your belief system. You truly believe all of this? That creative people, people with old souls, have been tasked with saving the world, with making it a better place for everyone, and to do so you must pay vast sums of money to study the writings of a Victorian lunatic, partake in bizarre courses and rituals, progress through the stages, so you can reach spiritual enlightenment?"

"Yes," though what had always sounded so magical and intriguing when Dante positioned it, just came across as a bit, well, foolish when laid out in Dwight's scathing tone.

"Ok, let's look at some other facts. I'll lay them out plain and simple and see how they sound to you," he reached for his notebook and started reading. "The Society has issued an order that its lower members cannot have children because there aren't enough souls to go around, and a growing population is resulting in increasing numbers of people being born without souls. Do you have any idea how nuts that sounds? How can you sit there and tell me you believe this shit?"

"Well, the population is growing too fast..." I said awkwardly.

"It's bullshit. I don't know if people have souls or not, but I do know that every child born is the same, so either they all have a soul, or none of them do. The Society treats its workforce, made up of, so they say, people with new souls, appallingly. I've spoken to some of the workers employed in Chyanvean. Most were too scared to say anything, but some talked. They suffer beatings and are sent to the hole for any minor thing such as failing to smile at guests. Their accommodation in the old servants' block is horrific. I wouldn't leave my dog there. They showed me. Tiny, cramped rooms, moldy, damp. I would expect you've never seen it being in the elite ranks, it would have been kept from you. While you were living in your luxury accommodation, you saw nothing of the suffering of those people serving you, or perhaps you just didn't care..."

The Society

"Wait a minute!" I protested. "You think we didn't suffer too? Sonny and I? You think we weren't beaten, sent to the hole, punished when we committed misdeeds, forced to sit for hours at a time studying, kept up until all hours of the night doing courses so that we were permanently sleep deprived? Because we were! In more recent times especially, Dante has been under so much strain, which I can only guess is from the pressure of the approaching enlightenment, and he takes it out on us too, not just on the workers."

Dwight folded his arms and gave me a self-approving look, "Is that a crack I see appearing? I thought The Society was wonderful, thought these people were your family, that you were happy there…"

"I was, I mean, look, you're confusing me!" I put my head in my hands as I struggled to regain control of my spinning mind. Images and feelings were flying out of control through my brain, and I desperately tried to employ the thought stop method to halt the negative emotions I was feeling towards The Society. "The Society is good; they do good work." I saw Dante kicking Sonny and hauling him off to the hole. I was filled with rage towards him. I stopped the thought in its tracks and recalled the euphoric feeling Dante instilled in you when he delivered a cleansing, how beautiful he was, like an angel. My mind began to calm. They loved me. They all did. Everything Dante did was for our own good, and soon we would be witnessing a marvelous event that would take The Society into a brilliant new era…

"No, it's all bullshit, an abusive, money and power-hungry cult," he insisted. "They kept your own mother's death from you, didn't even let you go to her funeral or grieve."

"We don't grieve the dead because we know they'll find their way back to us in their next life."

"Listen to yourself. This was your mother; you should have been there to say goodbye."

And that was how Dwight went on, for hour after gruelling hour.

*

The sun had started to rise. Through the small window I could see a patch of pink sky creeping along the line of the horizon. I was completely exhausted and broken.

"They stand for helping creative people, people with old souls, to flourish and fight back against a world driven by greed, war and big corporations," but I was just reciting dogma now, the words had lost all meaning.

"No Quinn," he said, "it's not about helping people. It's not about self-help, curing mental illness, overcoming addiction, spiritual enlightenment, standing up to the government, reincarnation, peace, a better world. This is just how they package it so they can sell it to people, this is just a sales pitch."

"That's not true, they do good work, they got me writing again and cured my depression," but my resolve was breaking.

"All The Society really stands for is controlling people and getting their money, raking in those huge donations you are all forced to give." Dwight fished around in the box of research materials and brought out some more papers. "Initial membership fee to join The Society and enter stage one: two hundred pounds. The cost to sit stage one exam and enter stage two: four hundred pounds. Cost to sit stage two exam and enter stage three: eight hundred pounds, and so on. Thirty percent of all earnings must be handed over as donations. And then there's the fees charged to low level parishioners and workers for various, mandatory services. They have to pay fifty pounds per disclosure, one hundred pounds per cleansing, and the different self-help courses all have varying costs too."

"Dante never charged me for cleansing or confessions," I insisted.

"No, because you are an old soul. Old souls get these services for *'free.'* Workers and low-level parishioners have to pay. I say you got them for free, but wait, how much money have you given them over the last five years?"

"I don't know," I said miserably, realising everything was falling apart around me.

"Come on Quinn," his voice had softened and he now sounded kind, "no one wants to admit they've thrown away tens of thousands of pounds and five years of their life on something that turned out just to be bullshit. I understand the need to justify what you've put into it, but it wasn't your fault. They used you. You are a victim."

"But it can't have all been for nothing. I can't stop now. I'm at stage five. I'm halfway to the top and true spiritual freedom. I'm so close to being allowed access to the secrets that the enlightenment will reveal."

"Quinn," he said gently, "it's all right, you can let go."

I slumped in my chair. I had no energy left at all. It hit me that he was right. It was all, as he said, 'bullshit.'

"How could I have been so stupid?" I said slowly. "I'm an intelligent person, how was I taken in by this?"

"You weren't stupid," he assured me, "like most of the people I help, you were vulnerable and sick, and that made you highly suggestible, a perfect target. I want you to say after me, 'it's all bullshit.'"

"It's all bullshit," I repeated.

"Now say 'I am a victim.'"

"I am a victim."

Dwight was grinning now, evidently very pleased with himself. It had only taken him eight hours to undo five years' worth of brainwashing.

"Can I see the others now?" I asked.

"As long as you're sure they aren't evil non-beings who are going to make you sick."

I managed a faint smile, "no, that's just bullshit too."

The moment I saw George coming into the room I got to my feet and flung myself at him, tears streaming down my face. I could feel it all sliding away, all the dogma and the lies. I didn't feel revulsion as he hugged me, he wasn't going to make me sick, I felt safe and loved and my soul felt lighter than it had in years as I was reunited with my old friend.

"Oh George," I cried, "I'm so, so sorry, I don't know what to say, you have no idea…"

"It's ok," George said, hugging me tightly, "we got you back, and that's all that matters."

I pulled away and there was my dear Emily, beautiful, kind Emily, sobbing her heart out. I went to her and as we embraced I felt all my old love for her come flooding back.

"It's you, you're back, you're our Quinn again. We've missed you so much."

She held me at arm's length and looked me up and down before she started to cry hysterically again and gave me another fierce hug. When we parted I noticed that my father was standing awkwardly in the doorway, watching us.

The Society

"Son," he said uncertain, "I'm so sorry for everything that happened between us. I hope you can forgive me."

I went to him and he took me in his arms. I thought my heart was going to break.

Chapter 32

2009

"And just like that," she commented in wonder, "five years of mind control erased."

Quinn twitched as if he had just been bitten by an annoying insect. "You make it sound as if that were the end of it, a nice simple conclusion."

"No, I know that wasn't the end," she had narrowed her eyes and the way she was now looking at him made him feel very uncomfortable. He shuffled in his seat, feeling as if he were shrinking under her gaze.

Although she was familiar with his case, there were details her research had not discovered. She had not had any knowledge of him being taken away for deprogramming until he had brought it up, and it certainly was a fascinating development. In her mind he had been an active and uninterrupted participant in The Society right up until the enlightenment. That he did not participate in these events as a practicing member came as a surprise to her. She knew he had been present that night, but that he had left, been deprogrammed, and retuned certainly put a new spin on things and made her even more eager to hear what he had to say about it all.

"So, you went back?" she prompted.

"I had to, didn't I? I couldn't abandon Sonny to those people."

"How courageous," she said.

"I thought after seeing what Dwight had done for me, that we could do the same for Sonny if I could get him out of there, and then we would both be free."

"I'm sensing it didn't work out like that?"

The Society

"I don't think I can do this, I'm sorry."

Quinn put his head in his hands and started to weep. His sobbing was so violent it rocked his body and made his shoulders shake. She got up and came round the desk so she could hand him a glass of water which he accepted gratefully. She crouched down in front of him and laid a friendly hand on his knee.

"You mustn't blame yourself," she said.

"God knows what you must think of me," he sniffed, before taking a long drink of water. "I'm so ashamed of myself for ever even being a part of it. What kind of idiot would allow themselves to be taken in by something so crazy? How could I just have turned a blind eye and pretended it wasn't happening when I knew how Dante was treating people? And of course I knew, I knew from the day I first saw those poor souls in the hole. And I did nothing."

"It's not your fault," she reiterated, patting his knee, "you know you were being controlled and manipulated. You believed in it all so much that you saw any punishment as being for the person's own good. Did you know that last year there was a police raid on one of their centres? They went in and tried to free the people who were supposedly locked away, and do you know what happened? It was exactly as Sonny told you it would be. They said they were there of their own free will, that it was their choice and they wanted to stay, despite the terrible suffering that was being inflicted upon them. So, you see, you couldn't have helped any of them any more than you could help yourself."

"Thank you," he said with a sad smile, "thank you for understanding, few people do."

"That's ok," she stood up and went back to her seat, "do you think you can go on or would you like another break?"

It was late. The bright day had gone and the sun had slid behind the horizon leaving the darkness to press against the window. She had switched on a single lamp which left the edges of the room in shadow and the formerly bright and airy office now felt oppressive and close. But he was nearly there and it would soon all be over. He knew with this unburdening would come a blissful shedding of his guilt and hopefully the closure he desperately needed would finally come.

"No, let's continue and get it over with, I *can* do this."

The Society

Chapter 33

1970

After Dwight was finished with me, and I had been reunited with my friends, I was overcome with exhaustion and went to bed in one of the rooms upstairs. It had become normal at Chyanvean for us only to get around four hours of sleep a night, as in the last couple of years Dante had increased the length of the study time and creative sessions, as he desperately pushed us to produce more work and progress faster though the stages. I had scarcely noticed how sleep deprived I had been, and it was wonderful to go to bed knowing I could sleep for as long as I wanted. I was so fatigued and burned out that I slept through the whole day, and when I woke up again in the early evening I felt better than I had in a long time. Once I was fully rested the ideas of The Society seemed even more crazy and far-fetched, and the thought of returning to that world and that way of life revolted me.

We ate a simple meal together in the kitchen of the cottage, and I was delighted by how at ease we all were with each other, as if no time at all had passed since we had last met. When we had finished our food I decided I would have to tell them about Sonny and my concern for him. I told them of my love for him, of my worries about leaving him at the house, and they listened empathetically.

"I'm sorry Quinn," Emily said sadly when I was done, "we had no idea."

She reached across the table and took my hand.

The Society

"I'm glad you've finally found someone who you care so much for and who cares for you," said George, "it's just a shame it had been under such screwed up circumstances."

I glanced at my father. Since coming out, I had never felt uneasy about who I was around George and Emily, there had never been any judgement, but with my father it was a different matter. There was that old sense of shame creeping back in, the awkwardness, the embarrassment, the feeling that I was a huge letdown and a disgrace to the family. I found I could not look at him and I quickly turned my eyes back to my empty dinner plate and started fiddling nervously with my fork.

"We need to get him out then," my father said slowly, "I want to meet the person that my son loves so much."

I looked up in surprise, sure at first that he must be being sarcastic. He smiled at me, and there were tears in his eyes.

"I'm sorry for the way I acted," he said. "I suppose losing you for so long has meant I've had a lot of time to think. There are far worse things in the world than having a son who is gay. Having no son at all, for one. Why should it matter? You can't help who you fall in love with. Oh, and another thing."

I watched as he went to a bag that sat in the corner and pulled out what appeared to be a book of some kind.

"I know you think I was never proud of you, and that I didn't show an interest in anything you did. I have a hard time showing emotions, it's just how I was brought up, it's not an excuse and I'm sorry I was such a rubbish father, but, well, here."

Raven Taylor

He handed me the book and I took it curiously. It was a large, plain covered notebook, but when I opened it up I felt the breath catch in my throat and my heart leap. I leafed through it slowly, tears welling in my eyes again, feeling like I was going to choke on my emotions. They were all there, taped to the pages, every story I had ever written for him as a child.

"You *did* read them," I managed to say.

"Everyone."

I glanced across at Emily who was grinning and crying at the same time as she watched this scene. The latter pages of the scrapbook contained press cuttings, reviews, articles all about me and my books from over the years.

We both stood up and embraced each other tightly while the others looked on.

"I've missed you so much," he said gruffly.

"I've missed you too."

"Ok, this is all very lovely, but if we're going to try and get this other guy out we need some kind of a plan," Dwight interrupted, "obviously I can't go and get him like I did with you as my cover is well and truly blown."

"No, and the house will be closed to visitors now as they'll be getting ready for the conference."

I sat back down in my chair. My father went to the kitchen counter, picked up a bottle of brandy and poured everyone a measure.

"It's going to have to be me, isn't it?" I said, and there was a chorus of protests.

"We just got you out, you can't possibly go back!" George exclaimed.

"Quinn, you can't, I mean what would you tell them, how would you explain your absence?"

The Society

"I'd have to tell a version of the truth," I said thoughtfully, "that the lot of you kidnapped me, but I escaped and made my way back. They can't possibly hold that against me."

"That would mean you'll need to go back as soon as possible," said Dwight.

"And what will you do when you get there? This is madness!" George insisted.

"That's definitely something you need to think about," Dwight agreed. "You won't have much time, you need to get away again as quickly as you can, and you might need to do what I did to your guy there; drug him, shove him in your car and drive like hell."

"This all sounds very dangerous," Emily said doubtfully. "Dwight, you have experience of this kind of thing, Quinn certainly doesn't, this could all go horribly wrong, and who knows what those people might do to him if they realise what's happening."

"Emily," I said, "I can't just abandon him, you must see that."

"Couldn't we just call the police?" my father suggested.

"On what grounds?" I asked. "You don't understand what it's like in there, everyone has consented to what's going on, they choose to be there, there's no crime being committed as far as the law is concerned. It has to be me, it's the only way."

"I don't like this at all," George complained.

"But I think I can talk him into leaving," I told them. "I did it once before. That would be a much safer option. I have just over a week before the enlightenment, I think if I can persuade him before that then we can slip away before they notice."

"A week!" Emily shrieked, "You can't go back there for that long, you'll get lost in it all again and never come back!"

"That's quite unlikely," said Dwight, "once a person has seen the light it's very, very difficult to trick them again."

"Even so…" she looked distressed.

"All right, but if you don't come out by the time that dam conference is over we'll be calling the police and sending them in to get you," George said.

"Agreed," I said.

It was a two-hour drive back to St Morlyn from the cottage. It was decided we should leave right away and we sat in tense silence for most of the journey. I could tell my friends were worried and anxious for my safety. Emily kept telling me how dangerous The Society could be. Apparently it had, at some point, come to their attention that George and Emily had been conducting research into them, and some workers had been tasked with following them, turning up at their home, sending threatening letters, and appearing at the publishing offices whilst George was working. All intimidation tactics designed to frighten them into dropping their investigations. I felt incredibly guilty that I had dragged them into all of this.

Dwight and my father sat up front while I sat in between my two friends in the back, with Emily clutching my hand the whole time. I could feel her shaking. She was so nervous. The plan was to drop me in the village and I would walk up to the house and tell them I had hitch hiked back after escaping my kidnappers. It suited our plan that I had not even had a change of clothes and was a disheveled mess. We made sure to find the others some accommodation in a guest house before I left them, so I would know where to find them when I came back out, and I said an emotional farewell to them in the street outside. Emily sobbed and pleaded with me to reconsider going back into that place and George wished me luck. My father said nothing, just hugged me.

It was a cold, clear night as I began my walk back to Chyanvean. The air was freezing and I wished I had my jacket as I made my way down the street. There was not a breath of wind and the path sparkled with frost underneath the streetlamps. I could hear the distant sound of the sea as the calm waves lapped lazily at the cliffs. I was terrified as I turned down the side road and came up to the gates. The house looked a threatening site, a huge, black monster whose presence seemed to pull me in, and for a moment I stood at the locked gates and considered just running. Everything about the place was sinister. Looking at it through clear eyes I realised what a prison it had been, and I really did not want to go back inside. My friends were back there waiting, my life could still be salvaged, and Sonny had managed all that time before I arrived, he could do it again…

Stop being such a bloody coward! I told myself.

I rang the buzzer on the intercom next to the gates and waited.

"I'm sorry but the hotel is currently closed," Magda's voice crackled through the speaker.

"Magda, it's Quinn, please open the gates."

The intercom clicked as it disconnected and the gates began to swing open with a loud, rattling screech. It was time for my performance to begin.

Chyanvean had never looked so foreboding as it did that night as I made my way down the driveway. The lighted windows watched me and the flag gave a tiny flutter as the house prepared to swallow me once more. Inside lurked a disease. A disease that they tried to disguise under a mask of birdsong and lavender, but the stench would always get through. Underneath it smelled of abuse and hopelessness. It was a place of suppression run by an evil dictator and the site of it made my skin crawl. I wondered how many people Dante currently had in the basement, driven half mad with The Society's delusional version of help.

As I approached, the front door flew open, and I saw Dante striding across the car park towards me. He did not look pleased to see me back, as I had hoped he would, but instead wore a lunatic expression of pure rage. I didn't even see the punch coming. Before I knew it I was sprawled on the ground, blood pouring from my mouth.

"Dissenter!" he yelled at me furiously as he delivered a sharp kick to my ribs.

I curled up into a defensive ball as pain shot through my body.

"Run away, will you?"

He kicked me again and I cried out. I could not even catch my breath in order to start telling him my story of being kidnapped. He grabbed me by my shirt and hauled me to my feet.

"What were you thinking?" He spat at me, his face mere millimetres from mine.

He dragged me to the door and flung me over the threshold. My legs did not want to support my weight and I crumpled into a heap on the floor of the foyer, gasping and dripping blood onto the polished wood. I had seen this side of Dante before, when he would just suddenly lose it over something one of the workers had done wrong, or because someone looked at him the wrong way, or didn't address him with the proper amount of respect. A switch would flip, and he would transform from charming gentleman to raving mad man. I think he had been getting steadily more and more deranged over the years as The Society grew, and his power with it, and such fits of rage had become more and more common.

"And now you come crawling back," another kick caught me in the back.

"Oh my God, Quinn!" a voice called and I heard footsteps hurrying towards us. "Dante! Stop!"

"Sonny?" I managed to croak through my swollen lips.

"It's me Quinn, I'm here," I felt his hands on me and I tried to open my eyes and focus, dreading another kick, but Dante was pacing now, clawing at his hair.

"Where the hell did you go Quinn?" Dante looked like a madman with his eyes wild and angry and a small line of spit running down his chin.

I tried to sit up, but waves of dizziness swept over me like the tide in the cove below. Sonny helped me and I laid my head on his chest, feeling his hands brushing my hair out of my bloody face.

"Calm down Dante, at least let him explain. Like I said to you yesterday, if he'd run away he would surely have taken his car! And his things! Nothing was missing from his room."

"The Pair of you make me sick," he raged, as we sat on the floor, clinging to each other like frightened children, "polluting my family's home with your vile ways, refusing to be cured, and all the while I give you a place to stay and you take advantage, you don't even try and straighten out your corrupt behaviour. How do you think that makes me look, if I can't even keep my own parishioners in line?"

"What on earth is going on?" I heard Kerrigan's voice call out, followed by a rapid, "Astrid, go back to your room darling, it's ok."

"Look who's back!" Dante yelled at her.

"Yes, I can see," she said calmly, "I think perhaps we should try and get to the bottom of all this, don't you?"

"Yes, yes, I think perhaps you are right."

Dante stormed across the room and grabbed me again, pulling me from Sonny's arms and hauling me across the foyer. I realised that he was dragging me towards the door to the tower, and the entrance to the basement. Whatever I had been expecting to happen on my return it certainly had not been this. Things really were going just about as wrong as they possibly could.

"I think it's time we had a little disclosure, don't you?" he barked, "Kerrigan, get the door!"

"Listen Dante," I pleaded, "maybe you're right, perhaps it's time Sonny and I stopped imposing on you, it's clear we aren't compatible with your beliefs and those of The Society, so maybe we should just go and leave you to it. It's simple really."

"I refuse to give up on you Quinn," he said, "that would make me look like a failure. Besides, I can't let you go, you know too much and we need Sonny."

Kerrigan was holding open the door to the basement.

"What shall we do with Sonny?" she asked.

"I don't know, I can't think, just keep an eye on him, don't let him out of your sight."

Dante shoved me and I fell down the stairs, banging myself in multiple places and certain I felt something crack in my chest. He followed me down, slamming the hatch shut above his head, and proceeded to drag me down the bright white corridor to the

The Society

treatment room. In the room were several parishioners, all of whom would have done something to disgrace The Society and been sent here for correctional treatment.

"All of you, out!" Dante roared. "Back to your rooms, go on!"

I watched as they scattered, and I was forced down into one of the chairs. I was still bleeding and bright red spots fell on the tables white surfaces looking like blooms of exotic flowers. Dante retrieved a textbook from a shelf and slammed it down on the table, opening it on a page that had a list of questions. Then out came the pendulum.

"Have you ever destroyed something beautiful," he read from the book.

"What? What has this got to do with where I was?"

"Answer the damned question!" he screamed. "Have you ever destroyed something beautiful?"

"No. I don't know. I don't understand."

The pendulum was shuddering and twitching maniacally, and this only seemed to fuel Dante's anger.

"Your mind and your energy are all over the place. I can't even get a reading from you anymore. It is very, very dangerous when a person's energy and thoughts are so out of control that he can't even answer simple questions."

"I didn't run away Dante, I was kidnapped!" I was finally able to say. "That man who came here, the American, he's a deprogrammer hired by my former friends to come here and snatch me. He drugged me and drove me away. I managed to escape and make my way back. It's as Sonny says, if I'd run away, I'd have gone in my car."

Dante's face was scarlet now and his breath came in ragged gasps. He stared at the pendulum as slowly, slowly it began to move in a clockwise direction. As its swings grew stronger his breathing began to slow and he began to relax.

"See, I'm telling the truth."

He dropped the pendulum onto the table and rubbed the bridge of his nose, screwing up his eyes.

"Perhaps you are, maybe I overreacted," he smiled at me.

I used to consider that smile beautiful, and that having him smile on me was like being bathed in radiant light. Now he looked twisted and I just felt revolted.

"Look at your poor face," I recoiled as he reached out and touched my cheek. "I've been under a lot of stress recently with the approach of the enlightenment, James-Anthony has been calling every hour, making demands, wanting to know that everything is going according to plan. You know how it's been; I've barely had time to eat or sleep, and I've been trying so hard to get you through your stage five exams so you can join us. It's so much pressure, so much is at stake, if things go wrong next week the very future of The Society, and of mankind, could be jeopardised and it will all be on my shoulders."

"What exactly is going to happen next week?" I ventured.

"Oh, that's right!" his eyes lit up and his grin became even more manic, "I didn't get to tell you that you passed your stage five exam!"

I no longer cared about stage five exams or being permitted to attend the enlightenment, but I tried to pretend that I was pleased. As I looked into Dante's eyes all I could see was complete madness. He was now well and truly unhinged.

The Society

Chapter 34

1970

Time does not pass in the hole the same way that it does above ground. For one thing, there are no windows, and the fluorescent lights are never turned off. The whole environment is an assault on the senses; the white walls, white floors, the smell of bleach; everything is just so sterile. Consequently, I quickly lost track of how long I had been down there. At first I was locked in one of the cell-like rooms alone, isolated completely from the other people who were being held there. It seemed like the longest time before I was even given any food or water, and when I was it was stale bread and cheese with mold growing on it, and a small cup of water, brought in by one of the workers who completely ignored me when I tried to talk to him. I attempted to console myself with the fact that I would be down here a week at the most before George and Emily would be coming with the police, but a week is a long time and a person could rapidly lose their mind if left in these conditions.

Dante visited me to carry out a disclosure, but I found that the pendulum no longer worked the way I had been convinced it had. It had all just been a trick. I told him what he wanted to hear about my kidnap, all lies of course, yet the thing indicated the truth. His clever tricks no longer held any power over me.

After a while I began to worry that perhaps I would never be found, even when George and Emily did return. I was also concerned that I might not survive that long without losing my mind or dying of dehydration. I

The Society

think that was the worst part of it; the maddening, persistent thirst that consumed me due to the tiny amounts of water I was allocated each day. I soon began to feel very weak from lack of proper nutrition. All hope of me having any means of getting Sonny away had almost entirely gone.

Some extremely bizarre things happened during my time down there that proved to me that Dante had either completely lost his mind or had always been this crazy and I just hadn't seen it. After a time I was allowed out of my cell to participate for several hours at a time in group activities with the other prisoners. We were made to partner up and quiz each other for hours on end using the question cards. There would always be a worker present, usually Aleksandra, standing over us, watching to make sure we were following orders. Once we were all made to stand with our hands on our heads for an indefinite amount of time to see who could last the longest. On another occasion, loud music was blasted into the basement at an insufferable volume, just the same song over and over again for hours, so now if ever I hear 'paint it black' by The Rolling Stones I have a panic attack. And I was, of course, beaten. All of that along with the sleep deprivation, and the lack of food and water, was enough to push me to the limits of endurance, and that was exactly what Dante was trying to do, to break me completely. He had to be certain that any ideas I might have gotten during my brief trip to the outside world were driven out and that he could restore complete power over me, and this was his way of doing it.

It must have been my final day in the hole, when the game of pass the parcel came. Sounds ludicrous, doesn't it? But that's finally how I got out, by winning what was clearly a rigged children's game.

It must have been almost a week since I had been down there (thought I did not know it at the time), when Dante appeared and told us we were going to play a game. Even in that short period I had deteriorated rapidly, had lost a considerable amount of weight, and was feeling weak and barely even able to stay awake. He set the whole thing up as some crazed excuse to let me leave the basement so I could attend the enlightenment.

He gathered us all together in the treatment room and told us to push all of the tables and chairs to the sides of the room to make some space. He then had us all sit in a circle.

"I'm sure you are all familiar with this simple children's party game," he was pacing slowly around the perimeter of the circle, hands clasped behind his back, looking every bit the perfect gentleman with his grey tailored suit and slicked back hair, "but we have a little twist this time."

I felt his hand brush the back of my neck as he passed by and his touch made me cringe.

"The one who wins the prize gets to leave this place, today, with a clean record and all past misdeeds forgiven. The losers will also get to leave, but they will be thrown out of The Society and put on our list of enemies, and if any of those people speak out about their time with The Society, well then they can expect all of their private disclosure tapes to be circulated among everyone they know and love."

I knew which outcome I was hoping for; to lose so I could leave this all behind. I should have known he would not allow this to happen.

"Something very important is to occur soon," he continued, "and I am making this gesture in honour of

The Society

this great event, so that we can all start anew in the new age. Of course, I can't tell you what it is given you are mere workers, and not worthy of the knowledge our high-level parishioners gain. With the exception of you, Quinn, you'll know soon enough"

He grinned a sinister and deranged grin at me as he dropped a parcel wrapped in brightly coloured birthday paper into my lap and walked over to the tape player on one of the tables.

"Let us begin," he said, and when he pressed play the room was once again filled with the sound of 'Paint it Black."

He did not even turn his back when he operated the music, and as the layers of paper disappeared, and we got closer and closer to the prize, the others began to grow desperate and anxious. At one point when the music was stopped, deliberately, with the parcel mid pass between two of the workers, a physical fight broke out. Punches were thrown, with the victor getting to tear off the next layer, disappointed to find there was just more paper. I could not believe that these people were actually coming to blows; they were so desperate to be allowed to remain a part of this madness. That scuffle summed up the whole thing for me and demonstrated the extent to which these people's poor minds had been warped. Would there have been a time when I too would have fought for the chance to be allowed to stay? Probably.

Then came the final layer. He did it on purpose and did not even try to hide it. He knew this was the last one and the bastard was looking right at me when he pressed stop, still grinning like a lunatic. I sat, looking dumbly at the small package in my hands. This layer had Christmas wrapping paper on it with pictures of snowmen. I felt like I was going to be sick.

"Well?" Dante called, "aren't you going to open it?"

My hands were trembling and I struggled to peel away the wrapping. Eventually I managed to tear through it and what I found was a piece of paper wrapped around a small block of wood. I stared at it while the room seemed to spin. All around me my fellow prisoners were gazing at me with looks of devastation on their faces. Some of them were crying.

Dante's polished shoes clicked on the floor as he crossed the now silent room and stood behind me. My whole body was shaking now, I was finding it hard to make my eyes focus on anything, and I felt dizzy and sick. He crouched down and put his hands on my shoulders. He leaned in and I could feel his warm breath on the back of my neck, and a knot of fear tightened in my empty stomach.

"Read it Quinn," he said in a tone that was soft and deadly.

With quivering fingers I peeled the small piece of sticky tape back and unfolded the paper from around the block. Dante's cursive script flowed elegantly across the paper as I struggled to bring the words into focus.

From the stage six prophecies, as written by our founder:

On the 21st of November 1970 I, William Thomas, will be reborn on earth after travelling for many decades on the astral plane, where I will have spent my time studying with the highest spiritual beings who have transcended the human form and become entities of pure light, or Gods if you will. I will bring with me all of the knowledge and power gained from

The Society

my time with these beings, to be imparted on all my followers; those old souls who have reached stage six and beyond.

I let the wooden block drop from my hand, and the hollow echo it produced when it hit the hard floor was amplified by the silence. Then I passed out and it all went black.

When I came round I was in bed in my room. The bed covers smelled clean and fresh and someone had dressed me in new pyjamas. The heavy curtains at the bay windows were pulled closed and a fire had been lit in the hearth. The lamp in the corner was turned on, spilling a soft pool of yellow light on the red carpet. The scene was a complete contrast to the jarring, sterile environment I had been living in for the last week. For a moment I just lay there, enjoying the warmth and the comfortable pillows, too tired to do anything else.

"Ah, you're awake," Kerrigan was sitting in a chair at my bedside and she gave me a warm, kind smile as she got to her feet and leaned over so she could look at me, "a little worse for wear perhaps, but you'll live."

I forced myself to sit up and she poured me a glass of water from a pitcher on the bedside table, which I drank thirstily. When I was done she took the glass from me and reached out and ran her fingers through my hair.

"I'm so sorry it has to be this way," she said, and she genuinely did look sad, "but I know what might cheer you up, give me a minute."

She left the room and I sat there listening to the crackling of the fire and the distant sound of the foghorn further along the coast. I was starting to drift off again when I heard the door open and Kerrigan announce, "you have a visitor."

Raven Taylor

"Sonny!" I cried when I saw him, feeling my spirits lift.

Kerrigan closed the door, but when I listened for her footsteps I did not hear her departing and I assumed she was standing guard outside.

Sonny jumped on the bed and hugged me, and for a while we just stayed like that in each other's arms.

"I'm so glad you got out in time," he looked extremely happy and excited, "tomorrow is going to be the most fantastic day ever."

"Sonny, listen to me," I pushed him away so I could look him in the eye, "this is very important. You and I are going to leave before all of that, we have to get out of here."

"But why?" trying to reason with someone so indoctrinated was infuriating.

"Because The Society, and everything about it is not real. It's all just about exploiting people for money and to satisfy Dante's and James-Anthony's sick need to control people."

"How can you say that?" he looked upset and I was struck for the first time by how childlike he could be at times, "they are our family."

"No Sonny, they aren't. Look, it's true, I *was* kidnaped, but while I was out there someone helped me to see this all for what it really is, just a lot of lies and manipulation. He can help you too if you come with me."

He looked pained, as if having to choose between me and The Society was too much to bear.

"But so many wonderful things are going to happen tomorrow. William Thomas is coming back and we'll all be set free, given knowledge and power beyond our wildest dreams; there will be no more illness, no more misdeeds, everyone will be forgiven, and we are

The Society

all going to reach ultimate spiritual enlightenment. He's going to grant us superpowers, psychic abilities, the possibilities are endless, don't you want to be a part of that?" he was looking excited again, like a child caught up in the magic of Christmas.

"Oh, for god's sake Sonny! None of that is going to happen," I insisted, "it's all bullshit."

Sonny was grinning serenely, "oh but Quinn it is going to be the most beautiful thing you ever saw," he stroked my cheek and my heart ached as I looked into his green eyes, "and you have to be there to see the part I'm going to play in it all."

"What exactly have they asked you to do?"

"I can't tell you that," he smiled, "all will be revealed tomorrow."

"Sonny, please try and understand that it's all nonsense. You've been brainwashed. Come with me and your eyes will be opened and we can live a normal life in the real world, you'll see that what we are living in now is just some deprived fantasy dreamed up by Dante and James-Antony."

"You're wrong," he said calmly, "you'll see."

He kissed me and I took a hold of him by the wrists.

"Do you love me, Sonny?"

"You know I do; I love you with all my heart Quinn."

"Then come with me. You are sick and you need to let me help you."

Chapter 35

1970

They let us have that night together, but with two burly workers now posted at the door and me in such an emaciated condition after my stay in the hole, making an escape was impossible.

They came for us at dawn. I had spent much of the night arguing with Sonny and getting nowhere until eventually exhaustion had overcome me again and we had fallen asleep in each other's arms and remained that way until they came to wake us.

Both Dante and Kerrigan strode into the room, flanked by the two workers who had stood guard.

"Good morning my friends," Dante cried jovially as he flung open the curtains, flooding the room with bright winter sun, "and what a beautiful, glorious day today is."

"Yes, and what a historical day it is going to be!" said Kerrigan happily.

She sauntered across the room and perched herself on the end of the bed, taking Sonny's hand in hers.

"My dear, sweet Sonny," she smiled at him, "today will be the most important day of your life, everything has been leading up to this, you are going to have the adoration of everyone in The Society after today, they are quite literally going to worship you."

Terror stuck in the back of my throat, but I dared not speak. Something was terribly, terribly wrong, and I simply had to get us both out of there. But how? Panic clutched my pounding heart as I watched Kerrigan pat his shoulder while he smiled right back at her, oblivious to the danger, like a boy staring up at his mother.

"Come on both of you, time to get up, there's much to do," she said breezily.

Kerrigan made her way back to the bay windows where Dante was looking out to sea, and she put her arm around his waist and rested her head on his shoulder.

"Today the sun rises on a new age and nothing will ever be the same again," she sighed dreamily.

I glanced desperately at the door but it was blocked by the workers. I wondered if the others would be able to talk the police into coming and how long they would leave it before doing so.

"There will be disclosures and cleansing all carried out by our glorious leader, and then great things will be revealed to all those who are worthy, and that includes you Quinn, as today you graduate to stage six."

"But what about Sonny?" I challenged. "He's only stage two."

"Sonny will be rewarded far beyond his wildest dreams, do not fear," as he spoke the two workers stepped forward and approached the bed. "Sonny my good fellow, you go with these gentlemen, they are going to get you ready for your big day."

"Sonny, don't," I said hopelessly, but he was already up and following them towards the door.

I jumped out of bed and hurried over to him. He paused and looked at me with a strange expression on his face that was a mixture of sadness and pure joy.

"Don't worry Quinn, nothing bad is going to happen," he assured me, as turned to follow the two men out of the door.

"No, don't take him, please, leave him with me," I rushed at him but Dante caught me and I did not possess the strength to fight him.

I struggled as Dante restrained me, and Sonny turned back to me and gave me a final kiss on the forehead saying, "it's ok, I'll see you tonight, it's going to be marvellous, you'll see."

"What are they going to do with him?" I asked fearfully as Dante released his grip on me.

"There's nothing to worry about Quinn, my dear friend Sonny is in an enviable position," he said as we watched Kerrigan follow the others out the door, "many of our congregation would give anything for the honours he is going to receive today."

I could not believe how normal and lucid Dante seemed today, back to his charming self without a hint of the madman who had terrorised us in the hole. He motioned for me to take a seat on the sofa, and he settled on the edge of my writing desk, lighting a fat cigar and looking at me confidently.

"But alas," he spread his arms and looked regretful, "it does mean that your time with him is over."

"But why? Why does it have to end?"

"You've had your fun, and now you are to go back to Lesley, and the two of you will settle down and start living like good parishioners. If this means resuming your treatment for your problems then so be it. There'll be no more of this nonsense in the new age, and you will get the help that you need. But don't look so distraught my friend, great things await us all."

"But none of this makes any sense…" I said more to myself than to him.

"Is your faith wavering Quinn?"

"I think I need to go now."

The Society

My only hope would be to leave now, find the others, and make sure we returned with reinforcements. I cursed myself for misjudging the whole situation so terribly.

"Yes, I do believe you would love the chance to run to those despicable friends of yours who I've seen skulking around the village this last week. But the thing is, I'm not going to let you go, because despite it all I still believe in you, and I believe that when William Thomas returns with his great gifts then you will no longer have doubts. I have confidence that you will never question The Society again after tonight."

He got up and went to the door.

"I'm going to send your wife along later to help you to get ready," he said, "she'll escort you to tonight's event. In the meantime, don't bother trying to go anywhere, the door will be guarded."

Chapter 36

2009

Quinn had fallen silent. Several minutes passed and he did not speak. She observed him quietly as he stared out of the window, understanding that this last past was going to be the most difficult. He was trying to gather his thoughts, to summon the strength to put into words what he had never spoken of to another living soul. Those memories of that last horrifying night in Chyanvean had been stuffed down and repressed so much that he had almost come to believe the lies he had told himself and George and Emily over the years. He had repeated this invention to himself so often, wielding it like a shield to fend off the demons when they attacked, battering them into submission each time. It had been difficult in the early days to smother the images that plagued his mind, but as time went by, the more he defended himself with the lies, the more he believed them, and his thoughts about what really happened became less frequent.

Going back there now would be like opening a dusty old box whose unpleasant contents had not been taken out in years. Sure he had peeked at what it contained often; small, stolen glimpses through a crack in the lid, but it had been years he had given it a proper viewing. Yet he knew that when he opened it the contests would be in pristine condition, he would be able to recall with absolute clarity what had happened. But if he unleashed it now it would once again consume his life. The lies were better. The lies he could deal with,

The Society

"Sonny didn't want to leave in the end," he said at last, "there was no convincing him."

Yet even as he spoke the words he could see the corner of the box was beginning to lift, and things were beginning to slip out and slither uninvited into his brain.

"And what about the enlightenment? Did William Thomas return?" she asked eagerly.

"No," Quinn struggled as his story started to fall apart. "The enlightenment was all just theatrics, a metaphor presented in a grand, carefully planned show."

"And then you just left the next day?"

"Yes," he said abruptly, "I tried again to talk Sonny into coming but it was impossible, and that's the end of it."

"Mr. Bergman!" she said sharply, abandoning all pretence of kindness. "We both know you are lying. It will do you absolutely no good to keep burying this. You have told me how much you loved Sonny, there is no way you just gave up and left without him. The only reason you didn't bring him is because you couldn't! What really happened?"

She watched his resolve crumple like an old paper bag before her. His shoulders slumped and he put his head in his hands as if he were trying to appear as small as possible. He suddenly looked very old and very frail. She could hear him trying to stifle his moans as he completely broke down.

"There was nothing I could do," he cried miserably, "they would have killed me if they'd thought there was any chance of me stopping the events from going ahead. I knew if I wanted to get out alive, and have even the tiniest chance of saving Sonny, I was going to have to play along with it."

She sensed this last part would be easier without the barrier between them, and she stood up and came out from behind her desk. For this part he was going to need a little human connection. She sat down next to him and poured him a glass of water. She handed him the box of tissues and he blew his nose loudly and took several long gulps of water. She laid a kind hand on his boney shoulder and he looked at her with red rimmed eyes.

"I never told anyone this, not even George and Emily. I told them what I just told you, simply that I could not persuade him to leave. I never told another living soul because I was terrified of what they might do to me. And what would have been the point? No one would have believed me."

"I understand," she took his frail old hand in hers, "nobody is blaming you. You are a victim too and isn't it time we tried to get justice for what happened?"

"You're right," he said determinedly, "it's time."

The Society

Chapter 37

1970

It was the longest day of my life as I waited in that room for evening to come and Lesley to arrive. I played out all kinds of scenarios in my head in which I managed to somehow get Sonny and myself away, to my car, and to my friends waiting in the village. I expected at any moment that the proceedings would be interrupted by the arrival of the police, and when that did not happen I truly began to panic. Obviously, something had gone wrong. I tortured myself with wild and farfetched possibilities such as Dante had somehow managed to capture and imprison my friends, or that he was actually crazy enough to have them killed rather than have them interfering with the enlightenment, or more likely The Society had already bought off the local law enforcement in some way, or that they simply refused to act on what was, after all, a rather wild story. Any number of things could be holding them up.

I was removed from my room briefly at around noon and taken to attend disclosure and cleansing which I wearily faked my way through, feeling absolutely nothing when James-Anthony put his hands on me. As usual I was given water beforehand but this time there was no high, I instead became quite sluggish and foggy and I was convinced that they had seen fit to feed me some kind of tranquilliser this time.

Back in my room as I watched the sun set over the sea, as I had so many times before from that window, I accepted that help was not coming.

*

The Society

At around seven Lesley arrived. I had a vague notion that maybe I could try and persuade her to help me get away, but it was too risky to express these thoughts to her, as to do so might have resulted in me not being allowed to attend the event at all, and I'd probably find myself back in the basement. She was dressed as if she were about to attend a film premier or some other fancy occasion in a floor length, midnight blue ball gown, which sparkled in the light, and her hair piled on top of her head. Expensive jewellery glittered at her neck and wrists.

"Hello, my love," she greeted me, placing her hand on my shoulders and kissing me on the cheek.

She smelled of musk and roses and I noticed she was carrying a suit bag. She stood back and looked at me critically.

"You look a bit worse for wear," she commented, "you've lost weight, and your face is a little bruised."

"Yes, well, the last week hasn't exactly been a picnic."

"I heard about what happened, about those dreadful people drugging you and kidnapping you and about Dante throwing you in the hole," she hugged me, "but it all changes today. In the light of the new age we are entering, the pair of us have to give up our wild ways and start behaving like good parishioners."

She released me and handed me the bag. I took it from her, feeling entirely numb and disconnected from everything.

"I'm quite looking forward to the next stage of our lives. We've had our fun, but it's definitely time we settled down. Come on, you need to get changed."

She strode over to my desk and sat down.

"This really is a lovely part of the world," she commented, "I think we should get a place of our own in the area."

I could scarce believe how deluded this woman was. Did she really believe that we were going to live happily ever after together in the Cornish countryside after tonight? I unzipped the bag and took out the customary white suite parishioners were always expected to wear at the annual conference.

"What do you think they are going to do with Sonny?" I asked tentatively as I started to undress.

"He's not your concern anymore darling," she said slowly, "I know he was your plaything for a while, but that part of your life is over. We're to be a proper married couple now."

"Yes, but they aren't going to hurt him, are they?" I asked hopefully.

"My dear," she crossed the room and picked up my tie from the bed, "Sonny has been well prepared for his part in tonight's proceedings. He has spent the last fifteen years being groomed for this. He will be absolutely fine, there really is no reason to be concerned. Sonny is in a very enviable position, for he is going to become a legend within The Society, his paintings will hang on the walls of every parishioner's home. Tonight, Sonny is going to get what he has longed for his whole life; he's finally going to join the ranks of the famous."

She wrapped the tie around my neck and tied it for me.

"Why, you are handsome, husband, despite what you have been through," she said, looking me up and down, "I really can't wait to start living as man and wife."

"Yes, dear," I forced a smile, "a new life together."

The Society
Always a sunrise, never a sunset.

The gathering for this event was smaller and more intimate than those of previous years as it was exclusive to those who had reached stage six and beyond. Few people had that amount of money to throw away in the pursuit of spiritual enlightenment and so not many had made it this far. I would say there were around a hundred people in attendance, all of whom I knew and recognised as prominent members of The Society, and who were, for the most part, well known celebrities. The chairs were not set in rows like they usually were but were instead arranged around circular tables of about ten to a table. The light was dim and there were beautiful centerpieces of red roses and lilies on each table, and candles flickering softly inside glass bowls. People were milling about and chatting excitedly, and I was struck by how normal the scene was. It could have simply been a fancy party, or a wedding reception, perhaps; there was nothing to suggest that anything sinister was going to happen. Benjamin Lovell even stopped us as we passed by to compliment me on my latest book and I forced myself to smile graciously.

I had Lesley on my arm as we entered the ballroom, and Dante was at the door greeting everyone individually.

"Quinn my good man," he said, shaking my hand, "welcome to this most glorious evening! And Lesley, you look stunning." He kissed both her cheeks. "I do apologise about your husband's appearance, but sometimes people have to be kept in line."

"Oh, I quite understand," she fawned, "it's all worth it if it means he can be here tonight."

They were both looking at me now, clearly expecting me to say something.

"Yes, well it wasn't anything I didn't deserve."

"Go and take your seats you two," Dante chuckled.

At our table we made small talk with our fellow artists, and when Alan Barnes, a celebrated concert pianist, commented on my face I tried to just laugh it off.

"I think we've all been on the wrong side of Dante's temper at some point in our lives," he laughed heartily.

Workers in their smart uniforms circulated the room, handing out glasses of champagne. Once this was done, they all left and the doors were sealed behind them leaving only old souls inside.

It's just a charade, I tried telling myself, *nothing bad is going to happen, it's just a bunch of rich people acting out a ritual, peddling their fanciful notions about reincarnation and people returning from the dead. You'll probably laugh about it all later when you're back with your friends.*

The inane chatter about how you found the last course, who gave the best cleansing, how was your last movie premier, died down as everyone sensed we were soon about to begin.

It was, as was the custom, Dante who took to the stage to open the event and introduce the Grand High Master of Souls, amid the usual wild cheering and applause. To begin with it followed the same format it always did, with James-Anthony running through the year's stats; telling us how many old souls had been recruited, or saved as he liked to call it, how many people had taken self-help courses at the community outreach centres. All the while I found myself desperately looking around for Sonny but seeing no sign of him. Lesley, on noticing how distracted I was, grabbed my hand and hissed at me to pay attention.

The Society

"And while all of this gives us reason to be immensely proud," James-Anthony continued, "we now come to the real reason why we are here tonight. Tonight, we will celebrate the rebirth of our glorious founder."

There was a lot of manic cheering, some of the guests looked deliriously happy and could hardly keep control of themselves.

"As you know, today is the day that our glorious leader is set to be reborn. He has completed his work on the astral plane, where he has been studying and gathering knowledge since he vacated his last body. When he returns he will impart all that he has learned onto his followers. The things that are to come you can scarcely imagine; we will have the power to heal the world on a grand scale, end all wars, put a stop to all forms of human suffering once and for all. And in time, all of mankind will progress up through the stages, and each and every person will have their chance to know him and learn his secrets. In these more enlightened times the population, which is dangerously out of control, will start to fall as people realise they cannot keep breeding at such an irresponsible rate, and with that will come a day when non-beings cease to exist, there will be fewer new souls and the world will become a beautiful, fully enlightened, cultured paradise.

"But first I would like to honour someone whose work has been instrumental in getting us to this point, my second in command, Dante Lewin-May!"

Dante joined him on the stage once again, with Kerrigan at his side in a stunning green gown.

"Fifteen years ago I set you a task," he began, "to take in and care for a troubled young man, to school him as per our founders' very specific instructions, and you have done so admirably. I appreciate that it has not been an easy task at times, and there have been many challenges along the way, and to show my appreciation I am awarding you this special medal of honour, in our founder's name."

The cheers erupted again, and James-Anthony pinned a gold medal on a grinning Dante's suit jacket.

"Thank you!" he beamed. "What an honour this is, but I can say, the real hour has been in serving The Society, and doing my part to ensure this long-awaited day goes to plan."

"And with that I would like to call to the stage the young man in question, Sonny Newton."

My heart skipped a beat as Sonny was brought from somewhere in the back and received on stage by Dante who gave him a big hug. Everyone was cheering madly, everyone except me. I sat feeling tense and sick, my stomach in knots, wondering what was going to happen. James-Anthony also embraced Sonny before stepping back up to the lectern. Dante and Sonny stood off to the side, both smiling broadly, and Dante had a fatherly hand on Sonny's shoulder.

"I am now going to read from the stage six prophecies as laid out by our founder," James-Anthony said. I recognised the words he read out as the same script that had been attached to a wooden block during the game of pass the parcel.

The room was silent, and the air was heavy with anticipation.

"To prepare for my return all misdeeds of my followers must be atoned for," James-Anthony continued in his booming voice, "the slate of every parishioner wiped clean, and to do so will require a sacrifice. Much like in the Christian religion when God sent his only son to die for the sins of mankind, so must the last of my family line die, willingly and without protest, on this night so that all misdeeds may be forgiven, and we can enter a new age of enlightenment."

"My god, they're going to kill him," I said softly, filled with disbelief and horror.

"Don't be silly," Lesley whispered sharply, "nothing is going to happen to him that he doesn't want."

"Ladies and Gentleman," James-Anthony boomed, "welcome to the enlightenment!"

Sonny had stepped up to the lectern and was preparing to speak. I was now on my feet, and when he noticed me he gave me a smile. It was all starting to make sense. The special training from which he would return talking about how death was not to be feared, rather viewed as a second chance. Had they really gotten to him that much that he thought he was simply going to die and start a new life?

"It has been a great honour to have been allowed the time I have had within this glorious group," Sonny began. "Without The Society I would have been dead a long time ago, I'm certain of that, and I would not have been able to experience the wonderful life I have had for the last fifteen years at Chyanvean. But I was born this lifetime into a faulty vessel which could not be repaired. I was burdened with a body and mind cursed with terrible afflictions. I have carried with me the misdeeds of all of mankind, and it is for this reason that I can enter into this knowing I am going on to better things, knowing that this life has imparted onto me all the lessons it has to give."

"Sonny, no!" I cried, rushing forward, my chair clattering to the ground.

Raven Taylor

The whole room was now staring at me. People were trying to grab me as I rushed by.

"Dante! Get him under control!" James-Anthony commanded, a furious look on his face.

Dante leapt down from the stage and hurtled towards me.

"You don't have to do this!" I cried as I hurried towards Sonny, who simply watched calmly from his spot next to the lectern.

Dante launched himself at me and tackled me to the ground. It was no contest really, and he soon had me pinned to the floor.

"This is murder," I protested, kicking and struggling against Dante's weight, "can't you see you've gone too far?"

"That's where you are wrong," Dante panted, twisting my left arm painfully behind my back as he straddled me and forced my face into the floor. "I'm talking about giving someone a release, a second chance. Sonny has tried to take his own life on several occasions, he understands that he has made such a mess of things this time round that there is really no going back for him. The chance at a new life really is his only hope. It's a mercy to put him out of his misery; he accepts all of this and he is more than willing, as the last serving member of the Thomas line, to do what must be done."

"Please, you can stop this now, before it's too late, because once you go down this road there's no going back, you'll be a murderer."

"There will be no murder my dear Quinn," he chuckled, "for Sonny is a true believer and is prepared to offer himself up willingly."

I twisted my head so I could get a view of the stage. James-Anthony was handing Sonny a golden goblet. Sonny took it from him, and I watched as he

The Society

whispered something in James-Anthony's ear before he began to make his way towards me.

"I know this must be difficult for you," Dante said quietly, "but this is his destiny, you must have known you and he could not continue."

Sonny was walking slowly towards us, looking completely serene. It almost looked as if he were gliding. Something about his demeanour terrified me. This was not Sonny. He was drugged, or hypnotised, or both, he had to be.

"Help me get him up," Dante ordered, and a large fellow from a nearby table came forward, and between the two of them they were able to pull me to my feet and restrain me so I couldn't break free.

"Quiet now, Quinn," Dante said soothingly as I tried to struggle, "try and conduct yourself with a bit of dignity and see this for the beautiful thing it is."

Sonny was close now, still looking placid and calm, and he stopped right in front of me and spoke in a low tone so that only those in the direct vicinity would be able to hear.

"My darling Quinn, please do not grieve for me. Do not be sad. It is my time to go. This is not the end, but a new beginning. Perhaps in a future life we will be reunited, but for me, it is time for me to depart."

I could feel the tears in my eyes as every last bit of strength drained from my body so that I sagged under the grasp of Dante and his helper.

"Be thankful for the time we had," he said as he put his free hand on my neck and kissed me briefly, "for it was truly beautiful."

"No, Sonny," my voice was no more than a strangled croak as he stepped back, and I looked into his eyes for the last time, "I can't lose you. I love you."

"I love you too, Quinn." He turned away and addressed the room at large, raising his voice so he could be heard. "I drink from the cup of our glorious founder so that the misdeeds of all his congregation shall be washed away, I die for your crimes, and so that he can re-enter the world and the new age of enlightenment can begin."

He raised the golden goblet to his lips, and as the light hit it I could make out the initials 'W T' engraved on it.

"NO!" I found my strength again and began to struggle violently against my captors.

I watched as Sonny started to cough and splutter, and then to foam at the mouth. I screamed until my throat was raw. Sonny fell to the ground and began to convulse, his eyes rolling back in his head. I kicked and yelled even though I knew it was already too late. I heard Dante say to his helper, "let him go now," and they released their hold on me.

I threw myself to the floor and gathered Sonny up in my arms. I even tried to stick my fingers down his throat in a desperate bid to make him throw up the poison that was already killing him. He thrashed and spasmed in my arms, blood welling from his nose and mixing with the white foam around his mouth. I clutched him tightly to my chest, vaguely aware that people were pressing in around me trying to get a look at what was happening; the country's rich and famous were all eager to witness a dying man's last tragic moments as he slipped away in the arms of his lover. Sonny had offered himself up as some sort of Christ- like figure, fully believing that he was atoning for the misdeeds of these people, and they would love and honour him as a god from this day. His movements were growing weaker as his body's last wretched attempts to cling to life slowly subsided. Within minutes he was as limp as a rag doll.

"No, no, no, no, no," I kept repeating to myself, as I wiped the blood and foam from around his mouth, knowing in my heart it was over.

I buried my face in his hair and began to wail uncontrollably. He smelled of the lavender that always perfumed the air in Chyanvean, and my head seemed filled with the maddening sound of birdsong.

"And so it is," I heard James-Anthony rumbling into the mic, "that we have assured we are all free from misdeeds, and secured the return of our glorious founder who will bring us knowledge from the astral plains that we can scare even comprehend."

My mind could not grasp what was happening. Where was he? Where the hell was William Thomas? If Sonny was to die then I expected a goddamn miracle; I expected to see William Thomas rise from the dead, or at least for them to perform some kind of illusion to suggest as much. But there was nothing. Just lots of people standing around looking high as kites, smiling deliriously.

"Well, where is he?" I yelled hysterically. "Where is William Thomas? I want to meet the bastard so I can tell him exactly what I think of his damn prophecy."

"Quinn, you're embarrassing yourself," Dante snarled at me, "you don't really expect to see him tonight, do you?"

"I do actually," I laughed the laugh of a man gone mad, "isn't that why we are all here?"

"We are here to bear witness to the sacrifice; we won't yet know where William Thomas is. His soul will return within the first baby born in Cornwall after midnight tonight. You'll learn all about that when you start reading the stage six materials."

"Of course! How silly of me!" I felt as if I were losing my mind.

"We need the body," Dante said.

"No. You can't have him. He's served his purpose, done what you wanted, now let me take him away so at least in death he can be free of this place."

"He'll be well looked after," Dante assured me, "he has attained the highest possible honour and we will take good care of his abandoned shell."

There was no shortage of volunteers to help prize him from my arms, and his body was taken from me and carried away. People had begun to return to their seats, murmuring excitedly, but I stayed where I was, howling in misery. Dante crouched down and tried to comfort me by putting his arms around me, and I found I was too exhausted to even push him away.

"Be brave, my good man, be proud of him, and be proud of yourself."

Lesley had joined us as she also sat down on the floor and attempted to console me.

"This is madness," I protested weakly, "it's sheer insanity."

"Come now my sweet Quinn," Lesley coaxed, taking my arm, "I understand how hard this is, really I do, I'm sorry you had to go through this, but it's all going to be ok."

Somehow I managed to stand up.

"I'd take him to bed," Dante suggested, "he has done us a great service, without him I'm not sure I could have kept Sonny alive these last few years, his love for your husband was often the only thing that kept him going. But I wouldn't imagine he'll want to stay and celebrate with us."

The Society

"Damned right I don't," I said, feeling some of my strength returning, and the anger welling up in me.

I shook away Lesley's arm. Her touch felt vile to me. I wanted none of them anywhere near me. On the stage Sonny's body had been laid out on a table, his arms folded across his chest, and parishioners were approaching one by one and heaping flowers around him.

"You're murders," I yelled at the room, "despicable murderers, every one of you."

James-Anthony was standing by the table where Sonny now lay, glaring at me with narrow eyes. I glanced towards the main doors to the ballroom. I would have no chance if I tried to make a run for it now with so many people around. I was going to have to let Lesley lead me away and I'd make a break for it once we were out of the ballroom. I had to fight the overwhelming urge to launch myself at Dante and cause him physical harm in whatever way I could. I wanted more than anything to feel his face break under my fists, to kick him until his bones cracked, but I understood my only hope of getting out of here was to go with Lesley, and so I tried to suppress my rage and attempted to look resigned.

"Get him out of here Dante," James-Anthony looked furious, evidently he had not been expecting such protest from any of his parishioners.

"Don't worry Master," Lesley called back to him, "I'm taking him to bed, I'll keep an eye on him for the rest of the night."

"No," James-Anthony said angrily, "the hole is a better place for one so corrupt who would seek to destroy this happy occasion."

Raven Taylor

James-Anthony ascended the stairs from the stage, and the whole room watched as he approached us.

"Might be the best place for you, also," he growled; he was now right upon us, his face mere inches from Dante's as he glared aggressively at him.

"Me?" Dante spluttered in surprise.

"You've really messed this up," he poked Dante hard in the chest, "he should never have been in attendance tonight, but for reasons I can't seem to fathom you rushed him through his exams so he could be here."

"But I..." Dante stammered. I had never seen him appear so small, so unsure of himself. There was not a trace of the self-importance that usually radiated from him.

Lesley had taken my arm again, and this time I did not shake her off. She was gripping me so tightly that her long nails were digging into me. I could feel her shaking with nerves over the unfolding conflict.

"I trusted you though, I thought your judgement was good, I reasoned you would never bring someone so unprepared, and who is blatantly allowing some sick and perverted love for our sacrifice to come above the needs of The Society. I assumed if you were bringing him in on this tonight then you had got him to a stage of good character. Evidently this is not the case. This man is not a good parishioner, and you have allowed him to attend this night. How could you have permitted this to happen?"

I was aware that every set of eyes in the room were upon us now. Dante threw himself to his knees at James-Anthony's feet and started to grovel and plead and make excuses.

The Society

"I can't have anything disrupt and befoul this night anymore, who knows what damage will occur from the trouble you have caused," James-Anthony was trembling with rage now, "I wouldn't be surprised if our founder deems us unworthy, not ready, after this complete farce."

On his knees, Dante was at the perfect height for James-Anthony to deliver a savage blow with his cane to his head. The sound of the wood connecting with Date's skull was sickening. He flew back and skidded along the polished floor, before coming to rest motionless at the feet of some gawking parishioners. Lesley had both her arms wrapped around my left arm now and was holding on for dear life. I looked in horror at the growing pool of blood on the floor around Dante's head. Nobody came forward to help him. My eyes scanned the room for Kerrigan, surely, she at least must have some concern for her husband. I saw her a short distance away. She wore a pained expression but made no effort to come to Dante's aid. I braced myself, ready to run, certain that I would be next to be on the receiving end of James-Anthony's fury. Sure enough, with Dante out cold, he turned his attention to me.

"I am sorry, Quinn Bergman," he said to my surprise, "Dante failed you. He was in charge of your treatment and schooling and he has let you down horribly."

I tried to find the words to answer but there was nothing. Lesley gave a small, relieved gasp.

"Some time in the hole should help to rehabilitate you, after that I will take you under my own guidance and see that you receive everything you need to become a proper parishioner and productive member of The Society. This man who I put so much trust in has clearly been soft, has overindulged you, and put your soul and spiritual wellbeing in the greatest of danger. But don't worry, I will personally see that this is all put right."

James-Anthony let out a long sigh and shook his head sadly as he looked from me, to Dante, who was just starting to come around, to Sonny's body on the stage.

"What a mess," he said regretfully, "come Quinn, you cannot stay here."

He strode over to Dante and hauled him to his feet where he swayed slightly, his face bloody from the laceration on his temple. He started to pull Dante across the hall towards the door. Lesley tugged on my arm and urged me to go with her as she followed. As we made our way to the exit I felt everyone's eyes follow us. I pretended to be complacent and obedient, making a show of leaning on Lesley as we walked. I would have to pick my moment. As we approached the doors I took one last glance over my shoulder at Sonny and felt tears once again burning the back of my eyes.

I'm sorry I couldn't save you.

James-Anthony banged on the door with his cane, leaving a small bloody mark on the surface, and the doors were pulled open by two workers who had been standing outside. He dragged Dante out into the corridor. Lesley and I followed.

It wasn't until we were back in the foyer that a horrible thought struck me. It would have been too easy to make a run for the front door where my car was waiting mere yards away, but I did not have the keys to the vehicle on me. I realised with despair that things were about to get a lot more difficult. I was going to have to run all the way into the village, and I did not feel optimistic about my chances given the state I was in. Still, I was going to have to try, because if I allowed them to get me down those stairs into the basement then I would surely be doomed.

    Taking a deep breath, I yanked my arm free of Lesley's hold, and, summoning every last ounce of strength I had, I hurtled across the foyer towards the front door. By some stroke of luck I found it unlocked.

    I did not look back when I heard James-Anthony's booming voice issuing instructions for the workers to give chase, not to let me get away, because I knew too much. I slammed the door behind me and began to sprint down the drive. It was cold outside and I was underweight and unfit. My breath came in ragged white puffs as I willed my legs to move faster. I could hear the heavy slap of the footsteps pursuing me echoing in the still night. I began to scream at the top of my lungs for someone to help just in case there was anyone from the village within earshot; a dog walker, someone walking home from the pub. The gates were looming up before me, barring my way, and I prayed that the code to unlock them was still Astrid's birthday.

    I risked a glance over my shoulder and saw three workers charging towards me, gaining on me rapidly. If only I could get out of the gates. I stopped and frantically keyed in the code, mistyping it twice and cursing loudly until finally they began to swing open. They were almost upon me now. Being driven by sheer adrenaline, I raced forward through the gap and out onto the road. I began to yell again, as loud as I could, hoping desperately to raise the alarm.

    I flew down the dark road, heading for the lights of the village. They were right behind me now. There was no way I was going to make it. They would be upon me at any second, and once they had me I would not be able to fight them off and would be dragged back to the house and thrown into the basement.

My lungs were burning and my legs ached. My energy was all but spent. One of them threw himself at me. I felt his fingers brush the back of my jacket, but he could not get any purchase and he crashed to the ground. He fell right in the path of the second man who tripped over him, spilling his heavy frame to the tarmac. I was jubilant as I realised this would surely buy me the time I needed to make it into the village, and I pushed myself harder. The lights were getting closer now; once I was among the buildings I would surely be safe.

The soles of my shoes pounded the ground and behind me and my pursuers were back on their feet and had taken up the chase once more.

I'm going to make it!

I passed the first house that marked the start of the village and I started to scream again. Looking back, I realised that they were still following and quickly making up the distance I had put between us. Somebody had to hear me. Up ahead I saw The Red Lion, where I had tried to get lunch when I first arrived in St Morlyn. A welcoming yellow glow spilled from its small windows, and I could hear the faint sound of happy chatter. Somebody with a deep baritone voice was singing 'Going Up Camborne Hill.' That was my salvation. There was no way they would follow me in there. I threw myself at the door to the pub and stumbled in, falling to the flagstone floor, the last of my energy spent, completely exhausted. I was right. The workers did not attempt to follow me inside. I wondered vaguely how they would be punished for letting me get away.

I lay on the ground, out of breath, and did not move. The merry banter and the singing had stopped as

The Society

everyone in the pub stared at me. What a sight I must have looked sprawled out on the floor in my white suit with Sonny's blood splashed on it and my bruised face. The gnarled faces of old fisherman with their knitted caps, leather skinned farmers, and the rosy cheeked women all stared at me in shock.

"What the bleeding hell is going on?" I heard a woman's voice enquiring from the back of the room.

"He's from that house, I think," a gruff and unfriendly voice said, "he's one of *them* I reckon."

"No, no, you have to help me," I tried to say, but the room was now filled with confused chatter as the silence broke and they began to crowd in around me.

"Watch out, the lot of you, let me through you daft old buggers," I heard the woman's voice again. "Charlie, Norman, out of the way!"

The sea of curious faces parted, and I recognised the blonde-haired woman who had refused to serve me on my previous visit years before.

"Judas! What happened to you?" she exclaimed as she surveyed my sorry appearance.

"I ran away," it was all I managed to say before the whole night, the terrible realisation of what had actually happened, caught up with me, and I became hysterical, crying and babbling incoherently as the villagers helped me to my feet and deposited me in an armchair by the fire.

Someone forced a glass of brandy into my hand. I was aware of them all crowding round me again, trying to talk to me, now sounding concerned and no longer hostile, but I could not hear what they were saying, nor could I speak. All I could do was sit and weep.

Someone had notified the local law enforcement. An irritable looking man in plain clothes pushed his way through the spectators and settled his ample frame into the chair opposite me, telling me that he was PC Trevor Andrews. By now I had regained a little composure and had stopped crying, helped in part by the brandy.

"So, what's going on here then?" he asked me, "where did the blood come from?"

"I came from Chyanvean, I ran away, my name is Quinn Bergman."

"Quinn Bergman?" he looked a little flustered, "do you have friends staying in the village? A young couple, a big black American fella, and an older gent?"

"Yes!" I said excitedly, sitting up straight, "George and Emily, and Dwight and my father. They were supposed to come and get me if I didn't come out of that place. You've spoken to them then?"

"I have," he said reluctantly, his cheeks starting to flush red, "a couple of days ago they came to the station with some rather wild story about that house and the people who stay there. Wanted me to go and see if I could talk to their friend, you."

"Well, what happened?" I asked, feeling myself growing angry again. "Why didn't you come?"

The whole pub was listening eagerly, clearly this would give them something to talk about for decades to come.

"Well, I did," he said defensively, "I went to the house and was met by a gentleman who told me the place was closed for a special religious ceremony that ought not to be interrupted. I asked about you and he said to come back in a couple of days when the house was reopened to the public."

"Pfft," a young man in a blue cable knit jumper and muddy overalls made a disapproving noise, "probably paid you off too, did he Trevor?"

The Society

The Policeman's face reddened again and he said, "Now listen here young Jonny, what exactly are you implying?"

"Oh, come on Trevor," said an old fellow in a flat cap, "we all know you've been up to that house before, trying to get in with the toffs, never listened to us when we made complaints about them trying to come into the school and corrupt the kids with their weird ways, or when they keep bombarding us all with their demented religious leaflets that they shove through every door in the village."

"Well, it's best just to keep the peace, isn't it? Especially with the neighbours," Trevor insisted, "I know they were a bit of a nuisance to begin with, but they've kept to themselves for years now."

"Yet you didn't see fit to follow up when this man's friends came here looking for him?"

"Not at all! I was going to give them a couple of days like they suggested, so as not to annoy them by intruding on their religious celebrations."

The young man snorted his disapproval and there was a general shaking of heads. I fell silent and felt my body growing numb, despite the heat of the fire. How different things could have been if he had just insisted on being admitted. Both Sonny and I could have been out before the enlightenment. Sonny might still be alive.

"Yet you choosing to wait made all the difference in the world," I said quietly, feeling completely drained.

"I should go and get your friends," he said, clearly feeling awkward and eager to get away.

"Yes, please do," I did not even possess the energy to be angry at him anymore.

As he left, the excited murmuring started again and I caught small snatches as the locals rambled to one another about how they had always known that something was not right about the people in that house, and how could a cult like that be allowed to practice right on their doorsteps? The blonde barmaid gave me another brandy, and in no time PC Andrews had returned with George, Emily, Dwight and my father.

"Come on folks, let's give them a bit of space," the barmaid urged, but the villagers all seemed keen to continue crowding us so they could hear more gossip. "Drinks on the house for all if you come this way!"

The offer of free booze got them all moving, and my small group of friends were able to gather round me, each hugging me in turn and making comments about how awful I looked.

"So, where's Sonny?" Emily asked, a concerned look on her face.

"Sonny wouldn't come," I lied, "things got dangerous, there was no more time, I had to get out."

"Are you hurt?" asked George, eyeing the bloodstains on my suit.

"No, I'm ok."

"Well, that's the main thing," he said, relieved, "don't worry, we'll find a way to get Sonny out, we won't give up."

"No," I said, "best just to leave it. It's finished. We can't help him."

And that did it. I started to cry again, and George pulled his chair closer so he could put his arms around me. I sobbed into his shoulder, and it felt like I might never stop.

The Society

Chapter 38

2009

"Even after you leave you are never truly free," Quinn said sadly, "they follow you, check up on you, intimidate you. They were terrified that I was going to speak out and talk about the murder."

She watched as he shivered and looked over his shoulder, as if expecting to see someone standing there.

"You don't need to worry anymore, you're perfectly safe," she tried to reassure him. "Here, drink."

She refilled his glass from the pitcher and he took a long, shaky swallow.

"I do have one more question, if you don't mind?"

"Please, ask anything you like."

"Do you know what happened to Dante? He was never seen or heard from again after that night."

He frowned. "I don't know," he admitted, "the last I ever saw of him was him being dragged away to the hole by James-Anthony."

"I've made enquiries," she said slowly, "he seems to have just diapered without a trace. People speculate about what happened to him, his wife Kerrigan insisted right up until her death that he was fine and living life away from the public eye, but if that were true there would surely have been some sightings of him. After what you've told me, I wonder, did that blow to the head kill him?"

"I wouldn't be surprised," Quinn said, "or perhaps he was just thrown into the hole and left to rot, never to be seen again."

The Society

"Possibly," she looked thoughtful, "do you know why I'm doing these investigations, why I have such an interest in all of this?"

"Why, to gather evidence of abuses and bring a case against The Society in court, that's what you told me."

"Ah but it's much simpler than that," she said, slowly standing up.

She crossed the room and pointed to a spot on the wall where a picture hook stuck out of the plaster.

"There's usually a picture that hangs here," she told him, "I sent it away to be repaired after the frame was damaged. I only got it back this morning, do you think I should hang it up again? It's in that cupboard over there."

A confused look passed across Quinn's face as he said, "if you like."

"Yes, I think I will."

Quinn watched, baffled, as she opened the cupboard door and took out a framed canvas. She reached up and hung it back on its hook and stepped back to admire it. Quinn's heart began to hammer in his chest and his stomach lurched as he looked upon the psychedelic landscape; the purple field of waving flowers, the green sky with the blue sun sinking, *no, rising*, on the horizon, and the black bird flying in the sky above. He sat, gaping, completely speechless as he stared at Sonny's painting.

"But how did you get that?" he asked when he finally found his voice, astonished. "Who are you?"

"Don't you recognise me?" she asked.

"I know you?"

"Yes," she confirmed, "you see, the real reason I'm investigating these matters is because The Society has tasked me with trying to find out what happened on that night. Until now no one has spoken about it, and those not in attendance were never even told there was ever a second coming predicted. There have been rumours; rumours that there was a big event in 1970, but what it was all about has been kept entirely secret. The information you have given me today is invaluable, the mistakes that were made that night could be the reason The Society is now starting to fail the way it is, but perhaps with this new information we can begin to rectify that."

"No, no, no…" Quinn muttered, a desperate and terrified look passing across his face.

She was one of them. He looked down at the glass of water which he was still holding in his hand. It was almost empty. He let it fall to the floor and watched as it rolled across the carpet, a dark, wet stain spreading around it. At Chyanvean there was always something in the water. How many glasses had she handed him since he had been here?

"Of course, for me this matter is also a personal one," she informed him. "I'm glad to finally learn why the nice young artist who was so good to me once simply disappeared one day and was never heard of again. I'm sorry to hear of what became of him, that does make me very sad, but that he died for our misdeeds is wonderful. This was never spoken of, but now I know of his sacrifice I will sing it to the congregation and he will be known to them, and his martyrdom properly celebrated, his memory revered. Take comfort in that, my dear man."

Quinn was horror struck. He was certain this must be some kind of terrible nightmare. It simply could not be happening. He had dreams like this, where they finally found him and caught him again.

The Society

"It is disappointing, however, that I still don't know exactly what became of Dante. I had rather hoped to gain some closure on that matter. When you're a small child and both your best friend and your father simply disappear, and you're forbidden from ever mentioning them or asking about them, it is rather disconcerting."

Quinn gasped in surprise, "Astrid?"

"There, you've got it now," she smiled at him.

Now that he knew who she was he could see it plain as day. He sat, hands trembling, desperate to be out of that claustrophobic room. He glanced at Sonny's painting and felt a stab of pain in his heart.

"Well, Astrid," he said, trying to sound calm. Was it his imagination or was he starting to feel a heavy drowsiness creeping over him? "I've never tried to harm The Society in all these years, I've kept quiet, and I wish you no personal harm either. You got what you want, I've told you all you need to know, I think perhaps it's time I was going."

He stood up, trying to hide the shaking in his hands as he put his cap on, but he felt sluggish and weighed down, like he was under water and the world was starting to slip away.

"Oh no," Astrid said, smiling sweetly, "you know too much, and now you've proved you are no longer afraid to talk, I can't possibly let you leave, Quinn Bergman."

Raven Taylor

The Society

Raven Taylor
Author Biography

Raven Taylor was born in South Shields, Tyneside in 1983. She now lives in rural Cumbria with her husband and two house rabbits. Raven has written a number of books, short stories and poems and has been doing so since she got her first typewriter as a young child.